NOTICE. THIS MATERIAL MAY BE
PROTECTED BY COPYRIGHT LAW
TITLE 17 U.S. CODE

RILEY LIBRARY
NORTHWEST NAZARENE COLL
NAMPA. IDAHO 83686

T·H·E
DREAM

D1052558

T·H·E
DREAM

HILDA STAHL

WHITE PINE CHRONICLES
BOOK 3

Thomas Nelson Publishers
Nashville

RILEY LIBRARY
NORTHWEST NAZARENE COLLEGE
NAMPA, IDAHO 83686

1403 40

Copyright © 1993 by Word Spinners, Inc.

All rights reserved. Written permission must be
secured from the publisher to use or reproduce
any part of this book, except for brief quotations
in critical reviews or articles.

Published in Nashville, Tennessee, by Thomas
Nelson, Inc.

Library of Congress Cataloging-in-Publication Data

Stahl, Hilda.
      The dream / Hilda Stahl.
         p.   cm. — (The White pine chronicles)
      ISBN 0-8407-3217-1 (pbk.)
      I. Title.   II. Series: Stahl, Hilda.   White
pine chronicles.
PS3569.T312D7   1992
813'.54—dc20   92–32276
                                      CIP

Printed in the United States of America

4 5 6 7 — 98 97 96 95 94 93

———————

Dedicated with love and pride

to a man with a vision

MARK AUGUST STAHL
(number four of seven)

———————

◊   With special thanks to   ◊

The Freeport Public Library
Joanne Hesselink
Keith Kirkwood
Jeff Stahl
Norman Stahl
Jane Jones

CHAPTER

1

♦ Her chin high and her fists doubled at her sides, Emily Bjoerling shouted up at the towering white pines deep in the Havlicks' forest, "I will not cry!"

But scalding tears welled up in her eyes and rolled down her cheeks. With a strangled sob she pressed her forehead against the nearest giant tree. How could she face her family and smile when they presented her with birthday gifts after supper? Could they understand how hard it was for her to be a year older and still an old maid? The tears fell faster and her throat ached with them. She should've married Bob Lavery before he went off to France to fight in the Great War no matter what Papa said!

She'd been in love with Bob since she was twelve. All she'd ever wanted was to be Bob's wife and raise a family with him. Papa had insisted they wait until Bob came home. Papa had said, "Emily, men return from war with only one leg or so injured their minds no longer work. I don't want that for you."

"I know I'll love Bob and he'll love me no matter what," she insisted. But eventually she agreed to wait, even though it was hard. Bob had been angry, but he'd agreed too.

She prayed for Bob every day, asking God to protect him and

RILEY LIBRARY
NORTHWEST NAZARENE COLLEGE
NAMPA, IDAHO 83686

bring him home safely. He hadn't written often in the two years he was away, at least not nearly as often as she wanted to hear. She knew that mail service in war time was irregular. Sometimes she wouldn't get a letter for weeks and then she'd get two at once. But never had more than two months gone by without a letter. Then she learned that Bob was on his way home. He was healthy and strong and excited about returning home. His ship had docked at a New York harbor and a few days later he had boarded a train. He was on his way home to Blue Creek!

She was all fingers as she dressed in her new lilac-colored dress. When would they be married and where? How would her wedding gown look? Where would they live? How soon could they have their first baby? She already knew the name— Bobby. They would be a family, Bob and Emily and Bobby. A year or so later they'd have Ned, and then Lilian and Betsy and . . .

She dreamed and planned as she walked to the station. She stood waiting on the platform a little off to one side so that when he came to her they'd have a minute away from his family and friends who were all there.

As the train screeched to a stop, Emily locked her hands together and stood on tiptoe. Finally she saw him and she ached to run to him. How could she hold herself back until his family had all greeted him? There was such a crowd around him, she could just barely see the top of his head. Such rejoicing, and hugging, and kissing! Tears blurred her eyes. She felt a little lonely just watching, but soon he would see her and then their reunion would be wonderful.

Slowly, as she watched, something began to register—Bob wasn't alone. There was a woman with him and she was being hugged and kissed by his relatives and friends. They were saying, "Congratulations!" and "Welcome!" and "What a wonderful surprise!" Emily gasped and pressed her hand to her mouth to hold back a cry. Who was the woman? Then Bob and the woman wrapped their arms around each other and, surrounded by his family and friends, left the station. Emily took a step after them, then stopped, her heart dead in her breast. The sounds of their laughter floated back to torment her like a poisonous snake about to strike.

Somehow she'd gotten through the next days and weeks. Somehow she'd managed to go on living, to stop crying, to go for five or ten minutes without thinking about Bob. She was certain he would realize his mistake. He'd send the woman away (his friends said her name was Monique and Bob had married her just before leaving France) and beg her to take him back. She would hesitate a little bit to make him understand how he had hurt her; then, of course, she'd take him back. She loved him. They belonged together.

Then today, very early on this morning of her twenty-fifth birthday, a day when she was supposed to celebrate and feel special, she'd heard the news: Bob and Monique were expecting their first child.

Emily moaned. "Monique! Always Monique!" After several minutes Emily pushed away from the pine. A breeze dried her face and ruffled her black hair. "I hate her," Emily whispered hoarsely. Then she lifted her voice and shouted, *"I hate her!"* The ugly words caught in the great sweeping boughs of the pines and seemed to block out the sun as much as the branches did.

Listlessly Emily walked through the forest. Patches of snow lay against the north sides of the trees. It was the end of April, but the sun couldn't reach the snow to melt it. Unconcerned about snakes this time of year, she walked without watching every step. She touched her side, and her heart skipped a beat. She'd run into the woods without her revolver. Papa would have her hide! He had so carefully taught her how to be safe, but she'd broken almost all the rules. If he learned she'd gone off the path and deep into the woods, he'd forbid her to set foot ever again in the Havlicks' forest.

Papa's job was to guard the ten sections of virgin pine forest that had belonged to the Havlick family since the early 1800s. He had been protecting the priceless trees since before she was born. It was the only stand of virgin white pine left in lower Michigan—six thousand acres in a totally natural state. Papa knew the dangers well. And so did she!

The first rule of the forest was: Never go into the woods without a weapon.

But she had.

A strange odor wove in and out of the overwhelming scent of pine, taking Emily's mind off her heartache. She sniffed; then sniffed again. "What is that?" she muttered. She knew all the smells of the woods as well as she knew the smells of her family's farm. She walked in the general direction of the odor, but it was gone. "Probably my imagination," she told herself.

Just then she heard a low growl. She tensed as shivers trickled up and down her spine. Suddenly her blue wool dress seemed too hot. Were the bears out of hibernation? Or was it a wildcat? She caught a streak of movement to her left. Was it one of the wild dogs Papa had told them about? Why hadn't she remembered her revolver? But she knew why—her birthday plus the news that Bob and Monique were expecting a baby had caused her to forget everything else.

Emily bit her lower lip as she pushed at the mass of black hair flowing over her shoulders and down her back. For the past three years she'd thought of having it bobbed, but each time she decided to do it, she lost her courage. She laughed ruefully. She had the courage to walk in the woods, yet she couldn't have her long hair cut. Maybe if she did, Bob would take notice. She frowned. *It's too late for him to take notice.* Oh, if only her heart knew that!

Slowly she walked toward home, forcing her senses to be alert to everything around her. The hair on the back of her neck prickled, and she stopped to listen. What was the danger?

Years ago tree robbers had given up trying to steal the trees for lumber. If this wasn't thieves, then what? "My imagination again," she grumbled as she started walking again. Perspiration dampened her skin and the wool dress made her neck itch.

She stepped around a tree trunk big enough to hide four people and gasped. She was staring down the barrel of a shotgun. Holding her breath, she lifted her eyes to see Jennet Havlick, a shotgun steady against her shoulder.

"Emily! I almost shot you!" Jennet lowered her gun, her lined face gray.

"You gave me quite a fright!" Emily was so surprised, and relieved, she thought her legs might crumple.

Jennet Havlick was seventy-four years old, slender, and sharp in her mind, but not as steady on her feet as she'd once been. She wore a blue serge dress, leggings, and heavy boots. A brown hat covered her white hair that was pulled back into two buns on the back of her head. She had been the first to inherit the white pines from Freeman Havlick's grandfather. Now the inheritance belonged to her grandsons Trent and Justin, twin sons of her son Clay and his wife Lark. "What *are* you doing this far from home?" Emily asked when she found her voice again.

"I could ask you the same," Jennet said stiffly. She observed Emily's wool dress with the loose belt at her rounded hips, and noticed she wasn't wearing a hat or leggings. "And without a weapon for protection, I see."

Emily flushed. "Don't mention that to my folks, please."

Jennet smiled and the strain left her face. "I won't. But you know they are right, Em. You shouldn't walk alone this deep in the woods."

"And neither should you."

"I know. It's just that I am drawn to these woods now more than at any other time in my life. They're in my dreams at night, my thoughts during the day. Free doesn't understand it.

5

But he's busy with his buggy making." Jen wrinkled her small nose. "There are still those of us who want a horse-drawn buggy instead of the gas buggy that's so popular now, so he has plenty of work!"

Emily chuckled. "Free doesn't want to admit automobiles are here to stay."

"I suppose. He says he is waiting to see if they catch on."

Jennet's gentle laughter died as she glanced around, once again looking worried. She shifted the shotgun nervously. "I know there's someone or something nearby that doesn't belong," she whispered.

Emily nodded, straining to hear unfriendly noises. She felt the same way. "Let's get out of here."

"No," Jennet shook her head, "I want to investigate."

Emily caught Jennet's frail arm. "Please don't. Send Papa out."

Stubbornly Jennet tensed. "I'll look. You run on home."

"And leave you alone? No! I can't do that."

Emily fell into step beside Jennet. She knew Deep Lake was ahead. She'd been there with her papa, but never alone. Maybe it was the lake she'd smelled. Even as she thought it, she pushed the thought away. The smell hadn't been that of water or fish. She quickened her steps to stay beside Jennet. Because it was early spring, the brush wasn't thick yet and walking was easy. The pine needles were several inches thick and their heavy walking shoes sank in deeply.

Jennet stopped, cocking her head. She'd heard something.

Emily narrowed her eyes as she turned in the direction Jennet was looking. She stiffened at the movement of something brown. Then a huge dog sprang into sight. Emily's heart zoomed to her feet. This must be one of the wild dogs Papa had heard. "Do you see it?" Emily whispered.

"Yes." Jennet's mouth turned bone dry.

Growling, the dog leaped toward them, its great fangs bared.

"Shoot!" Emily cried.

Jennet trembled as she tried to raise the shotgun to her shoulder. Shivers ran down her spine and fear pricked her skin. She was hurdled back to the time when she was a young mother and Willie Thorne had dragged her to the woods and left her to the mercy of the wolves.

Emily saw the terror on Jennet's face. The wild dog was almost on them. With a strangled cry, she wrested the shotgun from Jennet, aimed it, and fired. Instantly she knew she'd aimed too high, but the dog stopped a short distance from them and sank to its haunches. Saliva dripped from its yellow bared teeth. Its brown hair was medium length and matted with burrs and its black eyes never left Emily's face. Jennet whimpered in fear, her breathing growing shallow as a band of fear squeezed her heart.

Her hands icy, Emily fumbled with the pouch hanging at Jennet's side, trying to open it and get another shell. Why wasn't the dog attacking them? What was it waiting for?

Suddenly the dog stood, its short ears pricked. Then it turned and loped away, its tail hanging limply against its back legs.

Jennet sank to her knees and, trembling, buried her face in her hands. "I thought it was gone—that terrible day. But it was buried deep in my mind to torment me when I wasn't expecting it. I'm sorry. I was suddenly in another place and I couldn't move."

Still holding the shotgun, Emily knelt beside Jennet. "The dog ran away. But we have to get out of here in case it comes back."

Jennet lifted her face and looked as if she'd aged twenty years in the past few moments. "I was younger than you when it happened. I had come from Grand Rapids with Baby Clay to be with Free at the lumber camp near Big Pine. We were tucked safely away in his tiny cabin while Free was working. All at once the door burst open and in walked the devil himself—

that redheaded Willie Thorne. He wanted to know who I was and I told him. Clay was sleeping and I prayed he'd stay asleep. I knew Willie would kill him like he planned to kill me. He took me to the woods. I ran, but then he caught me." Jennet sobbed as if that long ago experience were happening right then. "He struck me, but my thick hair kept me from being knocked out. He left me for the wolves. I prayed. Oh, but I prayed! Then a wolf came. It growled and leaped at me. I felt its breath and I could smell its foul odor. I jumped aside, and it leaped again. Then Free was there. He . . . shot . . . shot it dead at my feet. I grabbed Free and clung to him like I'd never let go."

Emily's eyes smarted with tears, but her muscles were tensed, ready to spring away. "Jennet, please, we must get out of here."

Jennet focused on Emily's face and after a long pause slowly stood. She opened the pouch and handed a shell to Emily. "Load the gun in case the dog returns."

Emily nodded, glad to see Jennet was herself again. Side by side they walked back toward old Jig's cabin.

Jig was Emily's great uncle. He'd guarded the pines from the time Jennet and Freeman inherited them until he died in 1890.

Shivering, Jennet looked back over her shoulder. "Andree will have to be on guard so he doesn't get attacked by that dog."

"He will. Papa always takes great care in the woods."

"I know. Still, I worry. So many dangerous things are possible."

Emily breathed a sigh of relief as they neared the edge of the woods. They stopped near the stream between two giant pines at Jig's grave.

Jennet brushed pine needles from the tall marble marker. "I loved him, Em."

"I know."

Emily had heard stories of the old woodsman many times while she was growing up, but she never tired of them. She had grown to love Jig just from hearing about him. He'd died several years before she was born, but all her life she'd wished she could have known him.

"Why, Emily," Jennet turned to Emily with a gasp, "I just remembered! It's your birthday!"

Emily nodded, her heart sinking. She really didn't want anyone to go on and on about her twenty-fifth birthday.

"Happy birthday." Jennet squeezed Emily's hand. "I hope you have a happy day after that terrible adventure in the woods."

"Thank you."

"And Em, please don't mention me being here alone." Jennet's eyes darkened. "I don't want my family to worry about me."

"You really shouldn't go in the woods alone."

"I know. But I find such peace in there. I can't hear the noise of those infernal machines that crowd the roads or see the sadness in Clay's eyes because his boy is still gone."

The "boy" was thirty-year-old Trent Havlick. He'd been gone ten years. They didn't know if he'd gone to war and been killed, or if he'd simply disappeared in his great sorrow. Sometimes Emily thought of him and wept for him. They'd been good friends.

Emily and Jennet walked to the edge of the pines and, turning, looked into them again. Birds flew in the trees, singing lustily. In spite of their encounter with danger, there was peace in the forest.

"I have a dream for this place," Jennet whispered. "It began a few years ago and has been growing stronger and stronger. One of these days I'll tell my family." She turned toward Emily. "And I'll tell you and your family. But not today. It isn't the time yet."

Emily saw excitement deep in Jennet's eyes. She wondered

9

about the dream, but didn't ask. She knew Jennet would tell when she was ready.

"Come on," Emily said, "I'll walk you home."

"No. I can manage. You go on home and enjoy your special day." Jennet smiled as she took the shotgun. "Oh, Emmie, I remember the day you were born. Andree and Martha had been married a year to the day. You weighed no more than five pounds, and you had hair as black as coal and a face as red as oak leaves in the fall. I loved you from that first minute." Jennet brushed at a tear. "I was glad to see your two sisters and three brothers arrive too, but you were always special to me. You always will be."

Tears glistening in her blue eyes, Emily kissed Jennet's wrinkled cheek. "Thank you."

"I always hoped you'd marry one of the twins . . ." Jennet's voice trailed away. "But it didn't work out that way, did it?"

Emily shook her head. "Trent did marry my best friend, Celine, and I've been taking care of their child these past eight years." Her voice broke. Celine had died ten years ago, but sometimes the pain still struck her.

"And Justin married Priscilla." Jennet looked across the open field without seeing anything. "Things aren't right with them. I can feel it."

Emily had sensed it too, but she didn't say anything. Mama had taught her not to gossip.

Jennet patted Emily's arm. "See you soon, Emily."

"Goodbye, Jennet."

Emily watched Jennet walk slowly across the field toward the Havlick farm. Her son Tristan and his wife, Zoe, ran a big dairy there and Freeman still built his buggies in the workshop. Tristan's sons Wesley and Reed helped on the farm. Emily knew all the Havlicks, old and young, as well as she knew her own family.

Slowly Emily walked along the edge of the pines to the farm-house the Havlicks had built for her folks when they were first married. She was born in that house, and had lived there all her life. Maybe she'd even die there—an unhappy old maid.

Tears stung her eyes, but she blinked them away.

CHAPTER

2

♦ With Rachel Havlick's small hand in hers, Emily stepped out of the drug store where they'd just had a strawberry ice cream sundae. She stopped short. Bob Lavery was walking toward her, his light denim jacket flapping against his thin body. Her heart lodged in her throat and shivers ran over her body. She wanted to pinch her cheeks to add color to them, but she didn't. She watched as he passed the dress shop and stopped at the millinery store to look in the window. The smells of the Feed and Grain directly across the street blended with the aroma of freshly baked goods coming from the bakery. Two women emerged from the general store and stopped to talk. In the distance a saw shrieked at the lumberyard.

Emily nervously fingered the collar of her white dimity blouse and rubbed with a trembling hand at the waist of her blue pleated skirt. The hem of her skirt reached just below the calves of her legs and barely touched the tops of her shoes. The blouse and skirt were birthday gifts from Mama two weeks ago.

"Why're we stopping, Emily?" Rachel asked impatiently.

"No reason," Emily said hoarsely. She couldn't drag her eyes away from Bob even to glance down at her ten-year-old charge. Bob stopped to talk to Austin Jentry. His voice drifted to her, then was covered by the sounds of a horse and buggy moving down the street with a noisy automobile behind. The smell of exhaust hung in the air even after the automobile passed by and turned the corner.

"I want to go home. Amanda is coming to play dolls with me." Rachel tugged on Emily's hand. "Why do you always have to stare at Bob Lavery? Grandma Lark says you have a crush on him."

Emily's face flamed as she stared in shock at Rachel. "She didn't say that! Did she, Rachel?"

Rachel shrugged and tugged at the white collar of her rose-colored poplin dress. "She didn't know I was listening. Sometimes she forgets I'm ten years old and know all about love and things." She ran her finger around the loose belt that hung just below her waist, then flipped her long red hair over her thin shoulder. "I'm very grown up, you know and it *is* 1922. But Grandma acts like I'm still a baby. I just wish she'd let me cut my hair. I want to have it bobbed like Aunt Priscilla's. I want to look like the modern girl I am."

Emily was thankful to get onto another subject. It would be absolutely terrible if anyone knew she was still in love with Bob. She'd be humiliated if people were talking. She forced her attention back to Rachel. "I don't have my hair bobbed either and I am a very modern woman." Emily touched the mass of black hair pinned in thick loops on her head.

Rachel looked around, then whispered, "Sometimes I even want to smoke cigarettes just like modern ladies do."

"Rachel! Don't you ever take up that terrible habit! Modern *Christian* ladies don't smoke."

"I know," said Rachel with a loud sigh. "But it might be fun to hold that long holder and wear a short dress and dance.

Amanda told me about the dances. She even showed me how to do some of them. And I want to see a moving picture show with Mary Pickford in it."

Impatiently Emily shook her head as she pushed back a stray strand of hair, but she dropped her hand to her side as Bob walked closer. Could he hear the wild thud of her heart even over the clomp of his workboots on the brick walk?

He tipped his cap, revealing a thatch of wheat colored hair, and said, "Afternoon, ladies."

"Afternoon, Bob," Emily said, feeling more like a flustered teenager than a mature woman.

Rachel frowned. "Afternoon, Mr. Lavery," she said and tugged Emily's hand again. "Now can we go?" she whispered.

Emily's face flamed. If Bob had noticed her blush, surely he'd think it was from the heat. It was the second week of May but almost as warm as a day in June.

Bob paused and looked at Emily. "Any news about Trent?" he asked. Lately that was the only thing he ever said to her.

Emily shook her head. Where was her tongue? Couldn't she pass the time of day with Bob without getting weak-kneed and speechless? "No word yet," she managed to say finally.

"Sorry to hear that." Bob smiled and walked on.

Rachel tugged Emily's hand harder. "*Now* can we go?"

"You will not be rude!" Emily frowned down at Rachel as they walked away from the drugstore and down the street past the millinery, the dress shop, and the general store. Rachel was usually a very easy child to tend, but she had finished school the week before. Emily was finding it hard to keep her entertained while she adjusted to the slower pace of summer.

"I know my dad is better looking than Bob Lavery." Rachel ran to catch up and Emily, forcing away her embarrassment and impatience, slowed her pace.

"Yes, he is." Rachel had never seen Trent, but Emily and the Havlicks often talked to her about him.

"Mr. Lavery has light hair and blue eyes and is as thin as a rail. But my daddy has dark brown hair like Grandpa used to have, and he has dark eyes. He's tall and strong and smart as a whip." Rachel's brown eyes softened and she smiled dreamily. "I've got the best looking, the very nicest daddy in the whole, wide world!"

"He's a fine man all right," Emily said. A lump filled her throat. How could Trent stay away from his own child? Was he dead? He had walked away from his parents and his baby the day they'd buried Celine. Emily slowed her steps even more. A sharp pain at the loss of her best friend shot through her heart.

"And my mamma was the best mamma in the world," Rachel said, looking up at Emily. "Tell me about her."

"I've told you about her almost every day for the past five years."

"But I want to hear it again."

Emily's face softened. "I know you do."

They walked past the street that led to Havlick's Wagon Works, the sound of saws and hammers following them. Trent would be working there right now with Justin and Clay if he were home.

"Your mamma, Celine, grew up in the Blue Creek Orphan Home. She never learned anything about her family, even though she tried, and even though your Grandma Lark helped her check."

"Cause Grandma Lark was raised in the orphan home, too, and when she grew up she found her pa. And she wanted my mamma and all the other children to find theirs."

"That's right. Celine and I met at Sunday school when we were young. I was about four years old then, and Celine was six. But it didn't matter to either of us that she was older. We loved each other and played together as often as we could."

"And you saw each other in school. She was in third grade when you started first. And she finished school two years before you did."

Emily smiled. "Then what?"

"It's the best part. My momma and my daddy fell in love. And they got married and had me. And I have red hair like Momma and brown eyes like Daddy." Rachel leaned her head against Emily's arm as they walked. "Then the worst part happened, the very worst part. Momma died. She went to heaven to be with Jesus. And Daddy ran away because his heart was broken."

Emily nodded. She'd known Celine was in love with Trent Havlick long before he'd known it. She'd known Celine was expecting a baby before Trent knew. But she hadn't known Celine was going to die, or that Trent and Justin would have a terrible fight. And she hadn't known Trent would leave his home and family. In the past ten years he'd sent three post-cards to his parents to let them know he was still alive. The last one had come seven years ago when the United States declared war on Germany. Emily forced away the feeling of dread that often tried to overtake her. Only because she and Trent's family believed God answers prayer did they find hope enough to believe that someday he'd return.

As they walked past the Webber place, Rachel asked, "Why don't you tell Bob Lavery you love him?"

Emily stopped and stared in shock at Rachel. The aroma of coffee drifted out from the Webbers', and a cat meowed from the railing on the porch. "Rachel Havlick! You know good and well Bob is married! It would be a sin to speak to him about love!"

Tears welled up in Rachel's wide, brown eyes. "Don't scold me, Emily," she pleaded.

Emily bent down and pulled Rachel close. "I'm sorry, honey. I didn't mean to be so sharp."

Rachel touched Emily's arm. "Lots of times I have a won-derful dream about you. I dream Daddy will come home and marry you so you can be my momma."

Tears clouded Emily's eyes. "Honey, we all pray he'll come

home. And we all know God will answer. But I wouldn't marry him. We were always friends. We couldn't love each other as a man and a woman should when they marry."

"Why?"

"Because we were friends—your mamma and daddy and me." Emily didn't say she'd feel like a traitor if she married her best friend's husband, but that was what she felt.

Rachel brushed at her tears. "Will Daddy really and truly come home?"

"Yes. He will."

Rachel sighed loud and long. "You've been telling me that as long as I can remember."

"And I'll keep saying it until your daddy comes home."

Rachel gripped Emily's hand as they turned from Main Street onto Hickory. "Will he want me?"

A lump rose in Emily's throat. "Yes, he will."

"Will he love me?"

"Of course!" Emily squeezed Rachel's hand.

"You always say that," Rachel said with a catch in her voice.

"How could he not love you?" Emily asked. But what if something had happened to Trent, making it impossible for him to love anyone, especially his very own daughter, the only part of Celine that was left? Abruptly Emily pushed the terrible thought aside and smiled at Rachel. "We have to hurry. I have to help my mama and papa with the chores."

"Grandma Lark might not be back from the orphanage yet and Grandpa Clay will still be at the Wagon Works."

"Lulu will be there," Emily said.

Rachel sighed. "She won't let me in the kitchen when she's making dinner."

"Well, you'll be playing dolls with Amanda. And I'll be back in the morning. We'll make something special for Mother's Day for your Grandma Lark and your Great-grandma Jennet."

In silence they walked together from the brick sidewalk down the driveway leading to the large home Clay and Lark had

lived in since they were first married over thirty-one years before. Lilac blossoms covered a row of bushes to the left of the
driveway. Red tulips and yellow daffodils made a splash of color
beside the brick walk leading to wide steps and up to the front
door of the white frame and brick house. Emily's horse whinnied in the pen beside the large barn. Many of the barns in
town had been torn down, but Clay wanted to keep his. He'd
finally given up his milk cow when an ordinance was passed
banning cows within the city limits.

Rachel ran up the steps onto the porch and looked down at
Emily. "I will make something for you, too! And I'll pretend
you're my momma."

Laughing, Emily shook her head. She'd heard this often.
"Anyone would be proud to be your mamma, Rachel. You're a
dear, sweet girl."

"And you will marry my daddy and be my momma."

"No, Rachel."

"You can't marry Bob Lavery. So who will you marry?"

Emily's heart turned over, and she thought of August
Theorell in Sweden. She'd been corresponding with him for a
long time. Maybe it was time to agree to marry him, move to
Sweden, and begin a new life. "I'll see you in the morning,"
she said. Emily turned just as a dark haired girl, her arms filled
with dolls, ran into the yard. "Here's Amanda. Have fun."

While the girls greeted each other, Emily ran around the
house to the kitchen door and told Lulu, the housekeeper, she
was leaving for the day. Then she hitched her mare to her
buggy and drove along the brick paved streets lined with
homes and trees, across the railroad tracks and the bridge,
and into farmland.

She knew the entire area had once been covered with pine
trees. Her great-uncle Jig had once walked the woods with old
Clay Havlick, the fur trader. Later Jig had worked with old
Clay's grandson Freeman Havlick, the lumberman. Now the
land was farmland and in the areas that were too hilly for farm-

ing, second growth trees flourished. Papa had said that in another twenty years, the second growth would be big enough to lumber and he hoped lumbermen had learned the importance of replanting. Emily was thankful for the virgin pines still standing. Folks from all over came just to look at them, marvel at their size, and try to imagine that once the entire area had been covered with just such trees.

Emily turned off the road and onto the long lane that led back to her family's farm. The buggy creaked and swayed. She stopped near a shed and jumped to the dusty ground. Chickens, geese, turkeys, and ducks walked about searching for food. A colt nickered in a pen near the big red barn. In the field to the west of the barnyard Emily's brothers were discing. The ninety-five acres they farmed belonged to Freeman Havlick, but they lived there for free and kept the profit from the land. It was part of the deal to guard the white pines.

Emily quickly unhitched the mare and led her to the pen, then ran past several maple trees with tiny, new leaves just emerging to the back door of the house. The aroma of baking bread drifted out and her stomach grumbled with hunger. She walked through the enclosed back porch where a pile of wood was stacked against one wall and a wringer washer stood at the opposite wall. A round tub and an oval shaped copper boiler hung on the wall above the washing machine. She stepped into the warm, cheery kitchen and called, "I'm home."

Martha Bjoerling turned from the stove with a wide smile. Strands of gray hair had pulled loose from the bun at the nape of her neck and clung to her rosy cheeks. A plaid dress hung loosely on her slender frame and was partly covered with a flowered apron she'd made herself. Her blue eyes sparkled. "Another letter came for you today. From Sweden."

Emily wrinkled her nose and grinned. She glanced at the boiling teakettle, and then at her mama. "Did you steam it open and read it?"

Martha chuckled. "I wanted to, but I didn't." She studied Emily closely. "Have you decided how to answer August's proposal?"

"Do you want to get rid of me?"

"Of course not! You know better."

"Does it embarrass you that your oldest daughter is still unmarried?"

"Not one bit!" Martha rubbed her hands down her flowered apron, then shrugged. "Well, maybe just a little. Your sisters are married and having their families. You are every bit as pretty and bright as they are. You could be married if you wanted to."

"I just haven't found the right man, Mama." Emily hoped Mama never learned she was still in love with Bob Lavery.

"Maybe August Theorell is the one. God knows if he is, and he will let you know."

"You're right, of course." Emily hugged Martha, then picked up the letter from the square table that stood in the middle of the kitchen. "I'll read it after I do the chores."

Martha threw up her hands. "Did I get all the curiosity in this whole entire household? I want to rip the letter open and read it right now!"

Emily laughed and tapped the letter against her hand. "I'll let you know what it says." She started for the door that led upstairs.

"Honey," said Martha softly.

Emily turned, then tensed at the look in Mama's eye.

Martha licked her lips and cleared her throat. "Honey, I heard some gossip in town. About you."

"Mother! You know not to believe gossip." Emily tried to laugh, but it died in her throat.

"They said you were making eyes at Bob Lavery."

The strength drained from Emily's body and she gripped the back of a ladder-back chair. "Mama! I never would do that!"

"Emily, if you still have feelings for the man, force them out of your heart before they cause trouble. Loving a married man is wrong, and you know it is!"

"I would never, ever do anything to shame myself or my family."

"I know you mean that, Emily, but at times our feelings can make us do things we wouldn't normally do. It's time for you to seriously consider marrying August."

Emily hung her head. Water boiled out onto the range and danced across the top of it. A floor board creaked as Emily moved toward the doorway.

"For your own good, honey."

"I'll think about it, Mama," Emily whispered.

When her chores were finished, Emily walked past the cabin where Jig had once lived and into the Havlicks' pine forest. She thought of the wild dog she and Jennet had seen, but brushed the thought aside. It wouldn't come this close to the edge of the woods. The letter from August was in her hand, and his proposal weighed on her heart. Could she even consider leaving Michigan . . . and Bob? Tears pricked her eyes as she sank to the pine-needle covered ground and leaned against a giant white pine. It stood arrow straight, about a hundred and sixty feet tall and was about five feet across. Its long, sweeping green branches began about a hundred feet above the ground. Its needles were over four inches long with five in each blue-green bundle. The gray bark was thick and deeply furrowed with narrow scaly ridges. Pines such as the one she leaned against covered the six thousand plus acres of Trent and Justin Havlick's inheritance. Down through the years the forest had always been her refuge. She pressed the letter from August Theorell to her heart. The scent of pine hung heavily in the warm May evening and birds sang all around her, but she didn't notice.

"Is this really the way out?" she whispered through trembling lips. She pulled her knees up to her breast and smoothed her blue skirt down over her long legs. Could she leave? What if she couldn't grow to love August after they were married? She'd loved Bob since she was twelve years old. It wasn't easy to stop loving him. When he'd come home from France with Monique she hadn't stopped loving him. When she'd learned they were to have a child she hadn't stopped loving him. What made her think moving to Sweden and marrying August Theorell would set her heart free?

"I must do something," she whispered hoarsely. August's letter crackled in her hand. He'd be overjoyed if she would marry him, but he wouldn't wait forever for her answer. He dearly wanted a wife—and soon. If she hesitated too long, he'd find someone else. He wanted her to set a time, hopefully before the end of the year. The Great War had been over four years already, so once again traveling was safe.

"Please, Father God, help me to know what to do," she prayed softly.

What would she do if everyone in Blue Creek was talking about her love for Bob? What if Bob learned her terrible secret? She pressed her hands to her blazing cheeks. He'd assumed her love for him had died as easily as his for her. And she'd let him believe it to keep her pride.

"I will marry August," she said harshly. "I will marry him just as soon as I can make arrangements to leave."

Her heart sank and she covered her face with trembling hands.

CHAPTER

3

♦ With a groan that tore through his tight throat, Trent Havlick stopped his 1915 Dodge at the edge of Freeman and Jennet's property and stared across the freshly plowed field toward the large white frame house where they'd lived since they were first married more than fifty years before. Were they still alive? Were they home this Sunday afternoon just as they had been every Sunday all the years he was growing up in Blue Creek? Trent narrowed his dark eyes and tugged at his dotted blue and white tie. He had to expect changes in the ten years he'd been gone. He rubbed an unsteady hand over his clean shaven jaw, then settled his plaid cap firmly in place. He'd given up his slanted high heeled boots and his wide-brimmed Stetson when he left the Rocking R Ranch in Texas to come back to Michigan. The clatter of his car engine seemed loud in the silence of the countryside. He leaned forward and switched off the ignition, then slumped back in the seat. The silence after the engine died seemed deafening. He felt like an intruder.

The warm May breeze blew against him, bringing the heavy smell of pine and newly turned soil. He glanced at the acres and acres of forest to his left where he and Celine had spent hours walking and talking and planning their future together, then he looked quickly away before the pain of remembering overwhelmed him. His mother had taught him to walk the woods in safety; then he'd taught Celine. She had loved the flowers and birds and wildlife and woods as much as he did.

"I won't think about her," he whispered hoarsely as he gripped the steering wheel until the knuckles of his sun-browned hands turned white.

Why had he come back? There was nothing in Blue Creek for him but heartache and a rage so deep it frightened him.

"It's Mother's Day," Trent whispered. "I've come to visit my mother." Why had he suddenly felt he should be home this Mother's Day? When he hadn't come for ten years? But he knew why. Several of the ranch hands he worked with had talked about their plans for Mother's Day and suddenly he'd longed to see his own mother. Would he find her happy and well? Would she be glad to see him after ten years with little contact? He'd stopped at his parents' house in Blue Creek, but no one was home. He figured they were at Grandma's for dinner just as they had been every Sunday for all the years he was home.

Trent groaned again. Ten years was a long time in one way. In another, only a flash. Could he find the courage to drive the rest of the way to the farm house and face his family? Would he be able to get the money he needed to buy the Rocking R? It was home now. When the opportunity came to buy it, he jumped at it. Now, all he needed was money—money that was rightfully his.

For the first time he realized the road was smoother. Once it had been a corduroy road made of logs, but now it was covered with gravel, making driving less bumpy.

He heard the caw of a crow, the melodies of many birds, and the bawl of a cow with a new calf. He dared not let the memories the sounds were threatening to resurrect get past the block in his mind. He'd see his family and stay a couple of days, just long enough to convince Justin to buy his share of the pines, then he would head back down to Texas and buy the Rocking R. He had a life there that was different from the one he'd lived in Michigan and he was close to being happy.

Happy? How does happy feel? If he reached back into his memories he could remember that once he'd been happy, very happy. Blissfully happy. But remembering that would mean remembering Celine and he'd walled off all memories of her when she died. The pain of losing her had been more than he could stand. If he remembered their happiness, retracing their life together and their dreams for the future—dreams that died with Celine—eventually he'd have to remember how he'd felt when she died. He'd walled off those feelings, too. He'd simply walked away, leaving the pain here, along with his family, his friends—his life.

That was why he left and that was why he hadn't returned. Now, sitting in the quiet, staring down the gravel road leading to his grandparents' home, he couldn't stop the memories filling his mind. Sweat broke out on his forehead and he struggled to breathe.

He had kissed Celine and said, "Are you sure you'll be all right for a few minutes? I'll be back in less than an hour."

"I'll be all right," she answered with a tired smile. Her red hair was splayed across the white pillow under her head, and her face was as white as the pillowcase. Beside the bed in the wooden cradle Grandpa Freeman had built lay their tiny newborn daughter, Rachel—her hair as red as Celine's.

"Are you sure?" Trent ran a gentle finger down her pale cheek. "I shouldn't be leaving you, the way you're feeling and all."

"I'll be fine. Your mom is coming later today, if she can."

"But I told her I'd be home all day. She won't know there's a need to come."

Celine smiled weakly. "Women have babies every day. Don't worry."

25

Trent lifted Celine's small hand to his lips and kissed it. "I love you." His voice broke as a wave of love almost sent him to his knees.

"And I love you." Love blazed from her eyes as she caught his hand and pulled it to her lips. "You gave me a beautiful home and a beautiful baby. It's more than I ever thought possible."

"You're no longer an orphan without a family." He bent down and kissed her warm lips. "We're a family. The whole Havlick clan is your family now."

Celine laughed softly. "And we'll keep adding to it."

"Yes! We will! I give you my word. But I must take a contract to Justin to sign so it can go out in today's mail. It really won't take me long." He bent over and kissed her again. "I love you."

"I love you," she whispered.

He touched the soft fuzz of red hair on Rachel's tiny head, then hurried to his buggy to drive to town to the Wagon Works. The two huge factory buildings were buzzing with activity. The wide front doors were open to give the men fresh air as they built and painted the wagons.

Justin hurried out of the office to meet Trent on the lawn in front. He looked worried.

"Here's the contract," Trent said, handing a folder to Justin.

Even though both parted their hair on the right, they often made an effort not to dress alike so others could tell them apart. But still they would find they'd chosen the same clothes accidentally. This day they'd both chosen the same blue plaid shirt and dark pants. The difference was that sweat stood on Justin's wide forehead and soaked the front of his shirt. Celine said she could tell them apart because Justin usually had a worried look and Trent a smile.

"Gabe Ingersol is trying to back out of his contract and we have over half his wagons built." Justin gripped Trent's arm.

26

"Will you talk to him? Right now he's at the boarding house but plans to be on the five o'clock train." Justin rubbed an unsteady hand across his face. "We can't afford to lose Gabe's contract. You've got to talk to him. He'll listen to you. You have a way with people that I don't have."

"I can't," Trent said. "I have to get back to Celine right away." Already he was turning away. It was a fifteen minute drive to their farm and he couldn't leave her alone any longer.

Justin stabbed his long fingers through his thick dark hair. Deep furrows ran across his forehead. "It won't take you long. It's really important."

"Yes, but Celine is more important. And we both know Gabe. He's a talker. If I have to cut him off, he'll drop us for sure."

"But you have to see him, Trent! We can't afford to lose this contract."

Trent sighed heavily and nodded. "All right. I'll go see him if you'll ride out and stay with Celine. Or get Mom to go."

"I'll take care of it. Mom's gone with Dad to Big Pine, so I'll ride out myself. I'll stay with her until you get home."

Trent looked long and hard at Justin who often forgot everything when he got busy. "You won't get busy and forget, will you?"

"No. On my word as a Havlick, I won't forget. I have to finish one thing. Then I'll go."

Trent laughed and clamped his hand on Justin's shoulder. "Then I'll do it and get home as soon as I can. Thanks, Just."

"Thank you, Trent. We make great partners."

"That we do."

They smiled at each other and the strain left Justin's face.

Trent drove to the boarding house, his mind on Celine. He forced it on business as he met with Gabe in the boarding house lobby. Their business did indeed take longer than Justin had thought. But finally Gabe agreed to honor the contract and Trent drove home as fast as possible on the rough corduroy. At times the buggy bounced so hard he had to brace himself to keep his balance. The buggy top shielded him from the hot sun.

At home he stopped the buggy outside the white fence in front of the house. He looked around with a frown. Where was Justin's buggy? Feeling a sudden unease, he ran into the house, leaving the door wide open. The anguished cry of the baby sent chills down his spine.

"Celine!" he shouted as he ran through the hallway toward their bedroom. The baby's cry faded to a soft whimper.

At the bedroom doorway, he stopped short. Celine lay on the floor in a crumpled heap. She was surrounded by a pool of blood. With a cry of anguish, Trent dropped beside her and pulled her into his arms.

"Celine! Oh, Celine, what happened? You can't be dead! No! No!"

The next two days were a blur. The doctor came and looked at Celine. He said she'd hemorrhaged and died from loss of blood. Someone came and cared for the baby. Someone else came and cleaned the blood from the floor. Others brought food. Mostly people stood around crying, talking to him, patting him. He went for long walks in the forest. But he never went back into the bedroom where she died.

On the day of the funeral, they buried Celine's body in the cemetery in Blue Creek, and then they gathered at Trent's place. Justin pulled Trent outside away from the house bursting with friends and relatives.

"I'm so sorry about Celine," Justin said.

"I know you are."

Justin's face paled and he trembled. "I intended to drive right out to stay with her like I said I would, but I got busy."

Blood pounded in Trent's ears. Had he heard Justin correctly? "You mean you didn't check on her at all?"

"I'm sorry." Justin blanched as he shook his head. "I planned to."

Anger ripped through Trent and he clenched his fists at his sides. "Celine would still be alive today if you had!"

"Don't say that," Justin whispered, trembling harder.

"It's true! You know that, don't you?"

Justin hung his head. "I know," he whispered in anguish.

Trent leaped at Justin and hit him in the face. Justin jumped back, holding up his arms to shield himself from more blows. Trent lunged at Justin. They fell to the ground and Trent pounded his fists into Justin while Justin tried to get away without fighting back.

Clay and Freeman heard the fight and ran to them. Clay grabbed Trent while Freeman held Justin.

"Stop it, boys!" Clay cried. "Fighting on this day of all days!"

Trent ignored his pa and glared at Justin. "I'll never forgive you for this as long as I live!"

"What are you saying?" Clay asked in alarm.

Justin stood in silence with his head down.

Without a word of explanation or goodbye, Trent had left on the train that day and hadn't been back since, until now. He shuddered as he forced himself back to the present.

"I can't face him," Trent said with a moan. "I'll kill him if I see him." He rubbed sweat off his forehead and a steel bar tightened around his dead heart.

The quiet shattered as he started the engine and shifted into reverse, grinding the gears. He would leave this place and *never* return. There was nothing here but pain and anger. Let Justin keep the forest and the Wagon Works. Let Justin keep *everything,* including his guilt. He'd find another way to get the money he needed to buy the ranch.

Just as the car began to move, another memory settled in his mind—a tiny pink face surrounded by a fluff of red hair. Rachel. Tiny, beautiful Rachel. Celine's baby. His child. He'd left her, too, and for ten years he'd blocked all thought of her.

He stopped the car again, helpless to stop the memories.

It was early morning when Celine's gasp woke him. Quickly he turned to her.

"It's all right," she said. "Our baby is coming."

"Now?"

"Yes," she said, a broad smile covering her face.

He jumped out of bed and drew on his clothes. "I'll get help."

"No," Celine said. "There isn't time. Please stay with me."

He sat by the bed, holding her hands, stroking her hair, gently wiping the perspiration from her face, kissing her, and feeling helpless, until she told him it was time and what he needed to do.

He saw the red fuzz of hair, cradled the tiny head in his hands—amazed at how small it was, and gently guided the shoulders until he was holding a new life. With his own lips he sucked the mucus from the tiny throat and then he watched the tiny body turn pink as she began to breathe. He laid her gently in Celine's arms and together they counted the toes and fingers and kissed the tiny nose and eyes. She was the most beautiful creature Trent had ever seen and the love he felt for her and Celine overwhelmed him until tears of joy ran down his face.

In time he drove into town to get his mother, and Lark had cried, too. She went to his home with him and, while Celine slept, Lark bathed the baby, wrapped her in a pink blanket, and gave her to Trent with instructions to sit in the rocking chair and get acquainted with his daughter.

He held her nestled in the crook of his arm and when she opened her eyes, he was sure she could see his face.

"Hello, Rachel," he crooned. "We've been waiting for you. I'm your daddy and I'll always take care of you and your momma."

That had been the most wonderful day of his life and the next three days the most awful. When he learned his brother was responsible for Celine's death, he'd left Rachel as though she had died, too.

I'll have to see her, he thought. *Maybe that's really why I came back.*

He shifted into first and drove forward slowly. He'd come this far. He would see the family, talk to Justin, and then leave immediately. He didn't know what he would do about Rachel. Probably nothing. He didn't know her and he didn't think he could allow himself to get to know her. He certainly didn't know anything about little girls. Most likely she was fine with his parents and ought to stay there. The only thing he knew with certainty was that he would never forgive Justin.

Trent glanced at the dirt lane that led to Andree Bjoerling's home. Giant pines made a wall along the edge of the field. Pines on the high hills behind made the wall seem even higher. He pulled his eyes off the pines and saw a woman walking in the middle of the lane, a bouquet of purple and white lilacs in her hand. Something about her looked familiar. Trent studied her; then his eyes widened. "Emily!" he whispered. "It's Emily."

Trembling, Trent stopped the car and stepped out beside it. She was fifteen when he left, so that would make her twenty-five—five years younger than he. She was wearing a calf-length blue dress with a darker blue belt at her hips. Her long black hair flowed over her slender shoulders and down her back. She was probably married with children. A picture of her and Celine laughing and talking together flashed through his mind. They had been best friends.

Emily saw him and waved. "Hi, Justin," she called. "You're late for dinner, aren't you?" She'd been invited to join the Havlicks for dinner, but had declined. She'd felt a tension lately that she didn't understand. It seemed to have something to do with Justin, and wasn't just that he worked himself into the ground without a thought of his wife and children. Jennet had mentioned she felt the same tension. When she was only a

31

few feet away, Emily said, "I see you've bought another auto-mobile. You and your gas machines. You change so often, I can't keep up!"

Trent's nerves tightened. She thought he was Justin. Nervously he rubbed his clean shaven jaw. Justin had always talked about growing a beard, so Trent had never grown one. But when he left he'd tried to stop looking like his twin. Evidently he'd failed.

Emily's breath caught in her throat, and her eyes searched Trent's face. Was she seeing things? "You're not Justin," she said cautiously. "Trent?"

He nodded.

The lilacs tumbled from Emily's hands and scattered in the dust at her feet. "Is it really you?"

"In the flesh." Tears stung his eyes. Her face looked almost the same, but she definitely wasn't the teenaged girl she'd been when he left.

"Where've you been all this time?"

"Here and there. In Texas on a ranch the last several years."

"Why didn't you write?"

"I . . . couldn't." He'd tried often but, except for the three postcards, had crumpled all the letters and thrown them away.

Her lip quivered. "Is it really you?"

He nodded. "Yes, it's really me. It's good to see you."

"I can't believe it. Ten years is a long time. You still look like Justin. But your skin is as dark as an Indian's, and Justin doesn't own a suit like that." Her head was spinning and she knew she sounded silly. She'd waited so long for him to return, had prayed earnestly for his return. Now, here he was.

"You look ready to faint, Emily," Trent said as he stepped toward her. "Maybe you should sit in my automobile."

"No, thanks, but I'll be all right." She swayed and he caught her arm.

"Please, sit down a while."

She gripped his hand for fear he'd vanish into thin air if she didn't hold on to him. "You caught me by surprise. We prayed for your return. Rachel needs you."

His head spun. "Ah, Rachel. How is she?"

"Oh, Trent. She's beautiful! She has Celine's hair and your eyes. She's curious, and smart, and funny, and serious, and well-behaved, and naughty. She's a wonderful child. And she's very anxious to have her daddy back."

"Does she . . . hate me?"

"Oh, no. I've tried to help her understand the pain you suffered when Celine died."

Trent trembled. The pain was still as great as it was ten years before, perhaps worse.

"Are you all right?" Emily whispered, patting Trent's muscled arm.

He breathed deeply and forced back the anguish. "I'll be fine."

She looked into his face. How dark and handsome he was! "Are you sure?"

He nodded. "Tell me about yourself. Did you marry Bob Lavery?"

Emily flushed hotly. "He married a French girl, Monique, while he was in France during the war."

"But you still love him."

Emily ducked her head. "I can't help myself. It shows, doesn't it?"

He nodded. "Just as I can't stop loving Celine."

Emily looked into Trent's dark eyes. "You do understand! No one else does."

"I do." Trent's face softened. Knowing Emily understood his love for Celine would never die somehow made him feel better.

"I've missed you," Emily whispered brokenly.

"I've thought about you a lot." Slowly he pulled Emily close and they clung to each other, sharing the pain of loss. He felt the softness of her body and smelled the scent of lilac in her hair. She was no longer the little girl he'd played with. She was a woman.

She pressed closer to him and felt the thud of his heart and smelled a hint of sweat and leather. His chest was broader and his muscles stronger than when he left.

Finally he held her from him. "Since Bob is married, what does the future hold for you?"

She clung to his work-roughened hand. "I'm going to marry a man in Sweden."

"You don't say!"

Emily told Trent about August and even about the gossip around town that she was still in love with Bob. She tried to sound excited about a marriage to August, even though she didn't feel excited. She didn't want Trent to think she had no other choices. He listened quietly until she ran out of things to say. Her voice caught when she finished with, "But I do hate to leave Rachel."

"Why her especially?"

"I've been taking care of her."

"I thought she stayed with Mom and Dad."

"She does, but they needed some help, and hired me. I've been taking care of her for eight years. Oh, wait'll you see her! She looks a lot like Celine, but she's like you, too."

A muscle jumped in Trent's jaw.

"She's smart, Trent! And she has a sense of humor like yours. Her giggle is just like Celine's!"

He forced back a groan of anguish.

"Now that you're back, my leaving won't be so hard on her."

Trent looked off across the field, then back at Emily. "I don't intend to stay."

She stiffened. "What?"

"I only came to see the family and get some money."

"But why won't you stay?"

"I can't."

"Rachel needs you."

"She doesn't even know me."

"I've told her about you. She has even tried to understand why you left her."

Trent's jaw tightened. "I'd best be getting to the house."

Emily gripped his hand with both of hers. "Please don't break Rachel's heart."

"It's none of your concern, Emily."

His words stung her. She lifted her chin as pink stained her cheeks. "I love Rachel."

Trent sighed and nodded tiredly. "I'm sorry, Emily. It's hard for me to be here. I'd rather drive back down to Texas without seeing anyone."

"Don't you dare! Your family wants you back!"

"I doubt that." Trent took a deep, shuddering breath. "I came this far, so I'll see them. But I won't stay. I can't stay here. And I can't suddenly be a daddy."

Giant tears filled Emily's blue eyes and slowly ran down her cheeks. "We've all waited so long for you to come home. Please, please don't leave again."

"I can't stay."

"Stay a week. Only a week. And if you still must leave, then you can go."

Trent shook his head. He couldn't take the agony for an entire week.

"Then stay three days! You can do that. Can't you, Trent?"

He saw the pleading in her eyes and weakened. Then slowly he nodded. He pulled out his handkerchief and gently wiped away her tears. "Okay. I'll stay three days. But that's all."

Emily hugged him and smiled. "Thank you! You'll be glad."

"I doubt that." He looked toward the big farmhouse and realized he couldn't go alone. He turned back to Emily. "I need you to do something for me."

"Anything!"

"Go with me. I can't face the family alone."

Emily hesitated. "But I'd be intruding."

"I need you. This is going to be very hard for me. Besides, Rachel might need you. It'll be a shock to have me suddenly turn up."

"Rachel has looked for you every single day since she was old enough to know about you. She'll be thrilled to see you."

"Don't do this to me, Emily!"

"I'm sorry. I was thinking about her."

"I've come this far on my own, but I can't walk into that house by myself. Will you go with me?"

"All right. I'll go."

"Thank you." Trent opened the automobile door. "I'm glad to see you haven't bobbed your hair."

"I'm considering it."

"Please don't. I like the way you look."

"Things can't stay the same forever, Trent."

"I know."

Emily stood beside the running board and studied him. Fine lines spread from the corners of his eyes into his dark hair. The great sadness in his eyes tugged at her heart. "What about you, Trent? Have you found someone else?"

"No. Celine was my life. When she died, I died, too."

"It's been ten years! You need someone. You can't live your whole life without love and companionship."

"I can try." He'd had other women, but he didn't tell Emily that. It would shock her to know how he'd lived.

She saw the harsh look in his eyes and knew he was no longer the gentle country boy who'd left home at twenty. Weakly she stepped up on the running board and slipped onto the seat.

CHAPTER

4

♦ Dust billowed behind the Dodge as Trent drove slowly along the road leading to his grandparents' home. Bright green spring grass covered the ditches and a few dandelions poked out bright yellow heads. The tires crunched loudly on the gravel. He glanced at Emily sitting beside him with her hands locked together in her lap. "I don't know if I can do it, Emily."

She tensed even more. He musn't leave after coming this far! "You can face them, Trent. They love you."

"I doubt that."

"It's true."

He slowed the automobile even more. "How are Grandma and Grandpa?"

"Just fine. Free is still building buggies. It takes him longer, of course. But you know him. He hates to give in to the automobile."

Trent chuckled. "Sounds like him."

"And Jennet spends a lot of time walking in the pines. She has been waiting for you to get home so she can talk to you and Justin about an idea she has."

"What is it?"

"No one knows. She says it's a secret that she can tell only when you're here."

"What do you *think* it is?"

"I think it is about the pines, but I don't know what she has in mind. She says it is her dream, the fulfillment of Great-grandpa Clay's dream. When she mentions it, her eyes shine and she gets a little weepy."

"There are only two things to do with them—leave them alone or cut them down. Which do you think she'd want to do?"

"Well, she'd never want to cut them!" Emily hadn't meant to raise her voice, but she was almost shouting.

"Hold it!" Trent said. "I'm just discussing the choices."

"Cutting them isn't a choice." Emily managed to control the volume of her voice, but she couldn't avoid the angry tone. Hearing Trent say the words, even in passing, made her very angry. And when she thought of the sacrifices his family and hers had made and the danger they'd faced to protect and pre-serve the trees, cutting them was unthinkable.

"Do you have any idea what those trees would be worth if they were lumbered?" Trent asked. "Why, we could give away half the money—do all kinds of charitable things with it—and still be wealthy for many generations. But just standing there, they're not worth anything but trouble."

Emily was seething inside. She'd never thought she would hear a Havlick speak of lumbering the pines.

"They're your inheritance," she whispered. "Doesn't that mean anything to you?"

"No, not any more. Nothing means anything to me now. I want to sell them and use the money to buy the Rocking R. And since they're half mine, I intend to sell my half. If not to Justin, then to someone else."

"That would break Jennet's heart and your mother's as well, Trent. I don't know how you could even think of such a thing."

"I'm just being practical. We have to do something with them besides let them just stand there."

Emily's head was spinning and for a moment she had forgotten where they were going and why, until Trent stopped the car.

"What's wrong?" she asked.

"How can I face them after all this time?" Trent rested his forehead on the steering wheel. The anguish on his face broke her heart and melted her anger.

"You can." Emily patted Trent's hand. "Your family wants you, Trent. They've missed you more than you'll ever know. Just promise me you won't mention this crazy idea until you've heard Jennet's plan."

"What about Grandpa Baritt?"

"He and Mercy are on an extended trip out east. Your mom was sad to see him go. And he'll be sorry he missed you, but he wanted to take Mercy on a trip since he didn't when they were first married. They planned to go a few years ago; then the war broke out and they couldn't. This time your grandpa said nothing would stop him from taking his bride on a trip." Mercy Kettering had become the matron at the orphan's home just before Lark and Clay married. She was responsible for turning the home into a happy, loving place, rather than the dismal, harsh prison it had been for Lark. And then she'd met Matt Baritt and they'd fallen in love and married. Matt was Lark's father who had left her at the orphanage when she was an infant. When they finally got together again, he'd tried to make up for all he'd missed with Lark by helping Mercy with the children in her care. Together they had made many homeless children very happy. "He still refers to Mercy as his 'bride' even though they've been married twenty years," Emily said. "It's very romantic."

"You and Celine were so alike—always ready for a good love story."

"You have a soft heart, too, Trent Havlick."

"Not any longer," he said coldly.

A chill ran down her spine at the sound of his voice and the look on his face.

Trent drove slowly up the lane between lilac bushes in bloom and some young pines. He noticed several fruit trees in the yard that hadn't been there before. The barns, sheds, and house looked in good repair. Dairy cattle dotted a large green pasture that had been a cornfield when Trent left. "Dairy cows?" he asked as he lifted his dark brow questioningly.

Emily nodded. "Tristan and Zoe live on the farm with your grandparents and they run the dairy farm. They've been here for the last five years. My pa helps raise feed for the cows and my brothers help with the chores."

"Are those little guys big enough to do that?"

Emily laughed. "They're not so little any more. Lars is eighteen, Neil is seventeen, and Dag is sixteen, and all are almost as big as you are."

Trent stopped the car behind a black Ford and sighed. "They're ten years older."

"We all are," said Emily softly.

Trent gripped the steering wheel more tightly as he stared at the three story white frame house with the wrap-around porch. He and Justin had played on the porch during rainy summer days. They'd worked in the fields spring, summer, and fall. The Havlicks believed in hard work. Even though they had the money to hire their work done, they did most of it themselves. He was glad for that. Hard work the past ten years had kept him from ending his life. Now he was back to face the family again. Could Emily hear the wild thud of his heart? Did she know just how frightened he felt? She'd always been able to understand him. "I can't go in," he said hoarsely.

"Yes, you can, Trent. I'll be right beside you." Emily opened the automobile door and stepped out, then walked around and opened the door for Trent. "Come on. You can do it. You didn't come all this way to back out now. You always had lots of courage. I expect you still do."

With a loud sigh Trent stepped to the ground and stood beside Emily. Chickens cackled and a turkey gobbled in a pen beside the chicken coop. Wind whirred the blades of the windmill pumping water into a large tank. A Dalmatian ran up to Trent and sniffed his hand. "Sears, Jr.?" asked Trent, bending down to the dog.

"No. Junior died several years ago. This is Betsy, his daughter." Emily patted Betsy's head while Trent stroked her side. Sears had walked the line with Lark when she'd guarded the pines for Clay before they were married. He'd saved her many times. He'd lived to be fifteen. Junior was his pup and he'd learned to walk the line, too. Both dogs had a special place in all their hearts. "Betsy belongs to Tris and Zoe. Your mother did have her in town, but didn't feel right about keeping her there where she couldn't run free."

At the sound of an automobile coming up the lane, Emily turned and recognized Justin's car. Sunlight glinted off the windshield. Shivers ran down her back and she locked her hands together as he stopped the 1921 black Duesenberg behind Trent's blue Dodge. She darted a look at Trent and saw the stubborn set of his jaw and the angry sparks shooting from his dark eyes.

"Relax, Trent. It's your brother," Emily said. She hoped whatever had caused their fight just before Trent left had been forgotten. But Trent stiffened as he watched his twin step from the Duesenberg. His voice failed him and all the strength seemed to leave his body.

Emily looked from Trent to Justin and back again. They were identical except that Trent was wearing a suit and Justin a white shirt open at the throat and dark pants. Trent was dark-skinned from working outdoors. Next to him Justin looked almost sickly from working indoors behind a desk. She felt the tension grow between them as they studied each other. Would

Justin break the ice and give Trent a bear hug? She hoped he would, but as his eyes narrowed she knew he wouldn't.

"So you decided to stop pouting and come home to your responsibilities," Justin said sharply, his eyes boring into Trent's. "It's about time."

"Murderer!" Trent snarled as rage boiled up and out of him.

Emily frowned. What could Trent mean?

With a loud bellow Trent leaped at Justin, his fists flying. Justin dodged the blows and threw a punch that connected with Trent's shoulder.

"Stop!" Emily cried, helplessly wringing her hands. "Stop it!"

Trent flung himself at Justin again and they fell to the ground, rolling on the dusty lane, punching and shouting angrily. Betsy barked frantically as she raced back and forth from the men to Emily.

"Sit, Betsy!" commanded Emily.

With a whine and her head at a tilt, Betsy sat on her haunches and watched the fighting.

Emily doubled her fists at her sides and shouted louder, "Trent! Justin! Stop it right now!"

Trent tasted blood and dust, but his anger was too hot to feel the pain of Justin's blows or to hear Emily's shouts. In his mind he saw the shovels of dirt falling on Celine's casket, filling her grave. He grabbed Justin's throat and pressed both his thumbs into his brother's windpipe.

Justin struggled and broke Trent's hold, then broke free enough to get in hard punches to Trent's jaw and stomach.

Emily shot a look toward the house, expecting any minute to see the door fly open and the family run out. Maybe they were in the dining room, still sitting around the table, laughing and talking, and couldn't hear the racket. Or maybe they were gathered around the piano singing the way they liked to do when they got together.

Should she run and get Clay or Tris? No. She'd find a way to stop the fight without them. She thought of the dog fights she'd stopped in the past and wondered if it would work on Justin and Trent. She ran to the water tank and filled a bucket with the icy cold water, then ran back to the men, water splashing onto her leg and foot. With a mighty heave she flung the water onto the fighting men. They parted with strangled gasps.

"Stop fighting right now," she commanded in a no-nonsense voice.

Water streaming down him, Trent glared at Justin. "I didn't come to fight. I came to sell you my share of the pines." Trent slowly stood in the grass beside Emily, his clothes wet and muddy, his breathing ragged.

"Your nose is bleeding," said Emily, pushing her hanky into his hand.

His chest heaving, he held the small white cloth to his nose, all the while watching Justin.

With a groan Justin stood. His once white shirt was soaked with water and covered with dirt and blood. The buttons had popped off and it hung open, revealing his undershirt. His left eye was already swollen shut, and his nose was bleeding. He pulled out his handkerchief and wiped his face and nose. "I won't even talk to you about the pines," he snapped.

Anger churned inside Trent, but he managed to control it. "You're going to buy out my share so I can get out of here."

"Not on your life!" Justin knotted his fists at his sides. "You're going to do your share at the Wagon Works. I've worked like a slave the past ten years while you were off wandering the earth. And I'm tired of it."

Trent growled low in his throat. He wanted to knock the air out of Justin, but he didn't move. "I'll never work with you again. You saw to that ten years ago."

Emily looked from one to the other. What had happened ten

years ago besides Celine's death? What caused the rage between these two brothers?

"What's done is done," snapped Justin. "I need help at the
Wagon Works."

"Then hire somebody!"

"Nobody can do what you've been trained to do the way you
can do it, and you know it."

"Then let the business fail!"

Justin trembled. "It's come close to doing just that because
you weren't here. But I wouldn't let it. Nor would Pa."

Emily saw their rage was reaching the boiling point again.
"Look at you two!" she cried, waving her arm. "You're both a
mess! The family will see you like this. Is that what you
want?"

Trent tore his eyes from Justin and looked down at himself
with a scowl. He didn't want Rachel or Mom to see him in such
a mess. "I have a change of clothes in my Dodge."

"Then get them," Emily ordered. "What about you, Justin?"

"Grandpa always keeps clean clothes in the buggy shop,"
Justin said, his eyes hard on Trent. "We can change in there."

"I'll change in the barn," Trent said stiffly. He didn't intend
to be alone with Justin now or ever.

"Both of you get a move on," Emily snapped.

Justin limped to the buggy shop while Trent lifted his satchel
from his automobile.

"I'm sorry you had to see that, Emily," he said.

"I'm sorry it happened," she said sharply. "You both know
better. Fighting never solves anything."

"I told you I should leave."

"Well, you can't. You promised to stay three days."

Trent shrugged, then nodded. "Three days. It'll seem like
three years." He limped across the yard to the barn. Horses
nickered in the pen and a colt kicked up his heels and whinnied. The barn smelled just like it always had. He stopped just

inside, waited until his eyes adjusted to the dimness, and looked at the clean-swept wooden floor and the thick hand-hewn support posts. He'd kissed Celine for the very first time on the very spot where he was standing.

"You can't catch me, Trent Havlick!" Celine had called, gig-gling as she ran to the far end of the barn. She was fifteen and he was eighteen.

He put down the fork he was using to clean the stall. "And why would I want to catch you, little girl? I have my eye on a full-grown woman I met in Big Pine."

Celine's eyes flashed. "I'm not a little girl! I'm almost a full-grown woman." She walked slowly toward him, looking ready to cry. "Who'd you meet in Big Pine?"

"Marlene van Tol."

"Does she come from a fine family?"

"Yes."

"So, she's not an orphan like I am?"

"No."

"You plan to marry her?"

"Did I say anything about marrying anyone?"

The sparkle came back to Celine's eyes and she giggled again. "I'll bet she can't run as fast as I can!" She tapped Trent's arm, then dashed away. "You're It! Can't catch me!"

He ran after her and almost caught her in the last stall, but she scrambled up in the manger and ducked across into the next stall.

"Can't catch me, Trent Havlick!" Celine jumped from the manger and almost landed in a pile of manure. "You didn't clean this yet. Better get a move on before your grandpa sees this and thinks you've been playing instead of working."

"Grandpa knows I'm a hard worker." Trent stood outside the stall and grinned. He acted as though he didn't care if he caught her or not.

Celine stepped a little closer to him. "Emily and I have a secret."

"Oh?"

"She knows who I love and I know who she loves."

"Are you going to tell me?"

"No! And you can't make me!"

Quick as a cat he caught her and pulled her hard against him. His pulse leaped as they touched, startling him. She was little Celine Graybill from the orphan home and he'd known her all his life.

"You can't make me tell," she whispered, her hazel eyes wide in her pale face.

He looked at her moist lips and wanted to kiss her. He lowered his head, then waited for her to struggle to get away. She stood quietly in his arms, her heart beating against him. He touched his lips to hers. Sparks shot through him and he jumped away, alarmed at how he felt.

"I'm sorry," he whispered, struggling to keep his desire from her.

"I'm not sorry a bit," she had said, flipping her hair with a soft laugh. She'd run to the open barn door, turned, then blew him a kiss.

Now he closed his eyes and felt the warmth of her lips and the softness of her body. It had been ten long years since he'd kissed her. And no other woman had ever filled the need in him that she had. "Celine," he whispered raggedly.

His shoulders sagged and tears burned his eyes. Slowly he walked to the room where the hired man slept when they had one. He changed into a wrinkled, but clean plaid shirt and faded jeans he'd worn many times at the Rocking R. He brushed his hair, wincing when he hit a swollen spot. Fresh anger at Justin flared. He was without Celine because of Justin.

"I hate him," Trent said grimly.

He left his bag and wet clothes, then strode out into the bright sunlight just as Justin walked out of the buggy shop. They stopped and stared at each other. Betsy ran to Justin and pressed against his leg.

"No fighting!" Emily cried, running to stand between them. "Let's go inside and see the family."

"If he has the courage," Justin said, glaring at Trent.

Trent took a menacing step toward Justin, but Emily caught his arm and held him back.

"Please, no more fighting! At least not now."

"I won't fight again," said Trent harshly.

"If you ever do, you'd better plan to finish what you start," Justin said gruffly.

Trent reached for all the willpower in him, found it, and was able to keep from tearing Justin in two.

Her hand through Trent's arm, Emily walked between the men up the steps and onto the back porch. She smelled ham, but she knew dinner would've been over long ago. They were probably upset that Justin hadn't made it on time. She knew he was often late. They walked into the empty kitchen. Dirty dishes were stacked on the table for the hired girl to wash later. The aroma of coffee came from a pot simmering at the back of the stove. The kitchen felt too warm from the fire in the wood-burning cookstove.

"Is that you, Just?" called Freeman. "We're in the front room."

"Grab a plate of food if you're hungry," called Jennet.

Hearing their voices sent shivers over Trent. Many times in his dreams he'd heard them call him, only to wake up and find himself with strangers in a strange place.

"I'm not hungry," called Justin, darting a look at Trent. He lowered his voice. "It's not too late to go back where you've been."

Trent stiffened. "I'm going to see the family." He groped for Emily's hand and held on tightly.

She wanted to ease his tension, but couldn't find any words to speak that would help. Instead she prayed silently for him and for Justin and for Rachel and the others in the front room.

Justin scowled at Emily. "You always did take his side. You should've learned by now you can't count on him."

"Please, Justin," she said softly. "This should be a happy time for the family. Both of you work to put aside whatever is wrong for their sakes."

"He won't," Trent snapped, jerking his head toward his brother. "He's always thought of himself first and only."

"Just a minute, now." Justin stepped toward Trent, but Emily touched his arm and shook her head. He glowered at Trent, but finally turned away and headed through the wide hall that led to the front room.

His stomach a hard knot and holding Emily's hand in a firmer grip, Trent followed. He was too nervous to notice if the house looked the same. He heard the heavy tick of the grandfather clock, or was the sound he heard the pounding of his heart?

Justin stepped into the front room. Someone said, "Well, you're here!"

"I'm not alone," he answered over the noise.

Trent paused in the doorway, gripping Emily's hand so tightly she almost cried out in pain. A hush settled over the room. His glance darted around until he found his mother. She looked the same—soft brown eyes that could see into his heart, her hair pulled back loosely and pinned at the back of her head, slender build, and a spirit that couldn't be dampened. She wore a pale green dress and black, one-strap slippers. "Happy Mother's Day, Mom," he said with a catch in his voice.

Lark gasped and, for a minute, couldn't move. Then she shot from her chair, ran across the room, and flung her arms around Trent.

Emily stepped quickly to Rachel's side, who was staring speechlessly at Trent. Rachel pressed her face against Emily's arm.

"Son! You're home! At last, at last!" Lark kissed Trent all

over his face, then clung to him. Finally she stepped back and looked him up and down. Before she could speak again, Clay grabbed him and hugged him tightly. Gray streaked Clay's dark hair and deep lines were etched down the sides of his nose.

"Is it my daddy?" Rachel whispered loudly as she looked up at Emily.

"Yes," Emily answered, giving Rachel a hug.

"It is," Clay said as he stepped aside and gestured for Rachel to come to Trent.

Trent stared in shock at the red-haired girl. He was looking at Celine when she was a child! His head spun. "Celine?" he whispered.

"No, Daddy. Rachel. I'm your daughter. And Celine's daughter." She cocked her head and studied him. "Emily says I have your brown eyes and Momma's red hair."

Trent bent down until his face was even with Rachel's. Before he realized what he was doing, he wrapped his arms around her and held her close. She smelled like lilacs and soap and Sunday dinner. Her body was warm and firm as she returned his embrace. It was hard to believe the fuzzy-headed infant he'd left behind had turned into a real live child. What had he missed? Skinned knees, chicken pox, hurt feelings, laughter, pictures drawn lovingly at school, good morning Daddy's, hugs like this? A little piece of his heart began to thaw.

Emily stood back and watched the family swarm around Trent, while Justin sank into a chair off in a corner, his face a study of resentment. Priscilla started toward him, but he scowled at her and she turned back to Trent with sadness in her eyes. She was twenty-seven years old, but she looked younger with her light brown hair bobbed and curled and a light dusting of makeup on her face. Her rose colored dress complimented her slender figure, and stockings covered her shapely legs. Her black leather sandals with fancy Junior Louis heels were the latest grecian style. Emily had wanted a pair like them, but she couldn't afford to pay $3.19 for fancy, impractical shoes when she could get black serviceable ones for half the price.

Justin and Priscilla's four children swarmed around Rachel, asking her all kinds of questions while Jennet and Freeman hugged Trent, their faces wreathed with smiles.

"Our boy's home, Ma," Free said, tears of joy in his voice.

Finally Priscilla had her turn at Trent. They'd always been friends and he'd often tried to help her understand Justin's moods when Justin was courting her. "I'm glad you're home," she whispered in Trent's ear. "I need you—desperately."

Trent smiled down at Priscilla. He saw the sadness in her brown eyes. Was Justin ignoring her again as he had years before? He'd always had a habit of getting involved in his work and forgetting everyone and everything around him. "So you married him, in spite of everything?"

"I loved him."

"We'll talk later," Trent promised, giving her a gentle kiss on the cheek.

She nodded, suddenly close to tears. She introduced him to her four children, seven-year-old Ted, six-year-old Ryan, four-year-old Faith, and three-year-old Chloe. Then she backed away and made room for Uncle Beaver and Aunt Hannah.

Emily sat quietly near the door as she watched Red Beaver and Hannah. She'd often heard the story of their courtship, and how the family had been against Hannah marrying a Patowatomie Indian. But true love had won out, and through the years their marriage had been strong and enduring. Red Beaver's farm was prosperous, and he'd provided well for his family. They had five children and fifteen grandchildren, all living on farms around Blue Creek. Of all the married couples Emily knew, she thought this one might be the happiest, perhaps even happier than Jennet and Freeman whose delight in each other seemed endless.

After a long time Freeman said loudly, "Let's let the boy

sit down. We don't want to wear him out his first day home."

Everyone moved away from Trent except Rachel. She stood before him, looking up at him in awe. "You really do look like Uncle Just. But you look different, too. Emily said you were handsome and smart and strong. And she was right. Now that you're home you can be my daddy all the time."

Trent's eyes glistened with tears, but he refused to let them fall. "I won't be staying here," he said hoarsely.

Emily's heart sank. She'd hoped that once he saw the family he'd want to stay. She peeked at Justin through her long lashes and saw the angry set of his jaw. No one seemed to have noticed Justin's swollen eye. In fact, no one, except Priscilla, seemed to have noticed Justin at all.

Rachel stared at Trent in horror. "But why? What will I do for a daddy?"

Trent wanted to say something to make her feel better, but he couldn't. He knew she'd be fine without him just as she had the last ten years.

"Why can't you stay, son?" Clay asked softly as he held Lark's hand in his to keep her from crying out. He knew she wanted Trent home more than she'd ever wanted anything in her life.

Suddenly feeling all alone, Trent looked around. He spied Emily sitting near the door with an empty chair beside her. She patted the chair and smiled. Relieved, he strode across the room and sank down beside her, his legs too weak to stand any longer.

Rachel ran after him and crawled onto Emily's lap. "Daddy's home," she whispered in Emily's ear.

Emily smiled and nodded.

"I'll stay for three days."

"Three days?" Lark cried in alarm.

"Shhh." Clay patted her hand. "Let him talk."

Justin bit back an angry retort. He wanted to make them see what a waster Trent was, but he thought that nothing he might say would make a difference. They'd have to learn for themselves. Trent had always been their favorite.

"I have to get back to Texas," Trent began. "I'm buying a ranch there." He told them about the Rocking R where he'd worked the past several years. As Emily listened, she sensed the excitement in Trent's voice was not quite genuine. He seemed to be trying to make the work sound fun and romantic, but later all she could remember was talk of tumbleweeds, dust storms, northers, long, lonely nights spent riding the range, stampedes, cattle rustlers, and weeks-long cattle drives. She thought Texas sounded hot, dusty, and very, very lonely. She wondered why Trent would want to leave a loving family to live in such a place. Something must be terribly wrong to make him want to do it.

"The owner wants to sell," Trent said, "and I want to buy it."

"What about your business here?" Justin asked angrily.

Priscilla frowned at Justin, but he ignored her.

"I don't want it," Trent snapped. "It's your business. You can have it."

Emily laid her hand over Trent's. She could feel his tension and anger, and again she wondered why.

"Boys!" Freeman said, keeping his arm around Jennet. "We don't want harsh, angry words spoken."

"We'll settle this peaceably," Clay said.

Rachel slid off Emily's lap and stood at Trent's side.

Lark brushed a tear off her pale cheek. "Will you stay with us while you're here?"

"Please do, Daddy," Rachel begged with her hands clasped at her throat and her eyes wide.

Trent nodded. It would be easier to stay with his folks than to go to the home he'd shared with Celine. There were too many painful memories there.

"I hired a caretaker for your place," Clay said. "Gabe Lavery."

Emily flushed. Gabe was Bob Lavery's brother.

"It's ready for you if you ever want to move back in," Lark said.

"Kill the fatted calf," Justin said bitterly.

"Stop it," Priscilla snapped, frowning at Justin.

Justin scowled at her, but said nothing more.

Trent tensed, ready to leap up, but Emily gripped his arm. Finally he relaxed. "I plan to stay three days. I came to sell my share of the pines so I will have the money to buy the Rocking R and stock it with a new breed of beef cattle I've read about. I'd like to sell to Justin."

Jennet shook her head hard and jumped to her feet. "No! No, Trent! You can't sell your share."

"Easy, Jen," Freeman said, catching her hand.

"Why?" Trent asked in surprise.

"I won't buy it anyway," Justin snapped.

"You can't sell it and Justin can't buy it," Clay said.

Trent sank back as a cold chill crept over his body.

"It's in the will that if you die or if you refuse the trees, or want to sell them, they go to your next of kin. That's Rachel. They can't be sold, son, only passed on."

Trent groaned. It had never occurred to him that he couldn't sell his inheritance.

"The pines are for all people to enjoy," Jennet said firmly as she sank down to the couch beside Freeman. "Your Great-grandpa Clay bought them and passed them to me to save for future generations. I passed them on to your parents and now they belong to you and your brother. But they are for saving, Trent, not for selling. When you and Justin inherited the white pines, you inherited Great-grandpa Clay's covenant to preserve them in their natural state. And that's what we're going to do."

Bright spots of color dotted Jennet's cheeks. "I have a plan to tell all of you. It's my plan to make the dream come true. It's about letting people everywhere see and enjoy our beloved white pines."

"What's your plan, Ma?" Clay asked softly.

Trent looked longingly at the door, but he knew he couldn't leave. If he couldn't sell his inheritance, he didn't care what anyone wanted to do with the forest. But since he was trapped, he looked at his grandmother and waited for her to speak.

Justin moved restlessly. He didn't want to hear Grandma's idea either, but he also knew he couldn't leave.

Emily glanced at Trent, then settled back to listen to Jennet's plan.

From the couch Jennet looked around the room at her family. How it had grown since she'd given birth to Clay fifty-five years before! If all the children and grandchildren had been able to be home today, the house couldn't contain them. With effort she pulled her thoughts together. Her stomach fluttered with nerves. "I want to turn the pines into a nature preserve and logging museum."

Justin thought about the money the trees represented and his heart sank. The Wagon Works needed money right away or he'd have to go to the bank for a loan. And he didn't like to do that with the economy the way it was. For some time he'd toyed with the idea of turning those trees into cash, just as Trent apparently had. He also hadn't known he couldn't sell his inheritance. The news today had been a shock. All he could think of now was that Grandma's plan would cost more money and he didn't know where that would come from. Still, it was a nice idea.

Jennet nervously cleared her throat. She saw the looks of shock on different faces. She turned to Freeman. "I want us to build a logging camp just like you once had, Free."

"That's a tall order, Jen," Free said.

"But not impossible," Clay said. The idea appealed to him, even though it was a major undertaking.

Emily smiled as her heart leaped with excitement. Jennet's idea was the best she'd ever heard. It was past time for others to get as much enjoyment out of the forest as they did. But what would Papa think of the idea?

Jennet continued as if she hadn't been interrupted. "I want folks to see how the trees were lumbered out and how precious the ones are that remain. I want trails made through the forest so folks can walk them with a guide and enjoy what we've enjoyed all these years. School children can take hikes there and learn first-hand about all the wonders of nature. Families can visit on their vacations." Jennet leaned forward earnestly. "There are still bears in our pines and all kinds of wild animals that left other areas because civilization took their homes. We'd tell the people how years ago the wild pigeons blackened the sky because there were so many as they flew up from the trees. Now they're extinct because so many of the trees were lumbered. We'll tell them of the beaver and all the other fur-bearing animals that once lived in the woods. We'll make it come alive for them just as it does for us." She took a deep breath as she looked around at her silent family. "And we'll call it 'Havlick's Wilderness' because it's the last true wilderness in Lower Michigan."

"Havlick's Wilderness," Clay said, smiling and nodding.

Emily liked it.

Jennet tucked a stray strand of white hair into the bun at the back of her head. "It'll be hard work, but the whole family could work together. The small price we'd charge the visitors would help maintain the property and pay the taxes each year. We'd have benches scattered along the trails so folks could rest and enjoy the tranquility. We wouldn't allow anyone to pick a single flower or dig up any plants or kill any of the animals or birds. No one could leave litter behind, or take food to feed the birds and animals. We want the place left in its natural state. I want to know that fifty years from now folks will still be seeing the pines that've stood for hundreds of years. Our pines! Havlick's Wilderness."

Shaking his head, Free whistled softly. "That's a big dream, sweetheart."

"I know," she said, taking his hand. "But a Havlick always dreams big."

"You're right about that." Free looked around at the family. "What'd you think about your mother's dream?"

Emily blinked back tears. She wasn't part of the family, but she loved the plan. The trees had always been important to her. Sharing them with others was perfect.

Trent leaned back with a low sigh as he listened to the others all talk at once. He didn't feel a part of the discussion or of the decision. His name was Havlick, but he didn't belong here now. He belonged on the Rocking R in Texas. But how would he get the money to buy the ranch now?

Clay lifted his hand and called for attention. When everyone was silent he said, "Ma, I like your dream. I think my boys do, too. It'll take a lot of work, but I vote yes. Trent? Justin? What do you say?"

Justin shrugged. "It's fine with me."

Trent nodded. "Me, too."

"You boys are the owners of the pines," Clay said. "It'll mean working together to see it come to pass."

"No," Trent said gruffly. "I won't work with him. You'll have to get someone else."

"I'm too busy anyway," Justin said coldly. "I can help find someone to work the project, though."

"It'll have to be someone you both agree on," Clay said, studying his sons.

They both nodded.

Everyone started talking again, and Emily leaned close to Trent. "I'm going now," she whispered. "I'll see you tomorrow."

"Don't leave me," he said, gripping her hand. "Please!"

She sank back in her chair and let him hold her hand for comfort. Celine would've wanted her to do that.

CHAPTER

5

♦ His muscles tight from the stress of the day, Trent stopped his Dodge in front of Emily's house and slowly turned to her. "Thanks for your help this afternoon. I wouldn't have made it without you."

"I'm glad I could help."

He sighed. "If I remember right, you were always the one to help ease the way for me and for Celine."

She shrugged, but she was pleased that he remembered what she'd done for them. "I wish you would change your mind and stay."

"No." He looked down at his hands on the steering wheel. "Not with Justin here."

"What did he do to make you so angry?" Emily flushed. Of course that question had been on her mind all afternoon, but it slipped out before she thought. "I'm sorry," she said quickly. "It's none of my business."

Trent looked off across the farmyard without seeing the barns and sheds. He'd never told anyone that Justin was to blame for Celine's death.

"Don't answer that," Emily said as she fumbled with the door handle. "I had no right to ask."

He touched her shoulder. "You have a right to ask, and you have a right to know. But I can't talk about it. I doubt if I'll ever be able to."

Emily turned to Trent, her eyes full of compassion. "Have you asked God to help you with this, whatever it is?"

Trent's eyes pricked with tears as he shook his head. "Not even God can help with this."

She was shocked to hear him talk that way. He'd always had such faith. "He can help with everything. But we have to let Him."

Trent studied the curve of her chin, her rounded cheek, and the arch of her dark brows. He had forgotten her face. "You always did believe God is the answer to everything."

She locked her fingers together in her lap. "So did you."

"But that was a long time ago."

Emily's heart sank. She smelled the leather of the seats mingled with the pine scent that always filled the air. "You can't mean you no longer trust Him!"

"I guess I just haven't thought about Him."

"Then it's time you did. He loves you."

"When did you turn into a preacher lady?" Trent asked sharply.

"Don't get smart mouthed with me. I'm not Celine. She put up with it, but I won't."

He laughed, surprising himself. "And you never have. I'd forgotten that."

"Well, don't forget again." She lifted her chin and looked down her nose at him, then grinned. She caught a movement at the kitchen window and knew Mama had looked out. She was probably wondering what was going on. Most likely she'd think Justin was in the automobile with her. Wait 'til Mama learned the truth!

Trent watched a cat amble across the grassy road, then turned back to Emily. "You always could see right through me."

"And I still can."

"I hope not," he muttered.

"I know you're hurting badly inside. But for some reason you don't want to be free of it. You'd rather be in pain than ask the Lord to take it away and set you free." Emily shook her head. "From what you said, I can tell Justin did something that you won't forgive."

"You don't know the half of it!"

"Well, you have to forgive him, Trent." She shook her finger at him. "Unforgiveness eats away at you, and it will destroy you. It blocks your relationship with God, and with everyone else, too. That's why it's been so easy to lower your standards and live the way you do."

Trent flushed. "You don't know a thing about my standards."

"Yes, I do. I can see it in your eyes. Your parents and grandparents would be crushed if they knew what you've become. And it's all because you want to stay angry at Justin. It's not worth it, Trent."

He sighed heavily. "Some things can't be forgiven, Emily."

"*Everything* can be forgiven."

"No, not everything."

"If God can forgive us unconditionally the way He does, we can forgive each other. That's what it means to be Christlike."

He considered what she'd said and after a long time he said, "I'll give it some thought."

"Don't just think about it, do it. Forgive Justin and get on with your life. And while we're talking about your life, don't forget you have a daughter. It's time you took responsibility for her." Emily pushed her mass of dark hair over her shoulder. "When I leave, what'll become of her? She loves me, and it'll be hard for her to lose me and lose you, too, especially now that she has finally found you."

Trent shrugged. "Then don't go."

"I have to." Emily flushed painfully. "You know that."

"Well, I have to go, too," Trent said impatiently. "And I have to find another way to get the money to buy the Rocking R."

"Then take Rachel with you."

"To Texas?"

"Yes."

The idea was new to him, and frightening. "What about her friends and the family?"

"She can make new friends." Emily tapped his shoulder. "But you're her family and she needs you desperately. Now that she's seen you, she can't survive without you."

Absently Trent ran his finger around the smooth black steering wheel. A pig squealed in the pigpen and a robin sang on the branch of a tree. Trent shook his head. "The Rocking R is miles out in the country. She'd be isolated. She couldn't get to school or even to church. There'd be no one there but me and the hands. She'd be all alone."

Emily smiled as she leaned toward Trent. "You'll figure out something." Having Rachel go with him was a brilliant idea, and she wouldn't let it go.

Thoughtfully Trent rubbed his cheek as he studied Emily. He grinned mischievously. "I just had a real good notion, Emily."

She cocked her brow questioningly, not certain she wanted to hear it. Already she sensed she wasn't going to like it. He'd always known how to aggravate her with his teasing.

Trent folded his arms across his broad chest. The grin grew wider and his eyes began to twinkle. He paused dramatically, his eyes locked with Emily's. She felt the color rising in her cheeks, and little flutters began in her stomach.

"I'll take Rachel with me if you come along."

Emily gasped, then, unable to look away, sat mutely, her face flaming.

Trent threw back his head and laughed heartily. "Ah, this is

a first," he said when he'd caught his breath. "Always-ready-
with-something-to-say-Emily is speechless!"

"I confess—you caught me off-guard," she stammered
when she found her voice, trying to regain her composure.

"Excuse me." Trent reached for her hand, his voice gentle.
"But I haven't had a good laugh like this in years.

"Well, how about it?" he asked.

"Me go to Texas with you?"

"Un-huh."

"You can't be serious. Why would you think of such a thing,
even as a joke?"

Trent shrugged. "You're planning to go to Sweden with
some other man. Why not go to Texas with me? Besides,
Texas is a lot closer to home than Sweden is."

"I can't go anywhere with you. It wouldn't look right."

He laughed softly, thinking what he was about to say would,
as they say in Texas, "throw her for a loop."

"It would if you married me."

Again she was speechless, and Trent chuckled as he tugged
gently at a strand of Emily's dark hair.

"You planned on marrying that man in Sweden without loving him, without even seeing him before. You could marry me.
At least you know me."

"Stop teasing me!"

A tingle ran down his spine. Why should this be a joke? Why
not marry her? She already knew he would always love Celine,
and he already knew she was in love with someone else. That
wouldn't be a problem for either of them. "You could be Rachel's mother and see that she gets proper schooling and
everything else she needs. Even though it hasn't shown
much, I do want the best for her."

"This is just too ridiculous." Emily's heart raced and blood
pounded in her ears. Was he serious? She couldn't tell. What
had happened to her ability to read him like a book?

"It's perfect, Emily. We love each other as friends. That's all we need. But we'll give Rachel a whole lot more. And we'll both have answers to our problems."

Emily bit her lower lip. Was it possible? Would it work? "I don't know . . ."

"You'll have to decide fast. Remember I'm only staying three days."

"But, Trent, I can't make up my mind that fast."

"You did about this guy from Sweden."

"That's different."

"Sure. Because you've never seen him." Trent was pleased with his idea and his argument. "Talk to your parents about it and see what they say. They've always liked me and you said they love Rachel."

Helplessly Emily shook her head. "I couldn't marry you. We're good friends. We were best friends—you, Celine, and me. How could we be, ah, husband and wife?"

Trent saw her flush and understood the reason for it. "I didn't mean to embarrass you. We don't have to share a bedroom. We could live together as husband and wife without actually being . . . husband and wife. Does that sound better?"

"I don't know that it does," Emily said weakly. "I want children." And she wanted to know what it felt like to be held and loved by a man. But she couldn't say that to Trent without embarrassing herself even more.

He sank back against the seat. She'd surprised him. "Then we'll share a bed. You'll get the children you want and Rachel will get the mother she wants."

All the strength seemed to drain out of Emily. Was she actually considering marrying Trent? "What about you?" she asked weakly. "What do you want?"

"Celine," Trent whispered. "I want Celine."

Emily's eyes filled with tears. "I wish I could bring her back for you. But I can't. No one can. And I can't take her place. No one can do that either."

They sat quietly for a long time. The evening breeze blew cool air into the automobile. Sounds of birds and farm animals seemed to grow louder. Finally Trent said, "So, will you marry me and go back to Texas with me and Rachel?"

Emily took a deep, shuddering breath, then let it out. Should she? It seemed more appealing than going to Sweden. "Why not? I would rather marry you than August Theorell anyway."

Trent laughed. "Thank you, Emily. I'll see that you're not sorry for it."

"And I'll try to get used to living in Texas. I hear it's vast and empty."

"It's big all right. But I like it." Trent pursed his lips in thought. "This is Sunday. We'll leave Wednesday. Can you be ready?"

"Yes," Emily said breathlessly. Oh, how could she possibly be ready? Suddenly she laughed. "Rachel has been praying that I'd marry you and be her momma. I said it'd never happen."

"I guess some prayers get answered." Trent looked off across the yard without seeing a thing.

"Prayers get answered all the time," Emily said, smiling. "We prayed you'd come home and you did."

Abruptly Trent pushed open the door and stepped to the ground. After not hearing about spiritual things for so long, he was feeling uncomfortable. "Let's go talk to your folks. They may want to talk you out of this." He opened her door and helped her out, then stood with his hands on her shoulders. "I don't want you to be sorry for agreeing to marry me. If you want to back out, do it now before we say a word to anyone."

Emily's stomach knotted and for a minute panic seized her. Then she shook her head. She felt this was right for them. "I won't change my mind. We'll tell Mama and Papa. They'll really be shocked."

"So will my parents."

They walked together into the house and straight to the kitchen where she knew her family would be. Emily was shivering, not knowing if she was excited or scared to death. Supper was already over, but the aroma of fried potatoes and pork chops still filled the air.

Andree Bjoerling looked up from his newspaper. Laugh lines spread from the corners of his blue eyes to his gray-streaked black hair. He was tall and thin and dark from years of working outdoors. He'd come from Sweden when he was twenty-two, hoping to learn about Jig, his uncle, and had stayed to work for the Havlicks. He'd never been sorry.

"Mama, Papa," Emily called. "Look who's here. It's Trent, home at last."

"Trent!" Martha covered her mouth and stared. The boys just stared.

"Welcome, Trent," Andree said, jumping up. He gave Trent a bear hug, then stepped aside to make room for Martha.

"You're home again at last!" Martha hugged him fiercely. This was the man she'd always wanted to be Emily's husband. Martha turned to her three boys. "This is Trent. You knew him when you were little." She turned toward Trent. "That's Lars, Neil, and Dag. They're almost grown men now—they were little boys when you left."

Trent shook hands as the boys greeted him boisterously.

Emily stood to one side and watched her family talk to Trent, trying to catch up the past ten years in only ten minutes.

Finally Trent moved to Emily's side. "We have something to tell you," he said with a smile.

Emily's heart raced as her mother's eyes widened and her father's brows lifted questioningly.

Trent took Emily's hand in his. "I'm going back to Texas Wednesday and I'm taking Rachel with me." He smiled down at Emily, then looked at her father. "I've also asked Emily to go as my wife."

Emily saw the shocked looks on their faces. "I've agreed to go," she said softly. "Is that all right, Mama? Papa?"

"Well, I'll be hogtied!" cried Andree, slapping his knee.

"I say it's good news," Martha said, blinking back tears as she tried to read Emily's eyes. "This is so fast. Are you sure, honey?"

Emily nodded and smiled. "Yes, Mama."

"Good," said Martha. She hugged Emily, then Trent. "I want the best for you children. Even though I'm surprised, I'm very pleased."

"I always loved you as a son," Andree said as he hugged Trent again. "Welcome to the family."

"Finally we'll be rid of Emily," Lars said with a laugh as he shook Trent's hand.

"Thanks for taking her off our hands," Neil said, winking at Emily.

"I get her room," Dag said, grinning.

"Wednesday, you say?" Martha's eyes widened in alarm. "I can't be ready to give up my daughter so soon."

"Yes, you can." Andree slipped his arm around Martha's shoulders. "We'll send her off with a smile just like we did Betty and Lucille."

Emily looked at Trent and grinned. Now that they'd told her parents, it looked like she was really going to marry Trent Havlick.

They talked about wedding plans for several minutes before Trent said, "Now we must tell my family. I'll bring Emily back later."

Emily squeezed her mother's hand, then walked to the automobile with Trent. In silence they drove down the dusty lane to the gravel road, then on in to Blue Creek. The town was quiet. Lights shone from the windows of several homes. Main Street was almost deserted. Emily knew Rachel would already be in bed, and probably was asleep.

Trent parked where Emily usually parked her buggy. The

sudden silence with the automobile turned off felt good. "I think Mom and Dad will be happy," Trent said. "Don't you?"

"I . . . I don't know. I hope so."

"You aren't going to back out, are you?"

"No." Emily trembled. "I am nervous, though."

"Don't be." Trent jumped to the ground and ran around to open the door for Emily. "We're old buddies, remember?"

Emily laughed breathlessly. "Yes, you're right, old buddy."

They found Clay and Lark in the front room listening to hymns on the victrola.

"We've come to tell you something," Trent said.

Lark lifted the needle, stopping the music in the middle of a note, and moved the arm off the record. She faced Trent and Emily, her pulse quickening. She'd changed into a comfortable cotton dress that reached almost to her ankles. She couldn't get used to short dresses. "When you didn't come for so long, I was afraid you'd left again," Lark said as she kissed Trent on the cheek.

"We were talking about Rachel before you came," Clay said as he wrapped his hands around his black suspenders. "She's not going to be happy here with us if you leave again now that she's met you."

Trent cleared his throat. "That's what we want to talk about."

"Let's sit down." Clay tugged Lark down on the blue sofa beside him and kept her hand in his.

Her legs weak, Emily sat on the blue, tapestry armchair across from the sofa. A cool breeze ruffled the white muslin curtains at the windows. A kerosene lamp with white frosted globe and brass base sitting on the end table cast a warm glow over the room.

"Have a chair, Trent," Clay said softly.

Trent sank to the arm of Emily's chair. His mouth felt as dry as on a cattle drive. He ran a finger around the neckline of his shirt. "I don't know how to say this."

"Just say it, son," Lark said gently.

Emily shivered. She felt the heat from Trent's body. Was she doing the right thing?

Trent cleared his throat. "I want to take Rachel back with me. I know you'll both miss her a lot, but you can visit us and we'll come see you."

Lark's eyes filled with tears. "We want you to stay, Trent. Please, stay here!"

Trent shook his head. "I'm sorry, Mom. I can't stay. I'm leaving Wednesday with Rachel. And Emily has agreed to go with us. As my wife."

Lark gasped and Clay laughed in delight.

"Rachel will be glad," Clay said. Nothing ever surprised him, not even this. "She's been pestering Emily for years to be her momma."

Lark jumped up, pulled Emily to her feet, and hugged her. "This is so sudden. Are you sure?"

"I'm sure," Emily answered.

"She's sure," Trent said.

"Welcome to the family." Clay hugged Emily tight.

"Thank you." Emily's head spun. She was going to belong to the powerful Havlick family!

"I think we should go and tell Rachel," Lark said. "She's probably still wide awake day dreaming about her daddy."

Emily hung back as Trent and his parents started toward the stairs. What could she say to Rachel after telling her so many times that she'd never be her mother?

Trent glanced back and saw Emily hesitating. He motioned to his parents to go ahead of him, then waited for Emily. He took her hand and squeezed it reassuringly. "You said Rachel wanted this. Why be scared?"

"You're right, of course." Emily smiled hesitantly. She gripped Trent's work-roughened hand as they walked to Rachel's bedroom. The room was decorated in a delicate pink and white—not at all the colors Emily would've chosen for her.

When she saw them at her door, Rachel sat bolt upright in bed, holding a rag doll tightly in her arms. Her red hair hung in two braids over her shoulders. She looked at Trent fearfully. "Are you going away already? Did you come to say good-bye?"

Awkwardly Trent sat on the edge of the bed and gently took Rachel's hand in his. She was so much like Celine it took his breath away. He managed to say, "I didn't come to say good-bye. We came to tell you good news."

"You and Emily are going to get married!" Rachel said, her eyes large and full of excitement.

Trent stared at Rachel in shock. Suddenly the child seemed very much like Emily.

Emily laughed. "What makes you think that, Rachel?"

"It's because I asked God to arrange it. And I asked Him to bring my daddy home. He did that and now you need to get married. That's what it is, isn't it?"

"Yes, that's what it is," Trent said, shaking his head in amazement. "I've asked Emily to marry me and be your momma. She said she would."

Rachel cocked her head and looked at Trent. "Then will you stay here and always be my daddy?"

With Emily beside him and his parents standing at the foot of the bed, Trent told Rachel that he would always be her daddy and that he was sorry he'd missed so much. "I've let my grief keep me from you and that hurt both of us. I hope you'll forgive me."

"Oh, I will, Daddy, I will." Rachel threw her arms around Trent's neck and hugged him hard. Lark had to ask Clay for a handkerchief. He gave her his after he dabbed quickly at his own tears.

Then Trent told Rachel they would live in Texas on the Rocking R Ranch and they would be a family. "So, Tuesday Emily and I'll be married and Wednesday you and Emily and I will leave for Texas."

Rachel hugged them all and after a long time settled back on her pillow. "I want Tuesday to come fast."

Emily kissed her cheek, then turned away as fear pricked her skin. All at once she realized she was afraid for Tuesday to come.

* * *

Late Sunday afternoon Priscilla Havlick drove herself and her children home from Freeman's place. Her family lived only a few miles from the elder Havlicks' home. She was bone tired and she knew the children were, too. Little Chloe was almost asleep against Ted.

Priscilla parked outside the small garage they'd built the year before when she bought her black Ford. Lilac bushes at the side of the gravel driveway were in full bloom sending out their fragrant aroma. Red tulips and yellow daffodils swayed in the gentle breeze. They covered a wide patch of ground between the picnic table and the two story white frame house Justin had built for them the first year of their marriage. Then it seemed too large, but now with four children it often felt too small. She quickly looked around for Noah Roswell, their hired man, but couldn't see him in the pen feeding the pigs, near the large red barn, or at the wood pile splitting wood. He was probably already milking the cows. He'd worked for them almost a year, but only in the past few weeks had her heart skipped a beat at the thought of him. Seeing him and talking to him made her days worth living. At times she longed for him to take her in his strong arms and kiss her senseless. Flushing at the turn her thoughts had taken again, she said over her shoulder, "Run inside. I want to speak to Daddy alone. You may have cookies and milk at the kitchen table. Ted, help Chloe and Faith."

"I will, Mom."

"I don't need help," Faith said with a toss of her dark hair. "I'm not a baby like Chloe."

"Run inside," Priscilla said impatiently.

With happy shouts, the children ran up the back steps and through the back door. The screen slammed behind Chloe, then all was quiet except for the squawk of the windmill and the gobble of a turkey. Priscilla fingered the strands of white beads hanging down the front of her rose-colored dress. Waiting for Justin to pull up beside her, she angrily pressed her lips together. Once again he had embarrassed her by being late for a family gathering. Then he'd had the nerve to come in with a swollen eye after an obvious fight with Trent. The afternoon had been a strain for everyone with Trent's unexpected arrival. Justin's angry mood had simply made things worse.

As Justin stopped beside her, she walked around her automobile to his, her short skirt flipping around her slender legs. He still wore Free's blue work shirt and denim pants. "I want to talk to you," she said sharply.

Justin groaned. Once again he'd have to listen to her lecture about being on time and not making her look bad in front of his family. "Don't even start, Priscilla!" he said impatiently.

Sparks flew from her dark eyes. "How could you fight with Trent? What kind of homecoming was that?"

"He started it." Justin stepped from his automobile and carefully closed the door. His nerves were coiled as tight as the springs in the automobile.

Priscilla folded her arms and narrowed her eyes. "You don't want him to stay, do you?"

"I don't care what he does!" Justin started for the house, but she stopped him with a hand on his arm. He looked down at her small, well-manicured hand. Once a touch from her had sent his senses reeling. Now it only irritated him.

"Well, *I* want him here! Maybe then you wouldn't work so hard or be gone all the time."

Here it comes, he thought as his heart sank. How he hated to fight with Pris, but that seemed to be all they knew how to do. Occasionally a few days of being pleasant with each other would go by, but those days seemed to be happening less and less often. "Maybe I'd be home more if you wouldn't nag so much," he shot at her as he walked past.

Her face flamed. "Oh, what's the use? You don't care about me or the children. You care only about yourself and the Wagon Works." Priscilla stamped her small foot in the dusty driveway. "I don't understand you at all! If you talked nice to Trent, maybe you could convince him to work there again."

Justin whirled on her and doubled his fists at his sides. Priscilla had no idea the depth of Trent's anger, nor his, for that matter. "I won't work with him!"

"You are so stubborn!"

"I don't want to talk about it."

Priscilla tossed her head and her short hair bounced. "Then maybe you'll talk about Grandma's plans for the pines. Do you really think it'll work?"

"Probably. What Grandma wants, she gets."

"But the pines belong to you and Trent."

"If we can't sell them, we might as well do something to generate money from them."

"I suppose." She sighed heavily. "It just means more work for you. And I see so little of you now."

"It gives us less time to fight," he snapped.

Tears burned her eyes and she blinked them away. "Justin, I need you! I get so lonely."

"You have friends."

"I want a husband who loves me and spends time with me. I want us to have fun together! Please, Justin."

He saw the pleading in her eyes and he wanted to reach out to her, but he couldn't. "You already take more of my time than I can give. I took off this afternoon because you begged me to. If you had your way, I'd close up the Wagon Works and spend every minute of my time with you."

"You know that's not true."

"Do I?"

"I hate you, Justin Havlick," Priscilla whispered as her breast rose and fell in agitation. With a swish of her skirt she strode to the house and slammed the door hard behind her. Sometimes she wanted to scream.

Justin walked slowly toward the picnic table and sank down on the bench with his head in his hands. He winced as he touched his swollen eye. He winced more for what he'd done to Priscilla. He did love her, but somehow he couldn't let it show. What had happened to their happiness? Deep inside he felt the agony that was always there when he allowed himself to think about his life and what was happening to it.

Seeing Trent again had brought a fresh wave of despair over him. He was to blame for Celine's death, and he could never forgive himself. He was worse than the worst murderer he'd read about. A groan rose from deep inside him and burned in his throat.

A bee buzzed around his head but he ignored it as it flew off to the flowers. He smelled the lilacs that covered the bush behind him, but even their perfume irritated him. He heard Noah Roswell whistling in the barn, already at work on the evening chores. Noah was twenty-one years old, handsome, and scot-free. He was always cheerful and friendly, without a care in the world. Justin looked toward the big red barn. "I'd trade places with him in a minute," he muttered. But he couldn't. He was a Havlick and Havlicks were expected to succeed at everything while keeping smiles on their faces and in their hearts.

When was the last time he'd had a smile in his heart?

CHAPTER

6

♦ Monday morning while the children were still in bed and after Justin had gone to work, Priscilla walked outdoors. It was a chilly May morning, but the bright sun promised a warm day. A cat ran to her and rubbed against her ankle, purring loudly. A rooster flew to the top rail of the fence and crowed with its head back and its beak raised to the sky. The cool breeze ruffled her hair as she walked across the dew wet grass that dampened her walking shoes. She knew Noah would be milking. Her throat closed over and she stopped, her hand at her breast. What was she doing? She was flirting with danger. She should walk right back into the house where she belonged and leave Noah alone. But, lifting her chin defiantly, she said, "I don't care! If Justin won't love me, someone else will."

She took a deep, steadying breath and patted her fluttering heart with a trembling hand. She moistened her lips with the tip of her tongue as she stepped inside the barn and waited for her eyes to adjust to the dimness. The pungent odor was as familiar to her as coffee perking in the early morning. She'd grown up on a farm, then had moved here when she and Justin were married. A few months after the wedding her folks had decided to sell out and move west to Oregon. They hadn't been back since. She bit her lower lip. Right now she needed to talk to Ma. But Ma was far, far away. Besides, Ma would tell her to keep her eyes and thoughts only on her husband and off other men.

Priscilla walked to the great hand-hewn beam in the middle of the barn. Noah was perched on a one-legged stool milking a cow. He had strong, dark, well-shaped hands. He wore denim jeans and a blue work shirt with the sleeves rolled almost to his elbows. Black hair covered his strong, sun-browned forearms. His brown hair was short and thick with a slight wave. He rested his forehead against the cow's flank. Foamy white milk streamed into the pail between his strong legs. The cat ran to him, mewing lowly. He squirted milk at it and it opened its mouth to catch it. Noah laughed, and the sound sent a thrill over Priscilla.

"Good morning," she said, stepping forward so he could see her. She rubbed her hand at the waist of her flowered cotton housedress that she'd hemmed at a length of two inches below her knees.

"Morning." He winked at her and grinned, but he didn't take his hands off the cow. His eyes were as blue as the morning glories that climbed the trellis on her porch. "You look mighty pretty this morning."

"Thank you, Noah." She leaned against the wooden partition and watched him. "My brother-in-law Trent came home yesterday."

"You don't say. The Havlicks must be real glad."

"They are. But he plans to leave in a few days. He wants to buy a ranch in Texas." Priscilla liked the way Noah's brown hair curled against his neck and around his nicely shaped ears. "Have you ever been to Texas?"

"Nope. Been to Arkansas. You ever been?"

Priscilla laughed and shook her head. "I've never been out of Michigan. Can you believe that?" She knew his parents lived in Flint and that he'd left home at seventeen to join the army and fight in the war. He never did join the army, but he did travel all over.

"You seem like a real lady of the world. I took you for a well-traveled lady."

"I've been to Detroit."

"That's some city, ain't it? But I wouldn't want to live there."

"Me either. I've read about New York City and Chicago. You ever been there?"

"Yup. Wasn't impressed. They got big trouble with bootlegging in Detroit and in Chicago." Noah stripped the cow dry, then stood and put away the milk stool. He picked up two buckets filled with milk and headed for the door. "But what can they expect when they say no booze at all."

"Yes, what?" Personally Priscilla was glad drinking wasn't allowed, but she didn't say that to Noah as they walked outdoors. He carried the milk to the milk house. It was a small wood-frame building with room enough for a cream separator, washstand with a sink and hand pump, ice box, and rack to set clean buckets on. He strained the milk twice just the way she'd asked him to when he'd first started working for her.

"A man should be able to decide for himself if he wants to drink or not," Noah said as he washed out the milk pail, soapy water splashing against him. "That makes bootlegging all right with me. But it does cause a lot of stir."

"Oh?" She didn't care about bootlegging, but she wanted to keep him talking.

"Sure does. They got troubles all over Michigan." Noah glanced around as if he thought someone might hear. "Did you know there's a bar right outside of Blue Creek?"

"But that's against the law!"

"It's there anyway." Noah poured the milk into the separator, turned the handle and watched while cream came out one spout and skimmed milk the other. He put the milk and cream to cool in the ice box. "And I heard tell there's lots of bootlegging going on in the area. It wouldn't surprise me none if there're stills hidden around here."

"It wouldn't surprise me either." Priscilla hoped he wouldn't realize she was only making conversation with him. Actually she hated to think bootleggers had stills in their area. How handsome Noah looked as he stood with his hands resting lightly on the wide belt of his pants! She managed to say in great concern, "Yet Blue Creek has a good sheriff."

"You're sure right about that. I know Sheriff Spud Lamont pretty well." Noah grinned at Priscilla, sending her heart racing. "We sometimes play cards together."

Priscilla fluffed her hair. "I once tried to learn how to play bridge, but I couldn't get the hang of it."

"We play poker."

"Oh." Pa had said often it was a sin to gamble and she knew poker was a gambling game. Somehow it didn't surprise her that Noah played poker. Maybe he even visited the illegal bar. "I hope you don't lose your money."

"Not me! But I don't gamble heavy." He took the separator apart and washed it as they talked more about gambling and bootlegging. "Bootlegging would be a swell way to earn big money."

Priscilla tried to hide her alarm. "I guess it would be," she said weakly.

He dried his hands on a white towel and hung it neatly. "I'd best get back to the barn."

Priscilla couldn't let him go. "I have coffee in the house if you want a cup."

Noah caught her hand and squeezed it. "You're a real darling! I would like a cup. I make bad coffee."

He'd told her that and that's what had made her decide to offer him a cup. She'd been trying for weeks to find the courage. She looked at their clasped hands, flushed, and tugged hers free. "I have pancake batter mixed up. I could fix you a few pancakes."

"You're a woman after my own heart," he said, smiling down on her.

Her pulse leaped and she smiled up at him. He was a man after her own heart, too, but she didn't say that. He listened to her and he talked to her. And that was a whole lot more than Justin did.

A few minutes later Noah sat at the square oak table in the middle of the big kitchen with a mug of coffee in his hands while Priscilla quickly fried a stack of pancakes. Heat from the cookstove turned her cheeks pink. Having Noah watch her and talk to her about what President Harding was doing made her eyes sparkle. Since women had gotten the vote three years before, she'd tried to keep abreast of what was happening in the nation. It was hard to keep her mind on Noah's words when all she wanted to do was have him pull her close and kiss her.

Yellow curtains fluttered at the open row of windows beside the back door. A large white sink with a red hand pump was against another wall. Beside it were wooden pegs for hanging towels and jackets and hats. Crocks sat on the floor near a tall white cupboard between the hall door and the dining room door. Fire crackled in the cast iron range against another wall. On the far side of the woodbox were a row of shelves and a door leading into the spacious pantry.

Priscilla set the plate of pancakes before Noah, poured herself a cup of coffee, and sat with him at the big table. It had been a long time since she'd sat at her table with anyone other than her children. Justin usually grabbed a bite in town. Abruptly she pushed away thoughts of Justin and watched Noah. She liked the way he smeared butter on each pancake, then poured maple syrup over the entire stack. The butter melted and dribbled down the sides with the syrup. She'd helped make the maple syrup last February.

Noah cut off a bite and stuck it in his mouth. He rolled his eyes in pleasure and said, "Ummmm."

"I'm glad you like them," Priscilla said, smiling with pride. While he ate she told him about Jennet's dream of turning the white pines into a nature preserve and logging museum.

"Sounds good to me," Noah said in between bites. "But there'll be some folks that'll throw a fit."

"But why?"

"They don't want strangers nosing around. Because of the bootleggers."

"You sound so sure of yourself. How do you know that kind of thing?" Priscilla asked in surprise.

Noah shrugged. "I heard it around town."

"If so many people know about bootleggers and about the places that sell liquor, why doesn't anyone tell the sheriff?"

"Folks like to drink. They're glad for a chance to buy the stuff."

"Jennet and Lark Havlick would shut those places down if they knew about them."

"Nobody's gonna tell 'em."

"They don't believe in strong drink."

Noah shrugged. "A lot of folks think different. They get a kick out of drinking and hanging around together at them places."

"Do you?"

"I been in some, but I don't drink much."

Priscilla bit her lower lip. She'd never thought about Noah doing anything really bad.

Noah took a long swig of coffee, then wiped his mouth with the back of his hand. "Thanks for the fine food, Priscilla. It felt good to an old bachelor's empty stomach."

She flushed with pleasure. "You probably have women chasing after you all the time."

Noah grinned and shrugged. "I got my share."

Jealousy ripped through Priscilla and she quickly turned away to hide it. "The children will be waking up soon."

"Send 'em out later and I'll play ball with 'em."

Priscilla's heart almost burst with love. She turned back to Noah and smiled. "You're wonderful to play with them!"

"I figure kids need grown-ups to give 'em time or they have real problems when they grow up."

Why didn't Justin know that? She'd begged him to spend time with the children, but he was always too busy. "I'll send them out later, Noah. Thanks."

"You can come, too. Can you play ball?"

Priscilla laughed. "I haven't played in a long time."

"Then come on out." Noah caught her hand and squeezed it. Her very bones melted. His eyes softened and he squeezed her hand again. "Thanks for breakfast and for the fine talk. See you later outdoors." He strode out and she stood there with her hands pressed to her heart and her eyes sparkling.

* * *

Emily sank to the edge of her bed and groaned. She'd asked Lark to care for Rachel—Emily had a lot to do to get ready for her wedding the next day. Lark had quickly agreed. She was delighted that Trent was marrying Emily. "What have I done?" she whispered hoarsely.

The room suddenly seemed to close in on her. For twenty-five years this had been her bedroom. Three times she'd changed the wallpaper, curtains, and bedspread. Now lavender floral wallpaper covered the walls. White lacy curtains hung at the two windows. She'd made three small lavender pillows to use as decoration with the white pillows on her white bedspread. A large crystal vase full of lavender and white lilacs stood on her dresser, filling the room with their fragrance. After tomorrow this would no longer be her bedroom. Lars would change the room into a boy's room.

The door opened and Martha stuck in her head. "Can I come in?"

Emily nodded.

"You look like you've lost your last friend," Martha said as she sat on the bed beside Emily.

"I'm scared, Mama. Why did I agree to marry Trent?"

"Because you knew it was the right thing to do."

"Is it?"

"You wouldn't marry him if it weren't right."

"I don't know, Mama."

"He needs you, honey."

Emily sighed heavily. That was true. "But how can I get packed and ready by tomorrow?"

"That's why I'm here."

"You sure want to get rid of me, don't you?"

"No. I just want your going to be pleasant for both of us." Martha laughed as she walked to the dresser and pulled open the top drawer. "I'm doubly happy because you've given me a granddaughter without a waiting period."

Emily laughed and felt better. She opened the large trunk her brothers had brought to her room. "Mama, what do you really think about Jennet Havlick's idea for the pines?"

Martha turned from emptying a drawer. "I guess it'll work. I don't care for all those people that'll come traipsing around, though. Neither will your father. He likes his life the way it is."

"Sometimes change is good."

"Not when it makes you lose your privacy."

"I didn't think about that." Emily brushed a cobweb off the trunk.

"Jennet walked the line with your pa this morning. He's always glad for the company, but he says she's not as careful as she once was. Her reactions are slower because of her age. It's dangerous. But she won't listen to your pa."

"I heard Free tell her to take someone with her when she goes, but she usually doesn't."

Martha shook her head. "She loves the pines."

"That she does. It will be nice for others to enjoy the pines like we have all these years."

"I guess." Martha grinned as she held the blouse against her that she'd been folding. "I could take photographs of them with my new Buster Brown box camera and make pictures to sell. That way everyone could enjoy the view without coming here and bothering anyone."

"And we could send them pine needles so they could enjoy the smell," Emily giggled. "But that's not what Jennet has in mind."

"I know." Martha sighed and shook her head. "I think your pa might decide to take us all to Sweden to live to get away from the crowds of people."

"Who would guard the pines?"

"Who'll guard them once they're open to the public?"

Emily shook her head. "It will be hard to keep people from ruining the place. Jennet probably has it all thought out. She's a pretty bright lady." Emily pulled a box from under her bed and opened it. It held her treasures from childhood. She rummaged through the box, smiling at the memories its treasures brought back. She found a love note Celine had written to Trent when she was about thirteen years old. Emily pressed the note to her heart as she remembered the day Celine had written it. They were standing outside the school house after school.

"*You* give it to him, Emily," Celine had said breathlessly, her cheeks as red as her hair. "I just can't!"

Emily had laughed and had taken the note. "It won't bother me to give it to him."

"Then tell me exactly what he says and how he looks. Tell me every single detail!"

"I will."

Celine ran down the street toward the orphan home, then suddenly raced back. Her face was as white as the clouds in the sky. "I changed my mind, Emily. Don't give it to him. He might laugh. Or hate me. I am only an orphan. And he's a Havlick!"

"He won't hate you. And you're every bit as good as a Havlick!"

"No, I'm only an orphan. Tear up the note. Please!"

"All right."

Celine breathed a sigh of relief. "You're my very best friend, Emily, and you always will be."

"You're my very best friend and you always will be." Emily tucked the note inside her grammar book as Celine dashed away. At home she'd hidden the note in her special box in case Celine changed her mind. But she never did.

Now Emily opened the note.

"What is it?" Martha asked softly.

"A note from Celine to Trent."

"Read it to me, will you?"

Emily took a deep, steadying breath. "Trent, you are the best looking boy in all of Blue Creek, probably in all of Michigan. Do you like me for more than a friend? Does it embarrass you to have an orphan for a friend? The next time we go for a walk in the woods, will you hold my hand? Would it embarrass you to hold an orphan's hand? I would be happy and proud to hold your hand. Love. Celine."

Martha brushed tears from her eyes. "She was a precious girl. Rachel might like to have the note."

"I'll save it for her." Emily refolded it slowly, her mind still on Celine.

Martha sat on the edge of the bed and patted a spot beside her. "Sit down a while, honey."

Emily hesitated, but finally sat down. She knew Mama wanted to say something serious, but she didn't know if she was ready to hear it.

"Honey, I know you and Trent love each other and have for years."

82

"As friends, Mama."

"I know." Martha took Emily's hand in hers. They both had callused hands from hard work. "Don't be afraid to open your heart to a deeper love."

Emily gasped and shook her head. "It wouldn't be right!"

"Yes, it would. Celine is in heaven with Jesus. She wouldn't feel hurt if you grew to love Trent as a wife should love her husband."

"Trent and I are happy to leave it the way it is."

"There'll come a day when you won't be happy with only friendship. Friendship is wonderful and it's important, but it's only the beginning. Passionate love should be part of marriage. Don't feel guilty when you find your love growing deeper."

Emily flushed painfully. "I don't want to talk about it."

"You're going to live a long way from me, Emily. I need to tell you things now so when it happens you'll be able to handle it."

"It's not going to happen. Trent will never stop loving Celine."

"I know that. But that love will change. It'll become only a memory." Martha frowned. "It should be already. I don't understand what's keeping him from getting on with his life."

Emily knew it was his great anger at Justin and his great love for Celine, but she didn't say so. She didn't say anything about her great love for Bob Lavery either.

Martha wrapped her arms around Emily and held her close. "I want God's best for you, honey. I'll pray for you every single day. You remember that when you're way down in Texas."

"I'll remember," Emily said with a catch in her voice. She clung to Mama, suddenly afraid to let her go. She smelled Mama's skin that often smelled like vanilla and felt her soft hair against her cheek. Finally she pulled away. "I love you."

"I love you, too." Martha jumped up and wiped away her

tears with the corner of her apron. "It's almost time for you to meet Trent in town to get the marriage license."

Emily's heart jerked strangely. A marriage license!

* * *

At the Wagon Works Trent forced himself to stand beside Justin's large oak desk without breaking Justin's nose. Most of the factory noise was muffled by the closed door. Justin poised a pencil over a pad of paper as he looked up at Trent.

"I'll agree with anyone you suggest," Trent said impatiently. It took all his willpower to keep his temper. "It doesn't matter to me."

Justin snapped the pencil between his fingers. It was hard to be in the same room with Trent. "You are as much responsible for the pines as I am! If I had my way, we'd lumber them and be done with it!"

"That's fine by me!" Trent snarled. The pines meant nothing to him at this time. All he could think about was getting away from Justin, away from Blue Creek, and away from his painful memories.

Justin slammed his fist down on his desk, making the pad of paper jump. "But we can't do that, can we? We must do what Grandma wants."

A muscle jerked in Trent's jaw. Justin shoved back his chair and stood. They both wore white shirts and dark pants. Trent's dark tan and Justin's lack of one was the only difference in their looks. The tension mounted.

"I think Andree Bjoerling would be the best man for the job," Justin said in a crisp voice.

Trent cocked his brows and nodded. "I wouldn't have thought of him, but I agree. I think the family will, too." He pushed his hands deep into his pockets and hunched his shoulders. "I told Mom and Dad this already; Emily and I are going to get married tomorrow. We're taking Rachel and going back to Texas Wednesday."

Justin whistled in surprise. "You and Emily. I always thought there was something between you two."

"There wasn't! Only friendship."

"But she agreed to marry you."

"It's convenient for both of us." Trent turned toward the door. "Let's talk to Andree and be done with it."

"I've sent someone after him already. He should be here shortly."

Trent shrugged. He didn't want to wait even a minute longer alone with Justin.

Justin strode around the desk. "Aren't you interested in the Wagon Works at all?"

"No."

"We build chairs now," Justin said impatiently.

Trent turned in surprise. "How come?"

Justin forced his temper down. "Wagons aren't selling like they did before the war. There are fewer farms, you know. Since we have men here who know how to work with wood, I decided to go into building chairs. Simple kitchen chairs made of oak. I've built up quite a business. Every family needs chairs whether they live in town or the country."

"Chairs. That's a good idea."

"We need more lumber to fill an order that came in a few days ago. Oak, we need. Lots of it."

"You'll find it."

Justin's eyes flashed with anger. "Sure I will. I always do, don't I? I always have the answer. I always have the money."

Trent cleared his throat. "I know I said I wouldn't take any money from the business, but since I can't sell the pines for the money I need to buy the ranch, I want to know how much money is mine."

"It's all in a savings account at the bank," Justin said gruffly. The first few years he'd gladly put the money away for Trent, but as time passed and he had to work long, hard hours because Trent was gone, he'd grown very angry at sharing profits with an absent partner. Several times he'd even considered using the money, but his pride wouldn't allow him to. "Ten years' worth of money is a good piece of change."

"I told you not to do that! I never wanted anything from you."

"Dad worked the business too, so don't think it's me giving you a hand-out. You don't deserve one! You don't even deserve the money I put away for you. But it belongs to you as a Havlick. It's in the bank in your name."

Trent desperately wanted to refuse the money, but it was the only way to buy the Rocking R. "I'll get it before we leave." He couldn't bring himself to thank Justin.

Someone knocked and Justin opened the door. Andree stood there with his hat in his hands. He wore denim pants and a blue plaid shirt with wide black suspenders. His blue eyes crinkled as he smiled.

"Andree, come right in," Justin said.

"I'm glad to see you boys together." Andree shook hands with them, then sat beside the desk. Trent sat beside him while Justin returned to his chair behind the desk. "What business is so important that it can't wait until daylight is gone?" He'd planned to work all day in the fields after his daily trip through the pines to make sure the trees were safe from vandals.

"Grandma has probably told you all about her plans for the pines," Justin said.

Andree nodded.

"We want you to be in charge of it," Trent said.

Andree's eyes widened in surprise.

Justin fingered the broken pencil. "We'll pay you well."

"Money's not everything, boys," Andree snapped as he stabbed his fingers through his graying hair. "Them trees are almost as important to me as to your family. I don't like the idea of letting folks traipse through them woods and destroy all that I've been protecting. Your grandma don't think folks would pick the flowers or carve initials on the trees or throw trash in the streams, but I know better. I've seen how people are. I sure don't like the idea."

Justin hadn't expected Andree to be against the plan. "If you were in charge of getting the place done the way Grandma wants, you'd be able to keep people from destroying the trees."

"You'd be able to hire guards to keep the trees safe," Trent said.

Andree scowled and shook his head. "I don't like to tell you boys no, but I must. I don't want folks to have free access to the trees!"

"They wouldn't," Justin said, forcing back his mounting impatience. "Nobody could go out without a guide. *You* can hire the guides. Men you trust."

"Talk to Martha about it," Trent said. "Let us know tomorrow."

Andree smiled in relief. "That's what I'll do. I don't know if I can think about anything but my daughter getting married and leaving us." He slapped Trent on the leg. "Why don't you stay here, Trent? This is your home. If you want to raise beef cattle, do it here. You have enough land to feed a lot of cattle."

Trent's stomach knotted. He couldn't stay even if he wanted. It was too painful. "I have my heart set on the Rocking R, Andree."

Justin locked his hands around the arms of his chair. He couldn't tolerate having Trent here to remind him of what he'd done to Celine.

"I sure wish you'd stay," Andree said.

Justin stood up. "He's made up his mind. There's no changing it." He walked around to Andree and clamped his hand on his shoulder. "I hope you take the job. If you don't will you suggest someone? Grandma's set on having her way in this, so we'll see that it happens."

Andree sighed loudly. "You're sure right about her having

her heart set on what she calls Havlick's Wilderness. She was even talking about building cabins to rent out to folks who want to stay a week or two at a time. And a big resort cabin for rich folks with servants to wait on 'em."

"I didn't hear that part of the plan," Justin said.

"She even has the place picked out for the cabins," Andree said. "She told me this morning. It's by Deep Lake—the area covered mostly with oaks."

"I didn't know we had oaks," Justin said, alert and eager to hear more. "We need oak for chairs. I think I'll take a trip out there and check them out."

"Best way to go is drive up to Fromberg and take a boat across Deep Lake. You can get a clear view of the oaks and pines," Andree said. "I'd say there's about a hundred acres of oaks."

"I've never been in that part of the woods," Trent said. He and Celine had had a special spot near the creek where they sat and talked many times. A picture of them together flashed across his mind, and he bit back a groan of despair.

"We could use the oak," Justin said. He'd been wondering about cutting corners. Using their own lumber would save a fortune for them. Now with Grandma's plan for the woods, he wouldn't have to fight the family and Andree to cut trees. "We'll plan to take out only the trees that need removing to make room for the cabins."

Andree slapped his knee and stood up. "Boys, I've made up my mind. I'll take the job. I'd rather have the say about what trees come out than some stranger."

"Good!" Justin and Trent said together. They both reached to shake Andree's hand at the same time, and their hands brushed together. Both jerked as if they'd been snakebitten. They glanced at each other, then looked quickly away.

* * *

With a warm breeze flipping her long dark hair, Emily walked toward town, her head buzzing with what her future held. She stood on the bridge and looked down into Blue River. Water rushed between the tree-lined banks. Two ragged-looking boys fished off one bank, intently watching their lines. She'd learned to swim in the river when she was six. She and Celine had sneaked away when they were all having a picnic and Celine had taught her to swim.

"Just move your arms and legs like this," Celine shouted over the splashes she was making. "You can do it."

"I might drown." Emily was afraid of water because she'd fallen in over her head once when she was wading.

"I won't let you drown," Celine said. She held Emily around the waist. "Just lay down in the water and keep your face turned sideways. You can do it."

And she had. They'd both been proud, but couldn't tell anyone but Trent. They knew he wouldn't tattle.

After that they'd gone often. Many times Trent was with them. In her mind she heard their giggles and the splash of water. But that was a long time ago.

With a sigh she walked away from the bridge and past the lumber mill. The buzz of the saws cut off the sounds of the birds and even the sound of the train racing past. She glanced down the street that led to the orphanage where Lark had lived all her life until she'd married Clay and where Celine had lived until she married Trent.

"Oh, Celine. Do you mind that I'm marrying Trent?"

Emily walked down Main Street toward the courthouse. Lark and Clay had probably stayed home today to be with Rachel. It was going to be very hard on them to have Rachel leave them.

Emily's tan skirt flipped about her legs as she walked up the sidewalk to the large brick courthouse. Neatly trimmed grass wrapped around the building with flower beds scattered here and there, some in bloom and others waiting for summer. She brushed her shimmering raven hair over her shoulder with the back of her hand, then fingered the pearl brooch at the neck of her green blouse. She spotted Trent outside the courthouse. He looked handsome in his white shirt and dark pants. His hair was combed neatly. Should she tell him she'd changed her mind?

She considered it for a minute, but didn't. She walked to him, smiling hesitantly. She noticed the white skin showing near his sideburns. "It looks like you just came from the barber."

"Sure did," Trent said with a laugh. After he'd left Justin and Andree, he'd gone to the bank to see about his money, then right to the barber. He wanted to look his best for his wedding. His heart lurched, but he ignored it. He'd set his course and nothing would change his mind.

"Justin," called a man from the sidewalk.

Trent and Emily turned at the same time. Sheriff Lamont stood there with his hands resting lightly on his hips. He was in his forties and was beginning to get a paunch.

"Afternoon, Emily," the sheriff said, then he turned to Trent. "I'd like a word with you, Justin."

Trent frowned impatiently.

"This is Trent Havlick," Emily said. "Justin's twin. Trent, Spud Lamont."

"Trent, you say!" Sheriff Lamont lifted his hat to scratch his balding head. His hook nose was large on his narrow face. "Well, I'll be."

"Justin's at the Wagon Works if you want to speak to him," Trent said stiffly.

"You'll do just fine." Sheriff Lamont walked to them, his hazel eyes narrowed. "I heard a rumor a few minutes ago."

"What's that, Sheriff?" Emily knew he liked gossip as well as anyone. And he spread more than his fair share.

Sheriff Lamont settled his hat in place on his head. "About Jennet Havlick's plans for the pines."

Trent didn't want to take the time to talk about it, but he said, "We're going to make the woods into a nature preserve and logging museum. In fact, Grandma even plans on putting cabins in over by Deep Lake."

Sheriff Lamont clicked his tongue. "That sure sounds like more work for me, what with more people around. But I guess it means more money for the town merchants, so I can't complain. Just when will all this come about?"

"As soon as possible." Trent took Emily's arm as he turned to walk into the courthouse.

"Good luck," Sheriff Lamont said. "Nice meeting you, Havlick. It's always good to have another Havlick around."

Emily started to turn to tell the sheriff about them getting married and leaving, but Trent tugged on her to keep walking. She glanced at him from the corner of her eyes. He looked very determined. A shiver slipped down her spine.

The wooden floor of the courthouse was polished to a shine that reflected anything or anyone on it. Several closed doors lined the halls that went off the main entry. Voices drifted down the hall to Emily's left. A spittoon stood in one corner, a tall green plant in another. Pictures of lumbering in its heyday lined the walls.

Trent leaned his head close to Emily's ear and whispered, "If I hear another word about Grandma's plans, I'll belt somebody! I'm tired of the whole thing. I just want to get back to Texas where I belong."

Emily grinned. "You just didn't like being called Justin. Admit it."

Trent tapped Emily on the tip of her nose. "You think you're smart when you're right, don't you?"

"Of course."

"I was getting used to being the only Havlick around." Trent flung his arm wide. "Now here I am with Havlicks all over the place, and to make matters worse, there's one who looks just like me."

"No, Trent. You're much better looking," Emily said, laughing up at him.

He shook his head and chuckled. "You always know what to say, don't you?"

"Of course. The clerk's office is this way," Emily said, leading Trent toward it.

"I have news for you that might leave you speechless."

"Oh?"

"Your pa has agreed to head the project for Grandma. He said better him than a stranger who doesn't care about the trees."

"I am surprised," Emily said, her blue eyes wide. "Ma said he's against the whole thing. He'll do a good job, though. He loves those trees as much as the Havlick family does."

Trent's throat closed over. Once he'd loved the trees, but now he didn't care if he ever walked in them again. "Let's stop talking about the trees and get our marriage license."

Emily's stomach cramped, but she smiled and walked to the office with Trent, her head high and her shoulders square. She'd made up her mind and nothing was going to change it.

CHAPTER

7

♦ Jennet leaned against Free as they stood on the porch after supper, looking across the field toward the white pines. The temperature had dropped slightly and the breeze was pleasantly cool. The wind brought the constant aroma of pine along with an occasional whiff of the barnyard. The blades on the windmill squawked as they turned. A horse whinnied and another answered. Tears pricked Jennet's blue eyes as she looked up at Free. Sighing, she asked, "Is my dream too big?"

Free turned her to him and kissed her gently. "No, Jen. It isn't too big. It's a wonderful dream, and we're going to make it come true."

At seventy-four Jennet was as beautiful to him as she had been at sixteen. He'd bought her from a cruel uncle to whom she'd been indentured by her equally cruel father. Then when he'd learned he had to be married to inherit what his grandfather had left him, he'd married her. The marriage had started off rocky, but before the first year was over, they were deeply in love. They had six children; Clay, the eldest, had married Lark Baritt more than thirty years ago and she had given them the twins—Trent and Justin.

"I want to see Havlick's Wilderness finished before I die."

Jennet cupped her hand along Free's clean-shaven cheek. His sun-browned skin was etched with wrinkles and his once dark brown hair was gray. She saw the love in his dark eyes and it touched her deeply. He'd give her anything she asked for if he could. "Are you sure I'm not asking too much?"

"It'll take a lot of money—money we planned to leave to the great-grandchildren."

Jennet's blue eyes clouded. "I don't care how much money it takes! I want others to share the beauty we've preserved! Am I being selfish?"

"No, Jen. We all agreed to do it."

"Do you think any of the neighbors or the folks in town will object?"

"Why should they? We'll do our best to make sure nobody's privacy is invaded. And the merchants in town will be glad for the business. Tourism is growing in Michigan. Why not bring some of those folks here?"

"That's what I say!"

Free chuckled. "I know." They'd had the same discussion before, but Jennet seemed to need reassurance. She didn't want to do anything to cause harm to another person. "We'll call a meeting and talk to other farmers and the merchants. Then we'll know how they feel."

"Good idea." She stood quietly for a while. "The twins don't care about the pines." A tear slipped down her cheek. "But I *want* them to care! I want them to feel the same passion for the trees that we have!" She flicked away her tear and rubbed her hand down her flowered dress. "I thought working together on the project would do it for them. But they gave it over to Andree! I love Andree and I know he'll do a good job. But I want Trent and Justin to do it! Together! Oh, why can't they feel for the pines the way we do?"

Free held Jennet close and rested his cheek against her white hair. "They didn't get involved with them like we did and Clay and Lark did. Lark guarded the pines and grew to love

94

them. She took the boys to the pines when they were young, and they seemed to love them. But something happened when Celine died that drove the boys apart. If they'd give themselves a chance, they'd learn to care about the trees again."

"Yes, I'm sure of it!" Jennet pulled back from Free and spread her hands over the front of his blue work shirt. "I'm thankful Trent's going to marry Emily. Maybe she can convince him to stay here.

"I have a wedding gift for them. That's why I asked them to come this evening."

Free glanced at his gold watch, then slipped it back in his pocket. "They should be here any minute."

Jennet walked to a white rocker and sank down, her legs suddenly too tired to support her. "I had an architect draw plans for the cabins I want over at Deep Lake. Did I show them to you?"

"Yes," Free chuckled. "Twice." He patted her hand as he sat in the rocker beside her.

She laughed and wrinkled her nose at him. "You'll have to be patient with me. Occasionally I forget little details, but I still remember the important things! It's strange that sometimes I feel only twenty, then other times, I think I'm way over a hundred. It's a good thing we live by faith, not feelings."

They rocked in silence a while.

"I want the main cabin to be a place rich folks from Chicago and Detroit would come to and spend a couple of weeks or even the whole summer. If city folks could stay in our pines and rest and relax and take in the beauty and the serenity, they'd go back refreshed and ready to work again."

Free had heard it all before. Jennet had begun to describe to him her dream of Havlick's Wilderness some time ago. He knew it had been on her mind most of the time as she gradually envisioned a plan. And he was certain she'd shared her dream only with him. But now that she'd told the family and most of them had gotten excited about it, she needed to talk and he let her. She liked describing the small cabins for folks with modest income and the big cabin for wealthy people. And when she did, he could imagine it, too. She liked talking about her big dream. Often they'd sat on the porch after dinner and talked about it, getting eventually to the past. Jennet had helped free slaves through the underground railroad when they were first married. Those memories of danger and struggle would live again as they talked and he would remember his struggle making it as a lumberman. They would remember Jig, the old woodsman who could spout Bible verses as easily as he could name trees and birds. And they often spoke of the covenant they had with God and each other. Although their life together hadn't always been easy, it had been a good life. As Free listened to the soft melody of Jennet's voice, he was content. If only Justin and Trent could come to terms with whatever had driven a wedge between them . . .

A cloud of dust billowed on the road leading to the farm, and Free shook his head at the sight of it. If he had his way, everyone would still be driving horses and buggies. The new gas buggies made too much noise and too much dust and they left unpleasant odors hanging in the air. He wondered briefly if they could ban automobiles from Havlick's Wilderness. Then he supposed the family wouldn't allow it. They were all busy becoming modern. He still hated to admit that Clay had been right to get out of the buggy-making business and into making wagons, something many people would still need even when use of the gas buggy had become popular

"It's Trent and Emily," Jennet said, smiling as she slowly stood, shaking her cotton dress so it fell in graceful folds to her ankles. She made sure the cuffs of the long sleeves were still buttoned, then tucked a strand of hair into the bun at the nape of her neck. She walked down the porch steps with Free close behind her and stood in the yard to wait for them. Silently she prayed for Trent. She wanted God's covenant to be as real to him as it was to her. She wanted him to know all of God's promises were true and were for him. She turned to Free. "Remember when the twins were about ten years old and they made a covenant with each other just the way the Bible tells about the one Jonathan and David made?"

Free smiled and nodded. "They even pricked their fingers with a needle and smeared their blood together. They vowed to fight for each other, take care of each other, and always love each other."

"I think I'll remind Trent of that."

"Better not. He's too angry right now to be reminded. Let's pray for them both, and when the time's right, we'll bring it up."

"You're always right, Free." Jennet smiled at him, then turned to watch Trent and Emily walk from the blue Dodge toward them. Trent was wearing a white shirt and dark pants and Emily a peachy-pink dress that Jennet thought was much too short. Her long hair curled over her shoulders. Jennet was glad Emily had sense enough to leave it long, and not get it bobbed like Priscilla had hers.

"Hello, Grandma," Trent said, hugging her. She smelled the same to him, like bayberry soap. "Grandpa." He hugged Free, too, as Emily went into Jennet's arms. Grandpa smelled the same too, like sawdust and sweat.

They talked about the pleasant May weather and how the plans were coming along for their wedding the next day. Then Jennet asked Trent and Emily to sit on the porch on the bench between pots of ivy facing the rockers.

"I want to tell you both about my wedding gift," Jennet said as she slowly sank in her rocker and smoothed her long skirt over her knees. She refused to wear the new short style, and sewed her own clothes so she could make the skirts as long as she wanted.

"We don't expect gifts," Trent said as he and Emily settled on the bench.

Emily nodded her agreement as she folded her hands in her

lap and crossed her ankles. Gifts would embarrass her since this wasn't a usual marriage. "Please, no gifts," she said.

"You might as well make up your minds to take this gift," Free said with a chuckle. "Your grandma is determined. I know—she told me." It had taken Jennet years to find the courage to speak her own mind. Now she had no trouble letting everyone know her thoughts. She was even known to raise her voice now and then.

Smiling, Jennet nodded as she folded her hands in her lap. "I am giving you two hundred acres of land that joins the property you already own, Trent."

He flushed and shook his head. "Don't do it, Grandma," he said sharply. He knew she was trying to get him to stay. "I can't take it! I don't intend to live on that place again."

"Don't be so hasty, young man!" Frowning, Jennet leaned forward. "You don't know that you won't live there again. So, don't be so quick to turn down my gift. I am giving you that land."

Emily looked from Jennet to Trent and saw the identical stubborn set of their jaws. She knew Trent was sincere in refusing Jennet's gift, and she knew Jennet was sincere in saying she would give it.

"The gift is very nice," Emily said with a warm smile. "If we do take it, we'll sign it over to Rachel so that the land stays in the family."

"Do as you want." Jennet fought against tears of disappointment. "I just know I am giving it to you. It's almost covered with second-growth trees, and it has a wide valley that would be perfect for running beef cattle. And there's a spring-fed stream running through the place, so you'd always have plenty of water."

Trent tensed, but Emily's hand on his arm served to calm him. "Please try to understand, Grandma. I can't stay here. I have a life at the Rocking R Ranch. That's where I belong now."

"You're a Havlick!" Jennet jumped to her feet, her eyes blazing. Free tried to restrain her, but she brushed him aside. "You belong here, Trent! I don't know why you would ever think you don't."

Emily gripped Trent's arm so tightly she was sure she left nail prints in his skin. "We'll come back for visits," Emily said hastily.

Jennet shook her finger at Trent and cried, "This is Havlick land and a Havlick should tend it! Let Texas be tamed by someone who belongs there."

Free stood quickly and pulled Jennet firmly to his side. "Jen, calm down. Things are starting to get out of hand. Trent, accept the gift like a man."

Trent shook his head. "I will not take it! And I mean that. Give it to someone else."

Jennet's nostrils flared and she jerked away from Free. "All right. I'll do just that!" Her eyes locked on Trent's face, she studied him intently. After what seemed an eternity, she said, "I will give the land to Emily. She's going to be your wife, but a woman needs something of her own." Jennet had bought that very piece of land with money Free's grandpa had left her. She firmly believed other women should have the same opportunity. Jennet pointed at Emily. "It's yours."

Emily looked at Trent as if to ask what she should do.

"Don't you dare!" he snapped. How he longed to be back in Texas where he didn't have to face his family or his feelings.

Emily frowned slightly. His anger both alarmed and angered her. Why was he being so pig-headed? But telling her not to accept it was like saying "sic 'em" to a bulldog. She lifted her chin and turned to Jennet. "I'm honored to accept your generous gift, Jennet. Thank you."

Trent scowled at Emily. "What do you think you're doing?"

"Accepting your grandma's gift the way you should have."

He sputtered angrily, then stormed off the porch toward his automobile.

"He's angry." Emily fingered the brooch at her throat. Should she refuse the gift for Trent's sake?

"He'll get over it," Free said softly.

"He has to," Jennet said.

Trent stood beside his Dodge, his back stiff with anger. How dare Emily accept the land after he'd refused to? This was not the time to prove she had a mind of her own! Trent turned and impatiently called, "Emily! Are you coming or not?"

"She's not." Jennet caught Emily's arm. "She has papers to sign."

"I'll wait here." Trent slipped under the steering wheel, his head buzzing with sharp, angry words. He should never have returned home! He could've sent a telegram asking for money.

Emily followed Jennet and Freeman into their study where Jennet had spread out the papers to be signed and the deed for the land.

As Free held a pen out to her, she said, "Maybe I shouldn't."

Jennet tapped Emily's shoulder. "This is right, dear. Go ahead."

"Trent will get over it," Free said.

"You're right of course." Emily signed and dated the papers and put the deed in her purse. "Thank you, Jen. Free. This'll be Rachel's someday."

"No." Jennet shook her head. "It isn't for Rachel. I want it to go to your first son."

Emily turned crimson red. "As you wish." After today Trent might be so angry there wouldn't be a first son or any other children.

Several minutes later, Emily said goodbye and joined Trent in his blue Dodge. He drove away without waving to his grandparents. A huge cloud of dust billowed behind them, and the tires skidded as he turned on the gravel road.

"Why did you do it?" he asked through clenched teeth.

Emily shrugged. "Because it made Jennet happy." She jabbed Trent's arm. "It won't do you a bit of good to have a fit or pout or anything. The land is mine. So, that's that."

His nostrils flared in anger. "Have you always been this high-handed?"

"Probably."

He slapped the steering wheel with one hand. "How did Celine and I put up with you?"

Emily laughed, but it sounded strained. "You loved me. And I love you. That's how *I* put up with *you*."

"Emily, I don't know about you."

"Well, I certainly wasn't going to hurt your grandparents just because you're afraid you might be forced to stay here."

"I will not stay here!"

"I know. So relax, will you? Taking the land won't make us stay here."

His anger drained away and he chuckled as he carefully passed a pickup. "You're right, I guess."

"As usual."

He chuckled again. "I had forgotten."

"Don't let it happen again." She grinned at him and made a face.

"I think we just might end up having a very good marriage. Maybe friendship is more important than a grand passion."

"Maybe." Emily cleared her throat. Now was the time to discuss the delicate topic she'd been thinking about. She flushed as she said, "I want to say something but it's embarrassing to me."

"So?" He cocked his brow and glanced at her, then turned back to the road. "What is it?"

"Can we wait . . . to share . . . a bed . . . until we . . . get to Texas?"

He slowed the automobile, frowning. She never ceased to surprise him. "Why?"

"A new start in a new place." She fingered a fold of her skirt. "It'll be . . . easier for me."

Trent hesitated, then shrugged. "If that's what you want." Maybe it would be best. Maybe he wouldn't feel so guilty about sleeping with Celine's best friend once they were far away from here.

Emily sighed in relief. "Thanks."

He chuckled as he speeded back up. "You sure do embarrass easily, don't you?"

"Yes, about some things."

Trent laughed. "Good. Now I know just what to tease you about."

"Tease away. But if you can dish it out," she wagged her finger at him, "you'd better be ready and able to take it."

Trent laughed. She always could hold her own with him. "Bob Lavery was stupid not to marry you."

She turned away as sudden tears filled her eyes. For a while she'd actually forgotten Bob.

*   *   *

Tuesday at five in the little anteroom at the church Emily clung to a bouquet of lavender and white lilacs and lily of the valley. The Havlick and Bjoerling families along with a few selected friends sat in the sanctuary waiting. Organ music filled the air. Rachel, so excited she thought she couldn't wait, was squirming. Lark shushed her with a soft pat on her leg.

Clay smiled at Lark as he thought of their wedding day. He'd married her so he wouldn't lose the pines. He had mortgaged them to finance his business and was about to default on the loan. Willie Thorne was waiting to pounce when Lark's father turned up after a long, long absence and gave Clay the money he needed. But he said that to have the money, Clay must convince Lark to marry him. Feeling like a first-class cad, he'd done it. To his surprise, he'd discovered he loved her with a passion that startled him. He'd always wondered how Matt

Baritt knew something about him he didn't know himself. However Matt knew, Clay would be forever grateful. He couldn't imagine living his life without Lark.

Justin ran his finger around his collar and longed to be back at his desk working. He didn't want to see Trent or have to think about him. He glanced at Priscilla beside him and his pulse quickened. She looked beautiful and smelled like roses. After Trent left, maybe he'd make more time for Pris.

Priscilla moved closer to Justin as she remembered their wedding. They had married ten years ago, just after Trent left. They said their vows in this very church, and then went to Grand Haven for a honeymoon cruise. It was very romantic. Justin gave her his full attention and never once mentioned the Wagon Works. They were happy then. She'd almost given up hope they would ever be happy again. She glanced at their children to make sure they were sitting quietly. After the long lecture she'd given them, they were behaving.

With tears glistening in her eyes, Martha sat with her sons, leaving a space for Andree to sit beside her after he walked Emily down the aisle. They'd telephoned Betty and Lucille, with news of the wedding, but neither could come on such short notice. Betty's baby was due shortly and Lucille's husband couldn't leave his work. Martha prayed silently for her children, especially for Emily on this very special day.

Free slipped his arm around Jennet. He was remembering their wedding day. It had been a spur of the moment wedding and they were both dressed in work clothes. He prayed Trent and Emily would grow to love each other as much as they did.

Short and balding, Pastor Gray approached the altar with Trent walking behind him. Trent's spine tingled as he realized what he was doing, but it was too late to back out. The music swelled as the organist played the Wedding March.

Her stomach fluttering wildly, Emily slipped her hand through her father's arm and they walked down the aisle to join Trent. Emily had chosen a simple white dress and a roll brim, white, silk-velvet hat. There hadn't been time to get an elaborate gown even if she'd wanted one.

A pain shot through Trent as he thought of the day Celine had walked toward him down the same aisle. He'd been happier than he'd ever thought possible. This time was different. He wasn't expected to be happy. He wore a plain black suit that he'd bought just that morning for the occasion. He managed to smile at Emily and she relaxed enough to smile back.

She listened intently as Pastor Gray read the ceremony and then asked them to speak their vows to each other. Trent's voice cracked twice, but Emily managed to keep hers even and strong. Inside she was quivering, but she didn't let that show. As they exchanged vows, she remembered that Trent and Celine had exchanged the same vows, and she paled. What was she doing marrying Celine's husband?

At the correct time Trent slipped a wide silver wedding band on her finger and she glanced up at him in surprise. She hadn't thought about a ring, and she was surprised he had. Celine's wedding ring had been gold with three diamonds. It was in safe keeping for Rachel when she came of age. Emily stared at the wide silver band. Trent had actually taken the time to buy her a ring! A thrill shot through her.

At the end of the ceremony, Pastor Gray said, "You may kiss the bride," and Emily tensed. Her eyes opened wide in alarm as she met Trent's gaze. He stiffened, then brushed his lips against hers so quickly she barely felt the kiss.

"I'm proud to present Mr. and Mrs. Trent Havlick!" Pastor Gray said in a ringing voice. Organ music erupted in the silence, and Emily clung to Trent's arm as they fled down the aisle to wait outdoors to be congratulated. Emily had planned to drive right to Clay and Lark's home for wedding cake and punch, but Martha had insisted they greet their families and friends on the church lawn.

The guests swarmed from the church into the late afternoon

sunshine. Rachel dashed away from Lark toward Trent and Emily.

Suddenly a shot rang out. Rachel screamed and dropped to the ground. Women screamed and men shouted.

Emily swayed against Trent. Why had someone shot at them? What was happening? Maybe the shooter would shoot again.

Sweat soaking his body, Trent dragged Emily behind a giant oak. "Stay here!" he commanded and ran to Rachel, his heart racing, expecting a bullet to tear into his body. He scooped up Rachel in his arms and sped back to duck behind the tree with Emily while the others shouted to him to be careful.

"Is Rachel hurt?" Lark screamed as she huddled with the others at the side of the church building.

"We're all right," Trent shouted. Then he saw blood on Rachel and sank weakly to his knees. "She's been shot!"

Frantically Emily examined Rachel and saw she'd been wounded in her shoulder, her arm, and her leg. She was unconscious. Emily prayed that Rachel had only fainted from pain and fear.

"She's not dead," Emily called as she used her handkerchief to staunch the blood flowing from Rachel's shoulder. "But she needs a doctor."

"Oh, Rachel!" Lark screamed, struggling to run to her, but Clay held her back.

At the side of the church, Justin pulled Priscilla and the children close to him. "What is going on?" he wondered aloud. Who had shot at them and why? This was not the wild, wooly days of lumbering!

"Who shot that gun?" Freeman barked.

"I did!" a man shouted from behind a clump of bushes across the street from the church. "I didn't mean for nobody to get hurt. I just want all you Havlicks to listen to me!"

"Get a doctor! And the sheriff," Trent called frantically as he looked down on Rachel's pale face and the blood flowing freely. He couldn't lose his daughter now that he'd found her.

"Don't nobody move or I will shoot *to kill*," the man shouted.

"Everyone stay put!" Free cried.

"What's going on?" Justin shouted. "What do you want?"

"I'm tryin' to tell you!"

Trent looked helplessly at Emily.

She smelled his sweat and saw the pain in his eyes. "Who would shoot at us?" she whispered.

"I don't know, but I'll find out." Trent took a deep, steadying breath. "Then tell us so we can get my little girl to a doctor! She's bleeding bad!"

"I came to warn you not to build that tourist trap you're planning. We want things left the way they are."

"What business is it of yours?" Jennet cried, alarmed that anyone would want to cause them harm just because of her dream.

"I made it my business!" the man roared. He fired a shot into the air. It echoed; then all was silent. "Stop your plans or next time I'll kill me a Havlick or two!"

"You won't get away with this!" Jennet cried.

Free frowned at her and whispered, "Quiet! Don't antagonize him."

Jennet scowled at Free, but she was quiet, even though she seethed inside.

Emily held her breath and waited for a few minutes. When the man didn't speak again, she whispered, "I think he's gone."

Rachel opened her eyes and said with a sob, "I hurt all over."

"We have to get Rachel to a doctor," Emily said, patting Rachel.

Trent stood hesitantly and called, "I'm taking my daughter

to the doctor." When the shooter didn't shout or shoot again, Trent stepped from behind the tree. The others swarmed from the side of the church and filled the front yard.

"We're taking Rachel to the doctor," Trent said as he scooped her up. "Somebody go tell the sheriff what happened."

"We're going with you to the doctor," Lark said as she and Clay huddled over Rachel.

"I'll tell the sheriff," Justin said over his shoulder as he strode toward his automobile. "Pris, take the kids to Mom's."

Priscilla wanted to stay close to Justin where she felt safe, but she herded the children to her automobile.

"The rest of us will wait at Clay's too," Free said, his arm around Jennet to keep her from trying to follow the shooter. Fearful the shooter would return, he gestured for everyone to leave quickly.

Several minutes later the doctor bandaged Rachel's wounds. "She'll be just fine," he said. "Keep the areas clean and change the bandages every day. If you see any sign of infection, bring her right in."

"Is it safe for her to travel?" Trent asked.

"Safe, but not wise. Traveling's too dusty and too tiring. Rachel needs plenty of rest and her wounds tended regularly."

"Then we won't travel yet," Emily said.

His jaw set, Trent paid the doctor. Taking Rachel gently in his arms, he carried her outdoors.

"You'll be fine." Emily patted Rachel as she hurried along beside Trent. "We'll get you to Grandpa's and right to bed."

"I want wedding cake," Rachel said weakly.

Emily laughed softly. "We'll see."

Anger and resentment raged inside Trent. He should've taken Rachel and Emily and left yesterday. Whoever had shot his child was going to pay!

The sun had set and the temperature had dropped. Lights

shone from houses up and down the street. A dog barked and an automobile backfired.

"We'll have to put off the trip until she's better," Emily said.

"I know," Trent said grimly.

"You won't leave me behind, will you, Daddy?" Rachel asked, her eyes wide in her ashen face.

"No, I won't," Trent said around the lump in his throat. How long would it take Rachel to trust him not to leave her again? He set Rachel on Emily's lap on the front seat of his Dodge, then ran around the front and climbed in under the steering wheel. As he pushed the starter he said over the grinding noise, "We'll stay with Mom until we leave."

"That's fine," Emily said as he pulled away from the curb. She knew he wouldn't go to the home he'd shared with Celine. And she didn't want to. It didn't seem right. "Your mom has plenty of bedrooms for all of us."

Trent shot her a look of surprise. "Bedrooms? Who can think about that at a time like this?"

Rachel moved restlessly on Emily's lap. "I hurt," Rachel said, sounding close to tears. "Did somebody really shoot me?"

"Yes," Trent said grimly. "But we'll find out who did it so he can't do it again."

Emily shivered at the rage in Trent's answer.

Several blocks away Justin stood beside Sheriff Lamont as they looked around the area where the man with the shotgun had stood. The sheriff had picked up two empty shotgun shells, and they'd found footprints too obliterated to see clearly.

"Looks like you Havlicks will have to watch your step." Sheriff Lamont scratched his head, settled his cap in place, and rested his hand on the butt of his gun.

Justin shook his head. "Grandma won't give up her dream just because of this. I know her!"

"I don't know her all that much, but I bet you're right. If she wants, I can assign a man to keep his eye on all of you. It'd be a tall order, though."

"We can watch out for ourselves." Justin squatted down to look again for clues. The streetlight was too dim for him to see clearly. Tomorrow in the daylight he'd look the place over. He stood slowly, his eyes narrowed thoughtfully. "Why should anyone care what we do with the pines?"

Sheriff Lamont shrugged. "Might not be the pines at all. Could be the local farmers don't want strangers trespassing on their land."

"Grandma already talked to them. Nobody objected enough to want to shoot at us."

"Well, we'll find the man and put a stop to him shooting anyone. I sure hope the little girl will be all right."

"Thank you. So do I." Justin told the sheriff good night and strode to his Duesenberg. What would he have done if one of his children had been shot? His stomach knotted and he quickened his pace. Maybe he should try to talk Grandma out of her plans. He shook his head as he started his automobile. Grandma was stubborn. She wouldn't let tonight's shooting scare her.

But what if someone was killed next time?

"Then let it be me," he whispered hoarsely.

* * *

Emily pulled the covers up to Rachel's chin, then kissed her cheek. The lamp on the dresser cast a soft glow over the pink and white room. "Sweet dreams."

Trent knelt at the side of the bed and gently pushed strands of Rachel's red hair off her forehead. "Close your eyes and sleep tight, honey. Daddy won't let anything hurt you."

"You won't leave me while I sleep, will you?" Rachel asked, barely able to keep her eyes open. The medication the doctor had given her so she'd sleep soundly through the night had taken effect.

Trent kissed Rachel's cheek. "I won't leave you. I promise."

"We both promise." Emily knelt beside Trent. "Close your eyes, Rachel. Your heavenly Father is watching over you. He never leaves you. He loves you more than we do."

"I know," Rachel whispered as she finally closed her eyes. A few minutes later she was fast asleep.

Trent kissed her cheek again, then stood and lifted Emily up with him. He kept his hand on her arm. "She's so beautiful."

"Just like Celine," Emily whispered with a catch in her voice.

"She looks like Celine, but she sure acts like you."

Emily chuckled softly. "She does have a very strong will."

Just then Lark and Clay stuck their heads in the door. "Can we come in?" Lark asked.

"Of course," Trent said. "But she's already asleep."

"I'd like to stand by her side a while." Lark dabbed tears from her eyes.

"I'm thankful she's all right," Clay said hoarsely as he blinked moisture from his eyes.

"We all are." Trent kissed Lark and hugged Clay.

"I'll take my things to my room," Emily said. She'd explained to Lark that she wasn't sharing a room with Trent until they got to Texas. Lark had been surprised, but hadn't said anything.

"Your brothers already brought your trunk in," Clay said.

"Oh, good," Emily said. They were sure to tease her about not sleeping with Trent and she didn't want to face them.

"We'll see you downstairs later." Trent led Emily out so his parents could be alone with Rachel. Clay and Lark's room was directly across the hall from Rachel's. His was near the top of the steps and Emily's across from his.

She carefully pulled off her hat as they walked to her room.

The door stood open, but her trunk wasn't in sight. She dropped her hat on the flowered bedspread and looked around. "Where's my trunk?"

"I told them to put it in my room," Trent said.

Emily turned on him, her eyes flashing. "In your room? How could you do that? You promised! Did you forget?"

"Oh. Oh, yes." His temper flared. He'd told the boys to put the trunk in his room just to keep them from teasing Emily, but he wasn't about to tell her that now that she'd gotten so angry at him. "I guess I did forget."

"A person's word is his bond, you know," she said, keeping her voice soft so it wouldn't carry down the hall.

"You always were too trusting," he said, grinning.

"You always kept your word," she said stiffly.

"That was then. This is now. Times change. People change."

Was it possible he'd changed so much that she couldn't see right through him the way she had in the past?

"I told you people change. *I* changed!"

"I guess you have! You used to give your word and nothing could make you break it!" Emily knotted her fists at her sides and her breasts heaved in agitation. Spots of Rachel's blood streaked her wedding gown. "Do you think you can force me to share your bed?"

He gripped her arms. "I'm stronger than you are. I can make you do anything I want."

"No. No, you can't! You could make Celine do anything you wanted, but not me!"

He dropped his hands and stepped back from her. "You're the one who wanted this to be a real marriage. But this time, lady, you won't get your own way! It's either start our marriage tonight, or never!"

"Then it will be never!" She wanted to pound him with her fists or pull his hair out by the roots. "Bring my trunk in here and be done with it!"

He spun on his heels and strode across the hall to his room. He lifted the trunk to his shoulder easily, carried it to her room, and set it down with a thump. "Now, let's get downstairs and listen to our families wish us a happy life together."

With her head high and her cheeks flushed red, Emily walked ahead of him down the wide stairs.

CHAPTER

8

♦ Trent laid down his fork and patted his mouth with his white linen napkin. He'd changed from the denim pants and shirt he'd worn during the day, while looking for clues for who shot Rachel, to a white shirt and dark wool pants. He managed to smile at his parents, but he didn't bother looking at Emily. They'd barely spoken since the night before. When they had, Emily's anger was still evident. Rachel had eaten earlier and was already in bed.

"Fine meal, Mom," Trent said.

"How would you know? You barely touched your food." Lark frowned slightly. "And I made roast beef the way you like it."

"He has his mind on who shot Rachel, no doubt," Emily said. Her eyes were cold when she looked at him.

Trent flushed. Pete at the Wagon Works had talked about Gilly's Place where a guy could relax, get a drink, and find a girl. Without being too obvious, he had learned Gilly's Place was north of town, hidden among a stand of pines. Could Emily know he was planning to go there? "We still don't have a lead on who shot Rachel," he said. "The sheriff said he's been working on it, too."

Clay set down his glass of water. "I've heard some whispers

around town that it's the bootleggers who're worried about the tourists. From what I've heard, they think more people will bring more law. And that could shut down their illegal establishments and the sale of liquor."

Trent stiffened slightly. He had to be very careful of his reaction around Emily. She was too observant! "Have you heard about a speakeasy around here?" Was Gilly's the place Dad was talking about?

Clay shrugged. "None around Blue Creek, but I did hear there's one in Fromberg. And that's too close!"

"I'm thankful our family doesn't darken the doors of such places," Lark said with a shudder.

"Very thankful." Emily looked right at Trent. Would he go to a speakeasy?

"When I was a very young lady I belonged to the Temperance League and our group marched on a tavern that was trying to open right here in town. It was a terrible experience, but I'd do it again to close down those places." Lark's eyes flashed with indignation. "To think of people drinking and carrying on! I'm glad we're a dry state. I pray prohibition becomes a way of life for our country!"

"I'm afraid it won't," Clay said with a shake of his head. "There're too many people who want to have their liquor— right or wrong. That's why bootlegging is going on and that's why so many people are sneaking off to these places called speakeasies."

Lark lifted her chin high. "If I ever learn of such a place around here, I'll shut it down with my own hands!"

"And I'll help you," Emily said firmly.

Struggling with his conscience, Trent pushed back his chair and excused himself. "Don't wait up for me. I don't know how late I'll be."

"Where're you going, son?" Clay leaned back in his chair. "I could go with you, if you want."

Trent's heart lurched. "No need, Dad. You're tired after all that's happened the past two days. I'm used to being on my own."

Emily saw the guilt on Trent's face. What was he going to do? She wondered if he was heading out to his farm so he could reminisce about Celine and the happy times they'd had together.

"Good night." Trent kissed his mother's soft cheek, clamped a hand on his dad's shoulder, and gave Emily a brief nod.

Emily wanted to leap up and demand he stay home so they could talk and get the problem settled between them, but she sat very still and watched him leave.

Trent strode through the darkness to his Dodge. The night was pleasantly warm. Wood smoke from houses all around and the perfume of apple blossoms on the trees next door filled the air. Trent glanced back at the soft light shining from the windows. Did Emily suspect where he was going? "Forget her! She's too stubborn and unforgiving, and she deserves whatever I do to her."

Impatiently he opened the door. Maybe he should get a Duesenberg before he headed back to Texas. He could spare the money. Slowly he slid under the steering wheel. There was enough money in his bank account to buy the Rocking R and stock it with the cattle he wanted. He'd drawn it all out before the wedding, then had put most of it right back in when he learned they couldn't leave for a while. He took a deep breath and looked back toward the house. Should he go back inside? He thought of Emily's anger and his jaw tightened. He wouldn't spend the evening with her accusing eyes!

His mouth bone dry and his palms sweaty, Trent drove north out of town. He slowed as he neared the cemetery where Celine was buried. He groaned in agony. Without knowing he was going to do it, he pulled off the road and stopped. Slowly he walked through the cemetery. A twig snapped under his foot and he jumped. Moonlight gave him enough light to find the grave. Dad told him they'd added a monument after he left. He ran a finger over the engraved name. "Celine," he whispered and his voice broke. "I wanted you to live so we could grow old together." He knew only her body was buried there and that she was in heaven, but that didn't make her being gone any easier. Did she know the anger and bitterness he felt toward Justin for what he'd done to her?

He pushed the agonizing thoughts aside. He didn't want to think about that. He wanted to remember the fun they'd had together.

He squatted beside the grave and thought of Celine, but Emily's face kept getting in the way. And he could hear her speaking. "You're a man of your word, Trent. You must forgive Justin. Rachel needs you. God loves you. You're a man of your word, Trent."

He leaped to his feet, his fists doubled at his sides. "I gave my word to hate Justin forever! Is that the word you want me to keep, Emily Bjoerling?"

"Not Bjoerling. Havlick."

Her voice was as clear to him as if she were standing at his side. He whirled around, but of course she wasn't there. Like a mad man he ran from the cemetery to his automobile. He pushed the starter, and the noise exploded in the silence of the cemetery.

His wide mouth set in a grim line, he drove north until he found the turn off that led to Gilly's Place. He parked his Dodge away from the vehicles hidden behind a stand of pines. He didn't want anyone to recognize his automobile.

As he stepped to the ground, he saw the dark outline of Gilly's. It was a long wooden building without windows. The sight of it caused a chill to run through him. Did he really want to be here?

He stood in the shadows of the pines as three men who worked at the Wagon Works headed in. Already drunk, they were laughing and talking. What would he do if they saw him?

Of course, they'd think he was Justin. Four women in short dresses with several strands of beads draped around their necks stood in the lighted doorway, smoking and talking and laughing.

Maybe he should go home, but he'd come this far. He'd drink until he forgot his agony over Celine, over being home, and over getting married to Emily when he shouldn't have.

Trent took a step forward, then stopped. What would his family think if they knew he was here? He knew what Emily would think! She'd shake her finger at him and remind him he'd been raised with high standards. She'd say he was to abstain from even the appearance of evil. In his mind's eye, he could see her face and hear her words. He frowned.

"I don't care!" he whispered. "I'm going in!" He walked toward the entrance, but stayed in the shadows. He smelled liquor and heard laughter and bawdy talk. He would go in! So what if the family found out? So what if he spent the night with one of the girls just to show Emily that she couldn't run his life?

Then he heard Rachel say, "Daddy, where were you last night? I wanted you," and he hung his head. He couldn't go into such a place, especially one so close to Blue Creek where the story would spread like a forest fire. In Texas he'd been able to live like he wanted, but here things were different.

Deep inside a small voice said, "I saw you in Texas, too."

Trent felt hot all over. He knew the voice, but he'd stopped hearing it years ago. Being back home where everyone was always talking about spiritual things must have made him hear it again.

A man shouted, "Get your hands off me!"

Trent looked toward the door of the speakeasy. A large, burly man had a smaller man by the scruff of the neck and the back of his trousers. Trent recognized the smaller man was Lars Bjoerling, Emily's eighteen-year-old brother!

"Don't you never set foot in this place again, kid!" The big man tossed Lars through the door. He landed in a heap and rolled over on his side. The bouncer threw Lars' cap after him.

Lars leaped to his feet. "Send Suzie out and I'll leave."

Trent tensed, ready to spring to Lars' aid.

"Suzie don't want to leave." The bouncer's voice was sarcastic.

"Then I'm going in after her!" Lars lunged at the burly man, but was stopped by a powerful jab in the stomach and another on the chin. Again Lars fell in a heap.

"And don't come back!" The big man brushed off his hands and walked back inside, closing the door behind him and cutting off all but a faint sound of the music and laughter.

Trent ran to Lars and gently lifted his head. Lars moaned. "I'm taking you out of here," Trent said grimly.

Lars opened his eyes. "Justin?"

A muscle jumped in Trent's jaw. "Trent. Can you walk?"

"I guess so." Lars gasped with pain as he stood.

"I'll take you home where you belong."

"No! I got to get Suzie."

Trent gripped Lars' arm. "Hold it! You'll get tossed out again and maybe with a few broken bones this time."

"I can't leave Suzie."

"Who's Suzie?"

"My girl."

"What's she doing in a place like this? What're *you* doing in a place like this?"

"I heard Suzie was coming here with Ray Brookside. He doesn't know she's only seventeen. She said she wanted to go dancing, and she thought Gilly's was only a dance hall. But I'd heard different. I warned her this was no place for her to be. But she was mad at me, and she said she'd do what she wanted."

"Then leave her here."

Lars shook his head, then groaned and gingerly rubbed his jaw. "She wants to leave, but Ray won't let her go. He says she's staying with him until he's ready to leave. He's already soused to the gills, and he's a mean drunk."

Trent looked at the closed door. "Tell me where she is and I'll go in and get her."

"But you don't want to be seen in such a place, Trent." Lars looked at Trent sharply. "What are you doing here, anyway?"

"I heard about it and thought I'd check it out." Trent was thankful it was too dark for Lars to see his red face and neck.

"It's not the dance hall they say it is. It's a speakeasy and they sell bootleg liquor in there. I told Sheriff Lamont and he raided the place a couple of weeks ago."

"Then why isn't it closed down?"

"Because he didn't find any liquor. The folks were just dancing and having good clean fun. He said he ought to arrest me for giving him a false lead."

"Tell me where Suzie is and what she looks like and I'll get her."

"She's at a table to the right of the door. She has straight blond hair cut in a bob and is wearing a wide beaded band around her forehead. Her dress is blue and kind of shimmers when she moves. It's real short. Too short, but she doesn't care. She's out to have a good time."

"Who's the big guy who tossed you out?"

"Pork Lanski."

"You wait over under that tree. I'll be out shortly." Trent picked up Lars' cap. "I'll wear this."

"Take this too." Lars handed Trent a long, lightweight black coat. "I had the cap and coat so nobody would recognize me. I sure don't want Mama and Papa to know I been here!"

Trent chuckled and slipped on the coat. "I know what you mean." He pulled the cap down low on his forehead and turned the collar of the coat up. He was going to Gilly's and he was going to get a girl, but it sure was different from what he'd planned. "I'll be out as quick as I can."

"God is with you," Lars whispered.

Trent's heart jerked. He strode to the door and pushed it open just enough to slip inside. The room was dimly lit and filled with smoke and noise. Several people in the middle of the long room were dancing to the loud music. Two rows of round tables lined the walls and most of them were occupied by four or more people. The smell of liquor was strong, in spite of the heavy smell of cigarette smoke.

He spotted Suzie immediately. She looked lost and close to tears. The man beside her had his arm around her and was trying to get her to drink from the glass he was holding to her tightly closed lips. Trent saw the big man, Pork Lanski, who'd tossed Lars out. He was standing near the dance band, tapping his toe, with his arms folded as he watched the dancers.

Trent inched his way through the crowd until he stood behind Ray Brookside. He leaned down and whispered, "Pork Lanski wants to see you about bringing a minor in here."

Ray Brookside put his glass down so hard the liquor splashed up and out. He turned to look back at Trent, but Trent moved so that Ray couldn't see his face.

"Pork says if you pay him enough, he won't say anything. He wants you now." Trent moved again.

Ray shoved back his chair and started through the crowd.

Trent gripped Suzie's arm. "Come with me. I came to get you out of here. Lars is waiting outdoors for you."

Suzie gasped, her eyes wide with fear, but she jumped up and walked out with him. Just outside the door, she whispered, "Who are you?"

"Never mind. We have to hurry." Trent glanced down at her feet and knew she couldn't run on the rough ground in those shoes.

Lars leaped across to them. "Suzie! Are you all right?"

She stared at him, then threw her arms around him, sobbing hard.

"Get out of here fast," Trent snapped, clamping the cap back on Lars' head.

Lars scooped Suzie up in his arms and half-ran, half-walked to the shelter of the nearest pine.

Hurrying along beside them, Trent peeled off the coat and draped it over Suzie. "How're you two getting home?"

"I caught a ride here, so I don't have a ride back," Lars said.

"I'll take you then." Trent glanced back to see the door of the speakeasy fly open. Ray Brookside stood there, angrily looking around. Trent whispered, "We have to hurry."

Lars ducked around a pickup truck and broke into a run.

A few minutes later they climbed in Trent's Dodge and he drove away, the noise of the engine loud in the silence behind him.

"Suzie lives at Red Beaver's farm," Lars said. "Her pa works for Beaver."

"Is that Justin Havlick?" Suzie whispered.

"No. Trent," Lars whispered back.

Trent's stomach knotted. Justin indeed! Would it always be this way?

Trent drove into Beaver's lane and stopped when Lars asked him to. The moon was bright in the sky. An owl hooted. The smell of a pigpen was in the air.

"I'll walk Suzie the rest of the way so we can talk and she can pull herself together. I'll run home from here. Thanks, Trent. We appreciate all you did."

"I'm glad I could help."

Suzie climbed from the car and stood at Trent's window. "Thank you. If I can ever help you with anything, let me know."

Trent smiled. "No need. Just don't go to that place again. It's not for girls like you."

"That's what I told her," Lars said, putting his arm around Suzie.

"I believe you now," she said weakly.

"Don't mention about us being there," Lars said.

"I won't." Trent knew they wouldn't say anything about him being there either. They couldn't.

Trent made a turn-around, then drove slowly back to Blue Creek. Gilly's Place wasn't for him either.

Yawning, he parked the Dodge outside the shed at his parents' house and walked quietly to the bedroom he slept in alone. The house was quiet. The smell of coffee lingered.

He pushed open his door, then glanced back at Emily's. He saw a line of light beneath it. He hated being on the outs with her. Should he tell her the truth about the evening before—that he'd had her trunk put in his room just to keep her from being teased by her brothers?

He took a step toward her door, then stopped. Why bother? What did it matter if she treated him like a stranger? An enemy, in fact! For some reason it did matter.

Slowly he walked to his dresser and lit the lamp. He closed the door, then opened it, and stepped across the hall. He knocked before he lost his nerve.

Emily opened the door, the light glowing behind her. She wore a pale blue nightgown and a darker blue wrapper. Her feet were bare. She bit back a gasp. She'd thought it was Lark. "Yes?"

"I just wanted to let you know I'm back," he said stiffly. What was wrong with him? Was that the best he could do?

She tightened the belt on her robe. "Rachel will be glad. She asked about you."

"I'm sorry I wasn't here."

She suddenly realized her feet were bare, and flushed.

"Now what's wrong?"

She lifted her chin. "Nothing!"

"You're embarrassed about something."

She flipped back her mass of black hair. "If you must know, it's my feet. They're bare."

"I've seen you many times without shoes."

"Not since I grew up."

He chuckled under his breath. "I guess you're right about that."

She felt awkward. "Did you want something else?"

"I don't like it when we fight."

"Neither do I!"

"Let's forget what happened the other night and get back to normal." He waited for her answer, willing it to be what he wanted to hear.

She knew she should forgive him, but she couldn't. She wanted him to be a man of his word like he once was. Finally she said, "I'll try."

That surprised him. He'd thought she'd leap at the chance. "Don't make such an effort," he snapped and strode to his room, closing the door with a sharp click.

She stood with her head down. Her heart was racing. What was wrong with her? She knew Jesus said to forgive. Taking a deep breath she walked across the hall and tapped on Trent's door. "Can we talk?"

He sprang to the door, but didn't open it. "It's up to you."

"What'd you mean?"

"Come in all the way or not at all."

She whirled and ran to her room.

He pressed his ear against the door and listened. He heard her door click. Just as he thought. She had to have everything her way. Well, he didn't work that way, and she might as well find that out now.

* * *

Early the next morning Trent dipped the oars into the cold water and pulled, sending the rowboat gliding over Deep Lake, away from the dock at Fromberg toward the shoreline where their property began. Andree sat in the bow and Justin in the stern. Mist drifted up from the cool water. Quacking ducks flew low across the early morning sky. Men on the dock shouted to each other, but the sounds of their voices grew faint as the rowboat glided through the water toward the other side. Trent kept his eyes on the shoreline at Fromberg. He would not look at Justin, for if he did he knew his anger would erupt. Because of Grandma and the shooting a few days ago, they'd agreed on a truce while they investigated the shooting. Today they were going to check the oaks and help Andree mark the locations of the cabins.

Justin's stomach knotted so tight that pain shot through him. He knew he should've gone to work as usual instead of agreeing to go with Trent and Andree. At work he could forget everything except making wagons and chairs. As he braced his feet and gripped the seat on either side, he glanced at Trent, whose jaw was set. He looked ready to explode. Andree seemed relaxed as he studied the cloud formations. The silence in the boat pressed against Justin. He liked the noise at the Wagon Works. During a silence it was too easy to let his mind drift back to the failed areas of his life.

Trent dipped the oars deeper and pulled harder. Sweat popped out on his forehead and a dark cloud seemed to surround him.

Andree looked from Trent to Justin. Both had faces of stone. Silently Andree prayed for them. Trent was a far cry from being a happy newlywed. It was hard to get used to this angry young man being his son-in-law.

With a sigh, Andree looked over his shoulder at the approaching shoreline. Havlick trees looked like a solid wall beginning almost at the edge of the water. Pine tree covered hills jutted up to the right of where they'd land the boat. Giant oaks with leaves still as small as a mouse's ear covered several acres. Oak, maple, and walnut trees were mixed in with white pines in another area. It would be hard to decide which trees to cut. How could anyone saw down one of the giants that had been standing for hundreds of years? He turned back and the expression on Trent's face reminded him of something that had happened when the twins were about eight. He chuckled.

"Boys," he said with a hearty laugh. He didn't care that they were thirty years old—they were still boys to him. "I just thought about the time you went canoeing by yourselves for the first time. Remember?"

Justin shook his head. He didn't want to remember.

Trent remembered, but he didn't acknowledge it.

"You boys always did everything together," Andree said. "It was a great day to be on the river in a canoe. Your ma thought I would be with you, but you didn't let on none to her or me. I helped you with the canoe and you two got in and paddled away. You looked too little to do it, but you did it together. You boys always did everything together."

Trent bent over the oars, digging deep into the lake water. He would not think about that day! He'd close his ears to Andree's story!

Justin gritted his teeth as he recalled the day Andree was talking about. They'd tipped the canoe and he'd almost drowned, but Trent caught his shirt and held on tightly until he flipped the canoe and they could crawl back in. Even Andree didn't know he'd almost drowned. Scalding tears burned the backs of his eyes as Andree finished the tale.

Trent refused to listen and refused to see in his mind's eye two little boys paddling down the river. He glanced over his shoulder to see how close to shore he was. To his relief, land was only another minute or two away.

He rowed to the few feet of the shoreline where access was easy. Most of it was lined with rocks and trees. Birds sang in the tall branches and squirrels scolded.

Justin jumped into the cold water and tied the rope around the base of a young tree. He shivered as water seeped through his boots. He heard twigs snapping and the rustle of animals as they ran deeper into the woods. He caught a movement and watched closely until he made out a deer running away.

Trent waded to shore and stopped on the sandy beach, his boots waterlogged. He saw several animal tracks. Once he could identify every animal by its tracks, but he didn't know if he still could.

"Look at the beauty around us!" Andree cried, spreading his arms wide. Wet feet and pant legs didn't bother him. "The trees! The lake! And white clouds up above in a picture-perfect blue sky! It seems a shame to ruin this beauty by putting in cabins and a landing dock for boats."

Trent didn't want to notice the beauty around him, but he couldn't ignore it. The trees were indeed beautiful giants. He'd forgotten how big and magnificent the old-growth trees were. They were a far cry from Texas sand and sagebrush.

Justin walked several feet away to an oak and touched the rough bark. It was too large for the three of them to reach around. Its lumber would make many chairs after it had cured. Something stirred inside him as he looked up at the spreading branches covered with small leaves. High in the top he saw the large nest of a red-tailed hawk. He remembered that it came back each year to the same nest, repaired it, and raised its family. Could he destroy the tree and leave the red-tailed hawk without a home? He frowned. What was he thinking? Oak for lumber was more important than a nest.

The strong smell of pine made Trent think of the time he and Celine had brought a picnic to the side of the stream several yards past Jig's grave. They'd been married only a few months. They had spread the blanket on the pine needles, and he'd kissed her for a long time. They'd forgotten the picnic basket.

She'd curled tightly against him and said softly, "I have good news, Trent."

"You love me?"

"Always!"

"I love you?"

"Always!"

She lifted her head and looked into his eyes. "We're going to have a baby."

"A baby?"

"Yes. Are you glad?"

Tears had filled his eyes. "I want a girl just like you." And they'd had a girl just like her!

Trent knotted his fists as he struggled against the rush of tears he felt. He wanted to run back to the boat and row away. "Let's get on with it," he said sharply.

"You boys remember what I said about the wild dogs. Keep close watch." Andree led the way into the woods. He shook his head and clicked his tongue. "How can we cut any of these trees?"

"We have to," Justin snapped. He felt guilty about his tone of voice and tried to soften it. "Let's just mark a few, and then get out of here. I have work to do."

Trent bit back a sharp retort that surely would've brought on another fight. Sometimes it was very hard to be a Havlick and still be a man of his word. Was he a man of his word even though Emily didn't believe he was?

The massive branches blocked out the sun as they walked deeper into the woods. Trent smelled a strange odor. He sniffed and wrinkled his nose. Maybe it was his imagination.

Andree stopped in a small clearing and looked around. The ground was almost covered with pine needles. "This is a fine place for a cabin. It'll mean taking out only those two trees." He pointed to a maple and an oak.

Justin pulled a red marker out of his pocket and drew an X on each tree.

Farther in the woods Trent spotted a deep ravine with branches growing over it like a roof. It would be dangerous to build a cabin too close to it. He found another small clearing and called, "This is a good spot. It's far enough from the other for privacy." Grandma had said she didn't want the cabins on top of each other. She said folks deserve privacy while on vacation.

Several minutes later Andree found the right location on the side of a hill for the large cabin. Several trees would have to be removed, but the view of the lake would be perfect.

Justin marked the trees. To his surprise his heart sank lower and lower at the thought of cutting them. Once he'd loved the woods as much as the rest of the family, but then he'd gotten too busy to walk through them and enjoy them. Would he be able to stand seeing the area torn apart while the building was taking place?

While Andree and Justin walked around the area, Trent leaned against a maple. He and Justin had gone with Grandpa many times to tap maples. They'd never tapped this one, but he knew it would give gallons of sap to be made into maple syrup. When the Indians lived in these woods maybe they'd tapped this very tree. Red Beaver's people had lived in the area before they were sent to Oklahoma to live on a reservation.

"Does it hurt the maple to drill holes in it, Grandpa?" Justin had asked one chilly morning in February.

"It can't hurt," Trent had said. He and Justin were bundled up in the same kind of winter coat, warm red caps with ear flaps, and boots with wool socks to keep their toes from freezing. "If it did, Grandpa wouldn't do it."

"That's right. God made these trees so we could get sap from them to make maple syrup. Hang the buckets on these spiles." Grandpa had lifted Justin high so he could hang a bucket, then had done the same with Trent.

The first year he'd been tall enough to hang a bucket without Grandpa lifting him had been a milestone in Trent's life. And Justin had hung a bucket himself that same year. They'd looked at each other and grinned. They both knew it was a great occasion.

Impatiently Trent pushed away from the maple and strode through the trees to join Andree and Justin. He'd had enough of the forest and enough of the memories it brought back. He expected Justin had too.

Trent scowled. He no longer *knew* Justin's thoughts like he had in the past. The bond had been broken when Justin let Celine die. "Let's get out of here," Trent said gruffly. He'd had more than enough of the woods and the terrible memories.

He strode toward the lake with his shoulders bent and his head down.

CHAPTER

9

♦ Her black skirt swirling about her legs, Emily paced from one side of Lark's porch to another. Rachel and Amanda sat in the shade of a maple tree playing dolls. Clay was at the Wagon Works and Lark was inside talking to Lulu about supper. Emily brushed aside a gray and white cat winding around her feet. It leaped off the porch and ran to Rachel. Emily flipped back her mass of dark hair and continued pacing. For two weeks Trent had barely spoken to her except to tell her they had not learned the identity of the man who shot Rachel.

Emily bit her lip and swatted away a fly. She'd tried to tell Trent she was sorry for getting angry, but he wouldn't listen. She'd almost given in and moved into his room, but couldn't bring herself to. And he hadn't asked her to again. He'd been gone every day working with Papa on the plans for Havlick's Wilderness. Today he and Papa were planning the trails through the woods.

Lark stepped onto the porch and said, "Emily, I've been watching you for the last hour. You act like a caged animal. I think you need something to do."

Emily leaned against a support post and sighed. "I don't

know what's wrong with me." But she did know. She and Trent were no longer friends. He'd changed more than she'd known. Marrying him was a mistake. She thought he needed her. She thought she could save him—make him into the man he was before he left Michigan. How wrong she'd been!

Lark tucked a strand of gray hair behind her ear and smoothed the flowered apron covering her green dress. She hated to see the tension between Emily and Trent. "Why don't you take a trip out to the property Jennet gave you? It's a pleasant day for that."

"Oh, I don't know. . . ."

"You can drive my auto."

"I don't know how to drive."

"What? I thought you were going to learn!"

"I was." Emily didn't want to admit she was actually afraid to learn. Usually she didn't fear new things, but the gas contraption was beyond her powers of reasoning. How could it keep going? And how did a person know when to push down on what thing on the floorboard?

Lark shook her head and clicked her tongue. "I'm going to teach you to drive, or have Trent teach you."

Emily stiffened. She didn't want Trent to teach her anything. But she couldn't say that to Lark. "I don't know if I can learn."

"Priscilla did. She's a good driver."

"I'll think about it."

"Modern young ladies should know how to drive," Lark said, wagging her finger at Emily.

"I suppose."

"Take the buggy then."

Emily smiled and agreed. Maybe she did need to get out alone. She might even stop and see Mama.

They talked a while longer. Emily told Rachel goodbye, then she hitched a horse to the buggy and drove out of town toward Free's farm. The top of the buggy was down and the sun was warm on her bare head. She should've grabbed a hat, but once she'd decided to go, she didn't want to take the time to run upstairs for one. She turned on a tree-lined gravel road just before the turn off to Free's place. In the past she'd come this way often to see Celine. She'd spent a lot of time at the farm with Celine, but hadn't been back since she died. It would be hard to see it again.

The two hundred acres Jennet had given her butted against Free's place to the south and Trent's place to the west. She'd seen the property from the road many times before, but had never stopped to look it over. She waited for excitement to bubble up inside her, but she couldn't muster even a drop. If Trent were with her, it would be different.

"Oh, Trent, I miss you," she said loud enough to make the horse prick its ears. Trent was right—friendship was better than a grand passion. When Trent got home tonight she'd make him listen to her. She wouldn't let another day go by with them at outs with each other.

Several minutes later she turned onto her property and drove along a wagon trail winding around a hill covered with second growth pines and various hardwood trees. The oak leaves were small and the black walnut trees were covered with tight buds. Giant pine branches blocked the sun. The harness shook and the buggy rattled as the horse picked its way along the trail at the base of the hill. With loud cries birds flew up from the branches. After several minutes of driving through thick growths of trees she came upon the most beautiful valley she'd ever seen. She sucked in her breath as she stopped the horse, then gazed at the valley, her hand over her heart. The valley stretched on and on and was covered with lush green grass and yellow and white wildflowers. A deer grazing in the grass lifted its head, then leaped away with its foot-long white tail held high. It sailed over a stream running along the east side of the valley and disappeared among the trees. A bluebird flitted across in front of Emily and a robin sang nearby. A warmth spread through her. She felt as if she'd just come home after years away. It was a strange feeling, one she couldn't understand, nor did she try to. After a long time, she slapped the reins on the horse's back and headed for the stream. She pulled up beside a deer trail leading down to the water. Sparkling blue water rippled over stones and tree roots. A frog jumped off the grassy shore and landed in the water with a splash. She breathed in the heady scent of pine and the faint smell of the stream. She gazed around, holding firmly to the reins. In her mind's eye she could see cattle scattered across the valley, growing fat for market. It would be easy to fence the valley for cattle to graze. Her eyes widened and she gasped as she realized where her thoughts had taken her. She wanted to stay and make her home here, not in Texas. Could she convince Trent to consider staying?

"He'd never agree," she muttered. Then she lifted her head high. "But I'll try to convince him anyway!"

After a long time, she drove slowly out of the valley and through the trees onto Trent's farm. From the crest of a hill she looked down on the house and buildings. She knew Free had hired Gabe Lavery as a caretaker for the place. He was probably there right now. Smoke drifted up from the chimney and disappeared in the fluffy white clouds.

What if Bob Lavery was visiting his brother this afternoon? Emily's pulse leaped. She hadn't seen Bob lately. Truth to tell, she didn't think about him as often as she once had. His farm was one place over from Trent's, at the bend in Blue River. She'd dreamed often of living on his farm, tending to his needs, and becoming a mother to his children. Her muscles tightened. Monique was doing all that.

Abruptly Emily pushed away thoughts of Monique as she looked down on Trent's house.

The house was a four-bedroom, two-story white frame house with a wrap-around porch on the south and west sides. Trent and Celine had planned on a large family and had built the bedrooms large. Emily brushed away a tear. "Oh, Celine, I wish you were still here."

To the north of the house was a huge white barn. White sheds and a granary stood east of the barn. All the buildings were in good repair. Pigs rooted in a large muddy pen. It had rained hard two days ago. About twenty head of cattle grazed in a field in back of the barn. Chickens scratched in the yard and a turkey gobbler strutted from one shed to another. Maybe Gabe would let her look around inside the house for old time's sake. Lark had said Celine's things were still there.

Emily urged the horse down the hill to the road leading to the driveway. The buggy swayed and Emily braced her feet to keep from pitching out. Just then she saw a black Ford pickup truck pull into the driveway and stop. To her surprise Bob Lavery got out of the pickup truck and waved for her to stop. A blue chambray work shirt and heavy denim pants hung loosely on his thin frame.

Her breath caught in her throat and her heart hammered wildly as she pulled back on the reins. Was her hair a mess? Oh, why hadn't she grabbed a hat before she left Lark's? "Afternoon, Bob," she said with a slight catch in her voice.

He smiled and tipped his sweat-stained blue cap, showing his damp wheat colored hair. "Afternoon, Emily."

Emily struggled to keep from falling out of the buggy in a dead faint at Bob's feet. What had started out as a miserable day was turning into the best day of her life! "What brings you out here?" she asked, trying to keep her voice from cracking.

Bob rested his hand on the side of the buggy as he smiled up at Emily. "I came to see my brother, Gabe. He's taking care of Trent's place."

"Oh, yes. I heard that." She glanced up the long driveway to keep him from reading the love in her eyes. "I thought I'd take a look around. It's been a long time since I was here."

Bob cleared his throat as he squeezed the bill of his cap. "Is it right what I heard about you and Trent Havlick?"

Emily trembled. "Yes. We got married."

"Congratulations." Bob rubbed his calloused hand over his suntanned cheek and scratched the side of his thin nose. "It sure came as a shock to me."

"It did?" She looked deep into his eyes that were the color of the sky above. Just what did he mean?

"A terrible shock!"

"It was, ah, sudden."

"I heard about his daughter getting shot outside the church. How is she?"

"Fine. She was frightened more than hurt."

"I'm glad to hear that."

"Me too! It was frightening."

"I suppose you and Trent will be heading to Texas before long."

"I guess. Now that Rachel's well enough to travel."

Bob looked off across the field, then back up at Emily. "I sure was surprised about you getting married."

Emily moistened her dry lips with the tip of her tongue. "It was . . . sudden." She flushed as she realized she'd already said that.

He looked up at her, then off across the field again. "I heard . . . heard gossip about . . . about you being . . . in love . . . with me."

"Oh, dear," she whispered as her cheeks turned bright red. How she longed to sink to the sandy floor of the buggy and disappear from sight! She trembled so hard she dropped the reins.

He caught them, sprang up beside her, and looped the reins around the wooden brake handle. He turned to face her and caught her hands in his.

She stared at him in surprise, shivers running up and down her spine.

"I don't know if I can live knowing you're married," he said hoarsely.

Shock waves rippled over her as she swayed weakly. She felt the rough calluses on his hands. She smelled the tangy sweat of his skin as he leaned closer. "How can you say that?" she whispered weakly.

"Your love is real important to me, Emily."

"I . . . I didn't know. . . ."

He caught her close and kissed her roughly.

She gasped and pulled away, her eyes wide with shock, her mouth tingling from his touch. "You mustn't do that!"

"I couldn't help myself! You're a beautiful, desirable woman. I want you! I've always wanted you."

Her heart raced and the words sent her reeling. "But you married Monique."

"I was away from home. Lonely. And I couldn't live just on thoughts of you."

"Oh, dear."

"I hated myself for doing it." He ran a fingertip over her lips.

She groaned and leaned toward him for another kiss, but deep inside she heard, "Don't do it, Emily." She jerked back before their lips touched again. "I'm sorry," she whispered. "This is . . . wrong."

"How can love be wrong?" he asked in a voice hoarse with emotion.

Her eyes widened. "Love?" she whispered.

"Between us, Emily! You can't say no to it!"

Her pulse leaped. Since he'd returned from the war she'd longed to hear his declaration of love for her and feel his lips against hers! "I can't believe you're saying this." She'd dreamed of this very conversation. Or was *this* a dream? Maybe she'd fallen asleep. But no. Bob's face was indeed close to hers. She could see the splash of freckles on each cheek and the dark shadow of whiskers on his jaw. She could smell the tang of his skin.

"One more kiss and I'll let you go," Bob said, tugging her close again.

"No! Oh, we dare not!" Emily pushed against his chest until he let her go.

He rubbed an unsteady hand over his narrow face. "What will we do now?"

"Nothing!" she cried.

His face fell and he sighed unhappily. He sat in silence a long time. "Are you going back to town now?"

She nodded, not really knowing what she was planning to do.

He cupped her flushed cheek in his rough hand and leaned forward to kiss her.

She jerked back and his hand fell away. "Please. Don't. It's not right."

Bob sighed and nodded. "I know, but I couldn't help myself."

Emily pressed her hand to her racing heart. He couldn't help himself! Was it possible?

He tugged his cap low on his forehead. "I'll go about my business so you can get back to town. But I *will* see you again."

"I don't know. . . ."

"I must!"

She hesitantly unwound the reins and gripped them tightly.

He jumped to the ground and stepped away from the buggy. "Goodbye, my love. Until we meet again," he said softly.

"Goodbye," she whispered. She turned the horse and buggy and drove toward town, her mind in a daze. Would she let there be a next time?

His Adam's apple working, Bob stood quietly until she was out of sight, then he sprang in his pickup truck, drove to the house, and screeched to a stop, sending sand spraying. He jumped to the ground, startling chickens that were scratching in the driveway. "Gabe!" he called. "Get out here now!"

A shotgun in his hand, Gabe ran out the back door, slamming it behind him. He had the same wheat colored hair as

Bob, but his eyes were hazel instead of blue. His chest and arms were thick with muscles and his hips narrow. "What's wrong? Who was that?" He motioned toward the road with the shotgun.

Bob scowled at the gun as he said, "Emily Bjoerling. Emily Havlick now."

Gabe stood the shotgun on the ground and rested it against the pickup truck. "I had my gun on her when she came down the hill. I pretty near shot at her. And I didn't want to do that."

"It's a good thing you didn't!"

"It was bad enough hitting the little girl outside the church the other day." Gabe rubbed an unsteady hand over his day-old whiskers. "I still have nightmares over that one."

"Emily says the little girl's doing fine."

"It's a good thing. I'm no killer."

Bob slapped Gabe's thick shoulder. "I know you're not."

"It don't bother me none to break the law to make and sell liquor."

"The law's wrong," Bob snapped. "We already agreed it was."

Gabe leaned against the fender of the pickup truck. "Why was Emily here anyway?"

"She came to snoop, but I stopped her cold." Bob laughed wickedly. "I made a pass at her and scared her silly."

"You made a pass at that old maid?"

Bob nodded as he wrinkled his long, thin nose. "I had to do something to keep her away."

"All in the line of duty," Gabe said with a chuckle.

"It wasn't so bad," Bob said. "I planned on marrying her before I went to war. I could get her to warm up some if I worked at it long enough."

"Not if Monique ever heard about it. You'd be a dead man!"

Bob grinned and nodded. "She sure would get mad, but she won't hear nothing about it." Bob frowned. "Unless you tell her."

"Me? Never! She'd have my hide too."

Bob nodded. "I'm sure glad I was able to stop Emily from coming up to the house."

"She would've seen our cases of liquor and smelled the stuff cooking."

"It was a close call, all right." Bob hiked up his denim pants on his lean hips. "I came to pick up ten cases and take them to Gilly's Place."

"What about the sheriff?" Gabe asked as they headed for the house.

"He's gone for a while."

"How about Leroy? Is he having trouble with the still in the Havlicks' trees?"

"No." Bob stopped outside the back door. "But he will if the Havlicks keep on with their plans for the nature preserve. The place they want to build the cabins is too close to Leroy's still."

"He told me Jennet Havlick and Emily almost stumbled on it a while back." Gabe opened the screen door and the squack it made was a better alarm than anything else he could've planned. "He said he'll shoot anyone who gets too close. And he means it. It don't bother him none to kill. He's done it before."

Bob stopped just inside the back door and wrinkled his nose at the smell of brewing mash and the heat pouring out from the kitchen stove. A hundred pound bag of sugar leaned against a wall beside gunnysacks of ground corn. The smell of malt turned Bob's stomach. They'd had the sprouted corn ground by Logan Piper and paid him in finished liquor. Gabe had learned from Gilly which miller he could trust with his sprouted corn. Logan would keep his mouth shut for a regular supply of liquor. "I don't like working with Leroy, what with his quick temper. But he makes the best stuff and it brings high dollar."

"We don't want no killings," Gabe said.

"We only got to do this a few more months to pay off our farms, then we can quit. Maybe make just enough for our own use." Bob hoisted a case of liquor on his shoulder, steadied it, and carried it to his pickup truck. Gabe was close behind with another case.

In silence they loaded the cases, then pulled a black tarp over the back and tied down the corners. Bob gave the rope one last tug. It was easy for him to deliver the liquor because no one would ever suspect him—a good family man with a farm of his own. Since the Great War the farm wasn't paying enough to keep up his bank loan, so he'd taken to bootlegging. Gabe had started first to help pay off his farm, then brought Bob in on it when he'd seen his brother's need for extra cash.

Gabe pulled off his cap and wiped sweat from his forehead. "Is there any chance Trent Havlick will decide to stay in Michigan and want to move back here?"

"Not the way I hear it. Emily said they'll be going soon. If Rachel hadn't been shot, they'd already be gone."

"It almost did me in when I heard her scream and seen her fall."

"I'm just glad she didn't die."

"Yeah, me too. We don't want to do anything to make Trent stay!"

"I don't think Emily will come back here again," Bob said with a laugh. "I scared her too bad."

"I sure hope so. I wouldn't want to shoot nobody."

Bob stiffened. "Don't you dare shoot anybody! I mean it, Gabe."

"Only if I'm forced to, Bob. You would, too."

Bob shook his head, but he wondered if what Gabe had said was true. A few years ago he wouldn't have considered bootlegging, but times were too rough not to. Bob walked slowly to the cab of the truck and stepped up inside. "I almost forgot to ask you about Noah Roswell. I saw you talking to him at Gilly's Place the other night. Did he tell you anything important?"

Gabe grinned. "Give him more than two drinks and his tongue flaps at both ends."

"Did you learn anything?"

"Nothing worth knowing, but you never can tell when he'll tell us something important. I told him the Havlicks were trying to shut down Gilly's Place and we needed to know what they had planned. He says Priscilla Havlick is a real beauty." Gabe laughed and slapped his thigh. "I told him to play up to her and learn all he could about their plans. He said he'd be glad to. He'll do anything for a little money."

"When will you see him again?"

"Tonight. I set up a meeting twice a week. He knows how to get in touch with me if he learns anything important."

"It was a lucky day when you met him."

"You never know when a man working for the Havlicks will come in handy." Gabe scowled. "The Havlicks are too high and mighty for my blood. Always have been. They don't have a clue to all that's working against them to make them fall."

"Cut it out, Gabe. We agreed we ain't in this to ruin the Havlicks. We're in it to get out of debt."

Gabe shrugged. "If the Havlicks fall while we're getting ahead, well and good."

Bob sighed heavily as he started the pickup and drove away.

* * *

Emily's face burned with shame as she slapped the reins harder on the horse's back. It quickened its pace, making the buggy sway dangerously on the dirt road. How could she face anyone now that she'd allowed Bob Lavery to kiss her? She felt the kiss again and her blood surged and her lips tingled. With a frown, she gripped the reins tighter. How could part of her like the kiss and want more and part of her abhor it and be determined never to put herself in that situation again?

Without warning an automobile pulled from a side road onto the road directly in Emily's path. The horse neighed and reared, its eyes wild. The driver swerved in time to miss the horse's hooves. Emily sawed on the reins, trying to bring the horse under control. Shaking its head, the horse reared again and twisted enough that the buggy tongue snapped. Emily's heart thundered in fear as she pulled the reins harder. Finally the horse calmed. She wrapped the reins around the brake handle and jumped to the ground. Dust puffed onto her high-top walking shoes.

A woman jumped out of the open black automobile and walked angrily toward Emily. "You broke a lamp on my auto!" she cried, shaking her fist.

"Aggie?" Emily stared in shock at the woman she hadn't seen in two years. "Aggie Beaumont!"

"Emily Bjoerling!" Aggie stopped short and stared at Emily. "Imagine running into you this afternoon." Aggie waved a hand at her headlamp. "Just look at the damage you did. I expect you to pay me for it."

Emily lifted her chin and knotted her fists at her sides. "You pulled out in front of me. The accident was your fault and I will not pay a cent!"

"I see you're as sharp-tongued as you were in school!"

"I won't allow you to take advantage of me, if that's what you mean."

"And you call yourself a Christian." Aggie looked at Emily sharply. "You still claim to be a Christian, don't you?"

"Of course."

"Well, you'd still call me a sinner," Aggie said with a sharp laugh. She flipped her long strands of pink beads and patted her bobbed blonde hair that hung just below her soft pink hat with a wide turned-up brim. She wore a white middy trimmed in pink and a white skirt.

"I don't have time to argue with you." Emily unhitched the horse from the broken buggy. "I have to get back to town and send someone out for the buggy before dark."

Aggie swished her skirt and tilted her head. "Aren't you even wondering why I'm back?"

"No."

Aggie frowned. "I've moved back to Blue Creek. My dear husband died."

"I'm sorry to hear that," Emily said stiffly as she started to lead the horse past Aggie.

"Gossip around town is you married Trent Havlick for his money."

Emily stopped short as she held back her temper. "Not everyone marries for money."

"You and Celine made it hard on me for doing it." Aggie lifted her rounded chin and batted her dark lashes. "I'm not a bit sorry. But he didn't have quite the wealth I'd thought. I used his money to train to be a nurse. It'll give me a chance to find another rich man, this time one my age. And I will do just that!"

"Who could you possibly want in Blue Creek?"

"Maybe your husband."

"We're moving to Texas."

"Too bad. I could've taken him away from you. I've stolen my share."

Emily shook her head. "Don't brag about such a terrible thing, Aggie. You make it sound no different from when you stole mine and Celine's dolls."

Aggie shrugged and flipped her beads. "It's just as easy." Her short skirt swished around her long legs as she walked back to her car. She said over her shoulder, "I just might steal both the Havlick twins."

"How can you even say that? You and Priscilla were once good friends."

Aggie laughed softly. "All's fair in love and war."

Emily pressed her lips tightly together and gripped the lead rope as Aggie started her auto and drove away in a cloud of dust. "Now that she's back I'm glad we're going to Texas," Emily muttered.

She walked along the side of the road leading the horse. Since she was closer to Free's place than town, she stopped there and asked if she could leave the horse. Then she ran to her place and asked her brothers to get the buggy. As they hitched up their team she stood in the yard and told her mother what happened with Aggie.

"Are you sure you're all right, Emily?" Martha asked as she rubbed a hand down Emily's arm.

"I'm fine, Mama." Emily forced back a flush as she thought of Bob's kiss. Mama would never understand that. Actually, she didn't either.

"I hope Aggie doesn't try to make trouble for you the way she always used to do."

"We won't be here long enough for that to happen."

Martha narrowed her eyes thoughtfully. "I have this feeling that you won't move to Texas."

Emily's heart turned over. Mama's feelings often came true. "You're probably wrong this time."

"Would you be upset if you didn't move to Texas?"

Because of Bob's kiss she would, but she couldn't say that. "I looked at the land Jennet gave me. The valley is a perfect place for cattle. While I was there I actually wanted to stay. It was peaceful and very, very beautiful!"

As the boys drove the team and wagon down the lane, Martha walked to a bench under a maple tree and sat down. She patted the bench beside her and waited until Emily sat down. "Honey, God knows what's best for you and Trent—whether here or in Texas. Your papa and I are praying you'll both know."

Emily hugged Mama. "Thanks." All her life her parents had prayed for her and her brothers and sisters. Their prayers were as important to her as the food and shelter they'd provided. "I know Trent's mind is set."

"I'm sure he'll listen as God speaks to him."

Years ago Emily would've agreed, but now she couldn't.

They talked a while longer, then Emily walked toward town, her head buzzing with all that had happened. Once again she heard Bob's declaration of love and felt his lips on hers. She stopped on the bridge and leaned weakly against the railing. Water rushed down below and the smell of fish drifted up.

Bob had kissed her! Emily trembled and touched her lips. Her cheeks flamed at the shameless thing that had happened. "God, help me," she whispered weakly.

* * *

Priscilla leaned against the fence and watched Noah feed the pigs. His shirt sleeves were rolled almost to his elbows, revealing strong brown forearms covered with black hair. His gray shirt and dark pants were stained with dirt and sweat. Mud and manure covered the soles of his high-top work shoes. Just watching him work left Priscilla weak in the knees. "Did you have fun last night?" she asked. He'd told her he was going to the speakeasy near Blue Creek, and she was immediately jealous, thinking he would be with another woman.

Noah carried the bucket to the fence and easily jumped over. He landed beside her and smiled right into her eyes. "Sure did. Did you miss me?"

Priscilla stiffened and stepped away from him and the fence. He'd never been so forward and it startled her. "Why would I miss you?"

Noah grinned as he set down the bucket and leaned back on the fence, his arms crossed over his broad chest. "I hoped you would. I missed you."

Her legs weakened and she thought she'd fall. "You did?" she whispered.

"Sure did."

"You're just saying that. You probably had all kinds of pretty women hanging on you."

"None as pretty as you, Priscilla."

"Yes. Well. Thank you." She was at a loss for words. He'd never said anything like that to her before.

"How're the plans coming for the great Havlick's Wilderness you told me about?"

Priscilla shrugged. "All right, I guess. Justin's been working on the plans. He's going to have some oak trees lumbered out near Deep Lake and use them to make chairs in his factory."

Noah dropped his arms to his sides and stepped forward. "And when's he going to do that?"

"Soon, I guess. Why?"

"It'll give us more time together."

Priscilla's pulse leaped. "Oh?" she whispered.

Noah ran a finger down the side of her face, leaving a trail of sparks along her skin. "I don't like to see you so lonely all the time. Your husband is crazy for leaving you alone so much."

"He does have to work hard," Priscilla said weakly.

"Sure he does. He's a Havlick and he's got to make something of himself," Noah said dryly. "But he shouldn't ignore you or the children."

She knew that, but it felt strange to hear Noah say it.

"If you were my wife, I wouldn't leave your side," he whispered.

"Don't," she said weakly. But hadn't she wanted this very thing?

Just then Faith opened the back door of the house and shouted, "Momma, Chloe's being naughty again! Momma! Can you hear me?"

"I'd better go," Priscilla whispered.

Noah caught her hand and squeezed it. "We'll talk again."

She nodded, then ran to the house, her cheeks flushed pink and her heart racing. If Justin didn't come home on time maybe she would ask Noah in for coffee. She put the kids to bed early and put on her new green dress.

What was she thinking?

A black cloud settled over her and she whimpered.

CHAPTER

10

♦ Emily sank to the edge of the bed and stared at the half-packed trunk in the middle of her bedroom floor. It was going to be harder to leave Michigan than she'd thought. Absently she twisted a strand of blue beads around her fingers. Her mind flashed to Bob's kiss and she moaned. Getting away from the temptation would be the best thing in the world for her. She wouldn't have the strength to resist Bob if they stayed. She bit her bottom lip. She'd miss her family! She'd never been away from them.

A rag doll dangling from her hand, Rachel slowly walked in and leaned against Emily. "Amanda can't go to Texas with me."

"I'm sorry." Emily kissed the top of Rachel's head. "You know her parents couldn't get along without her just like I couldn't get along without you."

"But I can't get along without her either!" Rachel rubbed her hand up and down Emily's arm. "What friend will I have at Daddy's ranch?"

"I don't know. We'll have to wait and see. But your daddy will be there and so will I." Emily's heart turned over. Would Trent continue to be cold toward her?

"Grandma Lark and Grandpa Clay won't be there. I'll miss them a whole lot, Emily. And Grandma Jennet and Grandpa Free won't be there." Rachel went down the list of all the Havlicks who wouldn't be there. "And the Bjoerlings won't be there. What will we do without all of them, Emily?"

"I don't know." Loneliness smote her and she held Rachel close, resting her cheek on Rachel's head. "I guess we'll have to find new friends and new people to take the place of family."

"I wish I'd get shot again."

"Rachel!" Emily held her away and looked into her face. "Don't even say that!"

"But if I did, then Daddy would let us stay here longer. He might start liking it enough to want to stay forever."

Hesitantly Trent poked his head around the corner of the door. He was wearing a plaid shirt and denim pants. His heart jerked at the picture Emily and Rachel made. He walked in and even managed a smile. "Hey, why the long faces?"

Rachel ran to him and wrapped her arms around his waist.

Emily stood, her legs trembling. Was Trent ready to be friends again?

"Daddy, we're afraid to move to Texas. We won't have any friends or any family."

Trent shot a look at Emily, then knelt down to look eye to eye with Rachel. "We'll have each other. And you'll like my friends there. You'll have a pony to ride and a dog I named Cricket because he's as quick as one. You'll like Cricket."

"I guess I might."

"You'll like riding your pony."

"I guess I will."

Trent hugged her, then stood up. "Run downstairs and see Grandma so I can talk with Emily, will you?"

Emily's nerves tightened.

Rachel ran out and the room was quiet. From the open window distant sounds of the Wagon Works drifted in with the closer sound of a dog barking.

His dark brows cocked, Trent took a hesitant step toward Emily. "Are you afraid to move?"

She shrugged. "A little."

"You'll like it there." Trent folded his arms across his broad chest and frowned at her. "I heard you went out yesterday to look over the property Grandma gave you."

Emily's cheek turned bright red. Had he also heard Bob had kissed her? "I did." Her voice was sharp and she forced it to sound normal. "I thought it was beautiful land."

His eyes flashed. "I thought you'd have more sense than to ride out alone. After what happened to Rachel."

"I never thought about that."

"You could've been shot!" He dropped his arms to his sides and clenched his fists.

Suddenly it was hard for her to breathe. "But I wasn't."

He gripped her arms. "I don't want you shot, too! I don't even want to have to worry about where you are and what you're doing!"

"You don't need to." She twisted to free herself, but he was too strong. His fingers bit through her sleeves into her arms.

"Did you see anyone out there?"

Her face flamed.

He saw her red cheeks and let her go. "Just who did you see that makes you look that way?"

Her stomach fluttered. "Does it matter?"

"Bob Lavery!"

She flushed again.

"And you talked to him!"

"Yes," she whispered.

He felt her tension and saw her agitation. "Suppose you tell me about this meeting with the great love of your life."

Words caught in her throat but she finally managed to say, "He asked about Rachel. And wondered when we were leaving Michigan."

"Don't tell me he's sorry he married the French girl and now wants you?"

She lifted her chin defiantly. "Am I so unlovable that you think that's impossible?"

"Of course not!"

"Then what do you think?"

He nudged her trunk with his toe. "I think I'll be glad when we're in Texas. And I'm glad to see you're getting the packing done. We'll leave tomorrow morning as early as possible."

"Tomorrow morning? So soon?"

"Not soon enough for me!" He cleared his throat. "Mom said she'd get the family together to say their goodbyes. Your family too, of course."

The tension seeped out of her. "I hate to leave, but I will be glad to get to Texas where we can start our life together."

He gripped her arms again and looked into her face. "You think it's going to be that easy, do you?"

She stiffened. "Isn't it?"

"You're treating me like a Bolshevik and you think I'll be willing to take you as my wife with open arms?"

Flushing, Emily lifted her chin high. "I am not treating you like a Bolshevik! I've tried to apologize to you for not being your true wife, but you won't let me. You won't even take time to talk to me the way we used to."

He stepped away from her and looped his thumbs in his pockets. "Things are different now."

She bit her bottom lip and took a hesitant step toward him. "Why can't we be friends again? Like we were . . . before?"

His heart jerked. "I'll think about it."

"I miss you."

He'd missed her too.

"I wanted you to see the valley yesterday." Then she thought of Bob and her legs gave way. She dropped to the edge of her bed.

"What's wrong?" he asked sharply.

"Nothing." She forced a smile. "The valley is perfect for cattle just like Jennet said."

Trent waved the words away in exasperation. "Let somebody else put cattle on it! We're going to Texas and that's final." He strode to the door, then turned to face her again. "Don't go out alone again."

She pressed her lips tightly together and clenched her fists as he strode away, his footsteps loud in the hallway and on the stairs.

* * *

Jennet sat in the bow of the boat as Abel Grant paddled across Deep Lake. He was wide chested with thick muscles and ebony colored skin. His voice was deep and cultured and reminded her of the huge black man, George Washington Foringer, who'd saved her life when Blue Newmeyer, a slave hunter, had tried to kill her for helping in the Underground Railroad. She'd hired Abel this morning to guard this side of the forest without telling anyone else, not even Freeman. He wouldn't understand why she needed more than Andree Bjoerling. She couldn't understand it herself, but she'd felt compelled.

"Free would be very angry if he knew I was here," she said as Abel expertly dipped the oar in and shot the boat forward.

"You're safe with me, Mrs. Havlick," Abel said.

"I know I am." Jennet smiled. She'd met Abel purely by chance at Fromberg last month and had taken an immediate interest in him. When she'd decided to hire another guard, she'd sought him out and asked for his help. He was a thirty-five-year-old schoolmaster on summer break and had gladly accepted.

Effortlessly he rowed to shore, then tied the boat down. The water was cold on his feet and ankles. He waded back as Jennet stood. "Let me carry you so you don't get your feet wet."

"That's not necessary at all, but thank you." She rested her hand lightly on his shoulder as he swung her easily up into his arms. He took a step forward, then froze. He'd caught a movement and heard a low growl.

"What?" Jennet asked, looking around. The smell of the water mixed with the smell of pine. Birds flew from the trees.

He waited, but nothing moved. "Nothing, I guess." Slowly he waded to shore and put Jennet on dry ground covered with pine needles. He touched the butt of his revolver as he looked around.

"I think somebody will try to stop us from putting the cabins up," Jennet said as they slowly walked away from the lake and into the forest. She'd told him her dream. Several feet into the woods she stopped and turned to him. "I need you to watch the place, keep all intruders out, and destroy the wild dogs."

"I'll do the best I can."

Without warning a huge wild dog sprang at them, brown hair bristling, a mad glitter in its eyes, growling deep in its throat. Abel knocked Jennet aside, sending her sprawling to the ground just as he jerked sideways and frantically reached for his revolver. The dog barely missed him, then seemed to whirl in mid-air and hurled itself forward. Snarling, it struck Abel in the chest, knocking him to the ground. Abel felt the hot breath and saw the sharp fangs ready to sink into his throat.

Jennet pushed herself up, grabbed a branch, and whacked the dog hard across the back.

It turned from Abel with a ferocious snarl and, ears laid back, snapped at her. She jumped back, tripped, and fell down hard, knocking the air out of herself. With a deadly growl the dog turned back on Abel, ready to sink its teeth deep. He caught the dog by the throat in a deathgrip. Its coat was tangled and filthy, its breath like a rotted dead animal. Abel's heart roared in his ears as he tried to press the dog's windpipe to shut off its air. Its muscles contracted spasmodically. Its saliva dripped down on him. He pressed its windpipe harder while the dog jerked and growled deep in its chest.

Her breathing ragged, Jennet struggled to her feet and swayed over Abel and the dog. If she tried to strike the dog again, Abel might lose his grip and the dog would be at his throat with its razor sharp teeth.

Abel felt the strength of his arms waning. His face and chest were wet from the dog's foamy saliva. He heard the dog's breath rattle and he pressed tighter. All at once the dog went limp in his arms. With a cry he threw the dog from him and struggled to his feet. The dog lay in a ragged heap at the base of a pine. Abel swayed. Blood oozed from his face and arms where the dog had torn his flesh with his fangs.

"Are you all right, Abel?" Jennet whispered hoarsely as she plucked at his torn sleeve.

"I've been better," he said weakly.

"Thank God we're alive. Let's get out of here before we get attacked again."

Abel nodded. His legs felt almost too weak to walk, but he forced them to move. "Do you know how many wild dogs are in the pack?"

"No. But I've heard stories from the farmers who've had sheep killed. Maybe five dogs." Jennet stepped around a branch, then quickened her pace to stay close to Abel. "I don't want you to feel you must take the job after what just happened."

"I want the job," he said grimly. "A dog gone wild is very dangerous." He stopped at the edge of the water. The boat rocked gently, tugging against the line. He carried Jennet to the boat and sat her down, pulled the line free, and climbed in himself. Would he have the strength to row back across the lake? It stretched smooth and clear for what seemed miles.

Jennet looked back into the woods. Should she give up her dream? There were too many dangers to face, too much opposition. Softly she said, "Heavenly Father, thank You for Your help, Your strength, and Your wisdom to do what's right."

Taking a deep, steadying breath Abel started rowing toward Fromberg.

Jennet saw the pain on Abel's face. "I can take over," she said hesitantly.

"No need." Could he keep rowing? Muscle spasms made him jerk his arms. "I'll take it slow and easy." The boat barely crept forward.

Jennet wanted to demand to take over, but she knew she would have a hard time rowing. Oh, why had her body grown so old! Why wasn't she strong like she'd been during her childhood when she could chop wood all morning and still have strength to do the chores?

The morning sun burned down on her, making her head sweat under her bonnet. Her dress was dirty and ripped at the hem. Her mouth was bone dry.

At the dock Abel climbed from the boat and secured it, then reached to help Jennet.

Her legs trembled and she clutched Abel's muscled arm to keep from falling.

"You need a doctor, Abel." She glanced around to find someone who'd help, but the dock was empty.

He looked down at her and saw her wan face and felt her tremble. "Are you all right?"

"I'll be . . . fine." She tried to walk, but collapsed against him.

He lifted her easily and carried her to the first building, a warehouse with an office. He set her on a bench in the shade and found a drink of water for her.

She drank thankfully. "Please, sit down, Abel. You look ready to collapse."

He shook his head. His wounds hurt unbearably, but he didn't want her to know.

"Leave me and go get yourself taken care of."

"I can't just leave you!"

"You must! Look at yourself! You'll get infection in your scratches if you don't tend to them."

He touched his cheek gingerly and his fingers came away bloody. He sank down beside her.

"I must call my grandsons. They'll help us without worrying Free. Is there a telephone here?" She stood and the world seemed to spin. With a gasp she collapsed back on the bench. "I don't believe I can make it."

"I'll call for you."

"No. I must. Could you help me to the telephone?"

He lifted her again and carried her to the office where she got permission to use the telephone from a man too busy to notice the condition they were in. She had the operator ring the Wagon Works for her. Justin answered and for a minute she couldn't speak.

"Justin, I need you."

"Grandma?"

"Yes." She told him where she was and about the attack. "Bring Trent and come right away. Don't say a word to your pa or anyone else."

In his office Justin ran his fingers through his hair. What more was going to happen to them? He grabbed his hat and hurried into the factory where he knew Trent was talking with Dad near the outside door. Justin ducked around a finished wagon that had just been painted green. How could he get Trent without making Dad suspicious? In the past to get Trent to follow him without alerting Dad, he'd salute and keep on going. They'd made up the signal when they were seven years old and had used it until Trent had left. "I'll try it again," Justin muttered. He caught Trent's eye and saluted, then hurried out to his automobile.

Trent saw the salute and stopped talking mid-sentence. Had

he seen right? Did Justin want him? Justin had looked more upset than usual. "Dad, would you excuse me? I have to check on something. See you at home later."

"Is something wrong?" Clay asked, frowning.

"Not that I know about. I'll see you later."

Trent tugged his cap lower on his forehead as he dashed outdoors and looked around until he saw Justin just getting into his Duesenberg. A pain of anguish shot through Trent and he almost stopped. How could he be alone with Justin?

Justin motioned to him to hurry and Trent sprinted across to the auto. "What's wrong? Is it Rachel?"

"It's Grandma. Get in quick." Justin started the auto and backed out even as Trent was closing the passenger door.

"What about her?"

Justin told Trent what Grandma had said as he drove as fast as possible out of Blue Creek and north toward Fromberg.

"This is getting out of hand," Trent said, shaking his head as he braced his feet to keep from being thrown against Justin. "Why won't Grandma stay home where she belongs?

"I say we drop this whole Havlick's Wilderness idea." Justin cut the air with his hand to emphasize his point, then gripped the steering wheel with both hands. "I never did like it. It's not too late to drop it."

"But we both know Grandma won't." Trent stared out the windshield at the road ahead.

"Maybe she will after this. I hope she's not hurt. You know how she understates things."

Trent had forgotten that about her.

Several minutes later they found Jennet sitting in the shade of the factory with a black man in bad shape beside her. Trent and Justin exchanged startled looks.

Jennet hugged Justin, then Trent, and said briskly, "This is Abel Grant. We must get him to a doctor immediately."

Abel was too weak to object. He greeted Trent and Justin with a wan smile.

Trent's head spun with questions, but he kept quiet as he helped Abel to his feet.

Justin swung Jennet up in his arms and carried her to his auto. She seemed very frail. He wanted to suggest she see a doctor too, but he knew she'd object.

There wasn't a doctor in Fromberg so they drove Abel to Doctor Kyle Mewsac in Blue Creek and waited while he dressed the wounds. Medium height and leaning toward fat, the doctor was in his thirties with neatly brushed reddish brown hair and blue eyes. The office was quiet and smelled like medicine.

"What happened to you, Grant?" Dr. Mewsac asked when he finished.

"Got in the way of a dog," Abel said. He didn't want to give information Jennet Havlick didn't want known.

"Keep the bandages changed regularly." His white coat flapping around his thick legs, Dr. Mewsac walked Abel to the waiting room where the Havlicks waited.

Trent jumped up. "Doc, take a look at my grandma, would you?"

"Now, Trent," Jennet said with a frown. "I'm all right. Just tired."

"Did you get in the way of the same dog?" Dr. Mewsac asked with a laugh.

"I sure did." Jennet nodded. She'd known Dr. Mewsac for almost three years and admired him for his hard work. "But how about Abel? Will he be all right?"

"He's a strong man and shouldn't have any problem if he takes care of himself." Dr. Mewsac took Jennet's pulse as they stood there.

"That's enough of that," she said sharply, pulling away from him. "I'm fine, I tell you."

"Grandma, we want to make sure," Justin said.

"It won't take long to have the doc look you over," Trent said.

"There is no need, boys!"

They shrugged, knowing it was the end of the discussion.

"Just where was this dog?" Dr. Mewsac asked.

Abel shrugged as he looked to Jennet for the lead.

Jennet brushed back a strand of white hair. "We're having a problem with wild dogs in our old growth. We were there today and one of the dogs jumped us."

"I'm surprised you got away with your lives," Dr. Mewsac said sharply.

"Abel throttled the dog," Jennet said proudly.

Abel flushed.

"Let's go, Grandma," Trent said. He didn't want her to tell all their business outside the family. It wasn't safe.

"I trust folks will stay away from your woods after this," Dr. Mewsac said sharply.

"I hope so too," Jennet said. "We're going to be clearing out a few trees so we can start building cabins."

Trent tried to hurry her out, but she wouldn't be hurried.

"I thought you'd given up on that idea," the doctor said, his reddish brown brow lifted.

"I don't know where you heard that," Jennet said. "It's just not so. We will continue with our work."

"I hope no one else is hurt because of your stubbornness, Mrs. Havlick. First your granddaughter shot, now this."

"They are hardly connected," Justin said impatiently.

"Well, no. I don't suppose they are. But they both caused harm."

Trent looked at the man shrewdly. Was he warning them about continuing? Surely not! Trent relaxed slightly. He was seeing enemies where none existed. "We have to get you home, Grandma. And you too, Abel."

Justin shook hands with the doctor, paid the bill, and followed the others out to his car. "Where shall we take you, Abel?"

Before he could speak Jennet said, "To the farm. He has no family and he's staying with us."

Trent and Justin exchanged looks, but knew not to argue.

Abel shook his head. "I can't impose on you, Mrs. Havlick."

"You were hurt in my employ and I won't send you off by yourself. There'll be no more argument." Jennet smiled and patted his arm. "Let us do this for you, Abel. It'll help ease my conscience for what happened to you today."

Abel grinned and nodded. "You're very kind."

"Never argue with a Havlick woman," Trent said, laughing. He thought of Emily—now a Havlick woman—and the laugh died. She was probably the most stubborn one so far. What in the world was he going to do with her?

Justin helped Jennet into the front seat while Trent and Abel sat in the back. Justin patted Jennet's knee. "I'm glad you're all right, Grandma. But in the future you stay home where you're safe and let us make Havlick's Wilderness a reality. We don't want anything to happen to you."

Jennet caught Justin's hand and squeezed it. "I'll be more careful, but I won't sit at home and do nothing to accomplish my dream."

Trent shook his head. Just what was going to happen next?

Later as Justin helped Jennet to the house, Abel laid a hand on Trent's arm.

"I didn't tell Mrs. Havlick this, but I saw a man in the woods just before the dog attacked us."

Trent sucked in his breath. "Why didn't he help you?"

Abel looked worried. "That's what I was wondering myself. I think it'd be better to keep her away from the woods. She hired me to kill the wild dogs and keep an eye on the land around Deep Lake. I'll do that. But I don't want her in danger again."

"I agree," Trent said as a shiver ran down his spine. But

why was Abel so concerned? He barely knew Jennet Havlick.

Later as they drove away from the farm, Trent told Justin what Abel had said. "I say we should report it to the sheriff."

Justin nodded. "I wonder who could've been out there? Not Andree. He would've jumped to their defense. Maybe we should go have a look."

"Maybe so. It's a little late to go today, but we could do it first thing in the morning."

"I thought you were leaving tomorrow."

Trent groaned. "I was. But after what happened today, I can't."

Justin gripped the steering wheel tightly. He'd been holding his feelings in so Trent could leave without a big blow up. How much longer could he do it? "This could take a while," he said stiffly.

"I know." Trent's stomach knotted. Could he stay around Justin even a day longer and not kill him?

Justin slowed the auto as he glanced at Trent. "What about the ranch you're going to buy?"

"Cactus Pete said he'd give me until the end of summer."

Justin burst out laughing, surprising himself as much as Trent. "What kind of name is Cactus Pete?"

Trent grinned. "I had a chuckle over that one, too." He sobered. "I think I'll hang around another month to see Havlick's Wilderness get started. Then I'll head on down to Texas."

Justin bit his tongue to keep from crying out in agony. A month! Could he survive a month with Trent?

Just then Trent saw Gabe Lavery beside his pickup truck at the Feed and Grain. "Stop here, Just. I'm going to tell Gabe I'll be moving back home. You don't have to wait for me."

Justin pulled up behind the pickup truck and waited until Trent climbed out, then drove away in a daze. Trent had called him Just! Was Trent forgetting? Was it possible for them to work out their problems after all?

Trent walked to the man beside the black pickup truck, nodded, and said, "Afternoon, Gabe."

Gabe looked toward the departing auto and back to Trent. "Justin? Trent?"

"Trent. I wanted a word with you about my place."

"I've kept it up good." Gabe smiled even as he tensed for the worst. "You plan on selling it since you're moving to Texas?"

"Can't say yet. But I do plan to move back in. I'll be staying on here for a while."

Gabe paled. "And how soon do you plan to move back?"

"As soon as possible. Is tomorrow too soon for you?"

"I do have a few things to clear out of the house and some livestock to take over to my place. How about giving me a couple of days?"

Trent thought for a while. "Tell you what. I'll come out and help you move your things. I want to be in there tomorrow."

Gabe's temper flared even as fear smote him. "Don't trouble yourself on my account. I'll be out tomorrow afternoon. You can move back in then."

"Fine." Trent held out his hand and finally Gabe took it and shook it. "If you can't get your livestock out tomorrow, don't fret about it. Move it when you can." Trent felt the tension in Gabe and wondered what it was all about. Trent tipped his cap and walked away.

Gabe flung himself in the pickup truck and roared away. How was he ever going to get all his stuff out by tomorrow? Where would he move the still? He struck the steering wheel with his fist. Trent Havlick was going to be very sorry for booting him out like that!

Trent walked slowly down main street. A few buggies and automobiles stood outside the stores. Three women stood in front of the general store, talking and laughing. They smiled at him and called him Justin. He didn't correct them.

What would Emily say about staying on another month? He knew Rachel would be pleased. Would Emily find ways to be around Bob Lavery?

Trent doubled his fists. She was his wife and Bob Lavery had better stay away from her!

CHAPTER

11

♦ The smell of bread baking for supper followed Trent up the stairs. He stopped just outside Emily's closed bedroom door. Mom had told him she was there even though she'd finished packing. He wanted to tell her they were staying before he told anyone else. He reached for the doorknob, but stopped, afraid to walk in. Frowning at his own lack of courage, he knocked.

"Yes?"

"I need to talk to you."

"Trent?"

Impatiently he pushed open the door and strode in past the locked trunk. She was standing beside the bed, her hands at her throat. She wore a white blouse, a mid-calf length blue plaid pleated skirt, and ankle strap shoes with a low heel. Her red-rimmed eyes and sad face left him weak. "What's wrong?" he asked gruffly.

"Nothing," she said in a tiny voice.

"I can see there is."

She turned her face away, her black hair falling across her cheek. "You wouldn't want to listen anyway."

"Try me." He caught her hand and held it as he smiled.

She looked in his eyes and her pulse quickened. Was he ready to be friends again?

"Come on, Emily. Tell me what's wrong. Please."

"I . . . don't know if I can . . . leave my family. When will I see Mama and Papa again?"

Relief washed over him. He'd thought she was going to say she wanted out of the marriage. "Texas is a lot closer than Sweden."

"I know." Her voice rose in a wail. "But it's still a long way away."

"I'll make sure you get to see them."

"But it's still hard to leave them!"

"I'm sorry." He rubbed her wedding ring.

"Everything is different now." Tears filled her eyes. "And you're angry at me."

"Not any longer."

She opened her eyes wide in surprise and looked at him closely. "Aren't you still mad at me?" she whispered.

He shook his head.

"Are you sure?"

"Very sure."

"I am so glad!" She flung her arms around him and hugged him tight.

Startled, he just stood there, then hugged her and buried his face in her mass of black hair. He liked the apple smell of it and liked the feel of her soft body against him. "I have news that'll make you even happier."

His voice was muffled, but she'd heard him clearly. Trembling, she pulled away from him, but kept her hands on his shoulders. His hands at her waist felt warm and comforting. "What is it?"

"We're going to stay a while longer." He'd never noticed how dark and long her lashes were or how pretty her eyes were. "Maybe another month."

"Oh, Trent!" She laughed breathlessly. "I'm so glad!" She

hugged him again. She smelled the tang of his skin and felt the thud of his heart against her. Flushing, she jumped back. "Why'd you decide to stay?"

He pushed her hair off her damp cheeks and smoothed it down as he told her about Jennet, Abel, and the wild dog. He didn't tell her about the man Abel had seen or that Justin had gone to report it to the sheriff. "I told Justin I'd stay until Havlick's Wilderness gets under way."

"Are you sure?"

"I'd rather leave, but the family needs my help."

"You will be careful, won't you? I don't want a dog to attack you."

He smiled, pleased she cared. "I'm too tough anyway." He caught her hand and held it. "There's more."

Her pulse quickened. "Oh?"

"We're going to move to the farm tomorrow."

"To the farm? Oh, Trent! Can you handle that?"

A shudder ran through him. "Sure. You and Rachel will be there to help me."

"And that's a promise!"

He fingered the blue beads around her neck. "What about you? Can you handle running into Bob Lavery from time to time?"

She sucked in air. For a moment she'd forgotten about him. Could she keep him at arm's length if he wanted to be closer? She lifted her eyes to Trent. "If you'll help me."

He smiled gently. "I will. You can count on it."

Fresh tears filled her eyes. "Oh, Trent! I'm so glad we're friends again."

"Me, too, Emily. Me too." He'd missed her more than he'd realized and more than he thought possible.

"When do we move in?"

"Tomorrow afternoon."

"What about Gabe Lavery?"

"He's leaving right away."

"It'll be strange living at the farm."

Trent stiffened. Could he walk back in the room where he'd found Celine dead?

Emily saw the look on his face and knew what he was thinking. "Rachel and I will be right beside you, Trent. We'll help you."

"I haven't been there since the funeral."

She rubbed his arm. "I know. I know."

He bent his head as the agony swept over him again. She pulled him close and held him, soothing him with soft words. "Comfort his heart, Jesus," she whispered.

At last he stepped back, self-conscious for crying on her shoulder when it should've been the other way around. "I guess I'd better go."

"Does Rachel know we're staying?"

"No. I wanted to tell you first."

That pleased her. "Can we tell her together?"

"Sure. I know she'll be glad. She hates leaving Amanda and the family."

"She'll like living on the farm. She's pestered me often about going to the farm to see where she was born. And to see Celine's things."

Trent turned away. "Maybe you should take her alone for the first time. I don't think I could listen to and answer all her questions without crying like a baby."

"She'd understand."

"But I won't break down in front of her! I am her father, not some child!"

Emily cupped his cheek with her hand. "I know and so does she. If it'll help you, I will take her there by myself."

Trent covered her hand, locking it against his face. "Thank you." He liked the feel and smell of her skin. "I guess I'd better set you straight about our fight the day of our marriage."

She flushed and tugged at her hand, but he wouldn't release it.

"I had your brothers put your trunk in my bedroom so they wouldn't tease you."

Emily's eyes widened in surprise. "Why didn't you tell me?"

"I planned to, but you made me mad."

"So all this time we've been upset because of a misunderstanding!" She jabbed him with her free hand. "I don't like that a bit! I've been miserable without you, Trent Havlick!"

He caught her other hand, then held them both firmly in his. "I felt pretty bad myself. I guess all our secrets are out in the open now."

Bob's kiss flashed across her mind and she flushed scarlet. To cover up she quickly said, "You don't think I can tell you all my little secrets, do you?"

He chuckled. "You're an innocent girl. What secrets could you possibly have?"

"Not as many as you, I'm sure." She tugged him toward the door before he pursued the subject further. "Let's go tell Rachel and your mother."

* * *

The next morning, just after sunup, Trent picked up Justin at the Wagon Works and they drove to Fromberg. As they agreed, they both carried revolvers. Justin told Trent about his visit to Sheriff Lamont.

"He said Abel probably was only seeing things and to leave it up to him."

"Does he know we're heading there this morning?"

"No. I didn't figure it was any of his business. It is Havlick land."

"Maybe we'll run into him while we're there."

Justin shrugged. "Maybe."

Several minutes later they rowed across Deep Lake without talking. In silence they tied the boat securely and walked into the woods where Jennet said she and Abel had gone. Birds twittered in the high branches of the trees.

"Here it is," Trent said in a low voice. The ground was bare where Abel and the dog had fought. The broken branch Jennet had struck the dog with lay near the base of a pine. Wind whispered through the tall branches.

Trent shot Justin a startled look. "Where's the carcass?" he asked just above a whisper.

His nerves tight, Justin glanced around. No wild animal would eat a dead dog. A buzzard might pick its flesh off but the bones would be left behind. "Maybe Abel didn't kill the dog." His voice was low and terse. A shiver trickled down his spine. He turned to Trent. "Would Abel lie about killing the dog?"

"Why would he? Besides, Grandma saw it all." Trent walked away from the spot, his eyes on the ground for footprints or other signs to show that someone else had been there. He couldn't see anything. He glanced at Justin and shrugged. Would Abel lie about seeing a man here? Or had he been mistaken?

"Maybe the sheriff did something with the dog's body."

"Why would he?" Trent shook his head. "I doubt if the sheriff's been here yet. It's early."

"You're right. It sure is a mystery."

"Sure is." Watching his step in case of snakes, Trent slowly climbed a hill with Justin close behind him. They stopped in a spot where one of the cabins was going to be built. He heard a stream trickling through the woods to his left. It meandered down into a ravine and out of sight.

"I don't like this one bit," Justin said as he pushed his cap back.

"Something's going on. That's for sure." Trent looped his thumbs over his belt as he slowly looked around. He saw bushes leafed out, the ground covered with years of pine needles and leaves, and trees as far as the eye could see. He caught a flicker of movement and stood stone still. Had it been a deer? A bear? Or was it a man? Trent motioned in the direction and whispered to Justin, "I thought I saw something."

Justin narrowed his eyes, but couldn't see a thing. "Let's check it out." He led the way, his heart racing.

Just then a man stepped from behind a tree, shotgun pointed right at Justin's heart. "Hands up!" the man commanded. He wore high-top walking shoes, heavy pants, and a gray shirt. Black hair hung below a dark gray cap.

Trent wanted to grab for his gun, but he lifted his hands high as he stopped beside Justin.

Justin's hand itched to jerk his revolver out of the holster, but he also slowly raised his hands.

"Who are you and what're you doing here?" the man snapped. A white scar stood out boldly on his left cheek. "This *is* private property."

Trent narrowed his eyes. "And we happen to own it!"

"You're the one trespassing," Justin said coldly.

The man studied them several minutes. "Are you two Havlicks?"

"Justin and Trent," Trent said, motioning to himself and Justin as he said their names.

The man blew out his breath. Finally he lowered his gun. "Forgive me, men. I'm Pierce Lorraine, federal agent."

"What're *you* doing *here?*" Trent snapped, resting his hand on his revolver.

"Did our grandma hire you without telling us?" Justin asked sharply.

The man shook his head. "I'm a federal agent." He shoved his badge out to them and held it while they looked at it. "I work for the government to stop the making and selling of alcohol."

"But why are you here?" Justin waved his hand to indicate where they were.

Pierce Lorraine narrowed his eyes and a muscle jumped in his jaw. "There's a still in your woods."

"What?"

"That's impossible!"

"A man by the name of Leroy Bushnell operates it and several others around Fromberg and Blue Creek. He supplies liquor to Gilly's Place and a few other speakeasies on this side of the state."

Trent's stomach knotted. "How do you know this?"

"I followed him here. But I lost him before I could find the still. He's from North Carolina and he knows about moonshine and stills and revenue men."

Justin pushed his cap back. "Does he know you're here?"

"No. I don't think so. And I want to keep it that way."

Trent told him about the wild dog and the man Abel had spotted. "Did you see that happen?"

"No. But I did see Leroy Bushnell bury the dog. It belonged to him. He trained it to attack at his command, and return at a whistle."

Justin and Trent exchanged shocked looks.

"Why didn't you arrest this Bushnell?" Justin asked.

"He's working with someone in Blue Creek. I want them all, not just Bushnell."

Impatiently Trent brushed a bug off his sleeve. He wished he could rid the woods of Leroy Bushnell as easily. "Have you spoken to the sheriff?"

"No. In my business I can't trust anyone. I've told you fellas because I need help. You're Havlicks. If you know these woods you could help me find the still."

Justin moved restlessly. "Then what?"

"I'll keep an eye on it and on Bushnell so I can see who else is involved."

"How'd you get here?" Trent looked down toward the lake. "I didn't see a boat."

Agent Lorraine chuckled dryly. "I rowed out from Fromberg

like I was going fishing, then rowed close to the bank along your woods. I hid the boat behind an outcropping of rocks and climbed up there. Bushnell hides his boat near where yours is tied up. He's got it hid so well it took me a while to find it among the bushes. He takes a different route to the still so he never makes a trail."

"Smart man," Trent said, shaking his head.

"We heard tell about a pack of wild dogs. Have you seen them?" Justin asked.

"No. I think it was just a rumor Bushnell spread. But keep your eyes peeled in case he has more than one dog." Agent Lorraine explained to them what they were looking for and that Bushnell's still would be near a stream or creek. "Whatever you do, don't jump the man. He's dangerous. I'll be in the boarding house in Blue Creek tonight, Room 10. If you learn anything, stop in and tell me. I checked in as Joe Bent, a salesman."

Nodding, Trent and Justin walked silently away, watching for signs of trespassing.

About two hours later they found the still hidden in a ravine with branches growing across to make a natural hideaway. The smell turned Justin's stomach. Trent watched a tiny trickle of smoke rise and dissipate in the tree branches.

Cautiously they crept away from the ravine and back to their boat. They didn't speak until they were in the middle of the lake.

"I plan to tell Andree what's going on," Trent said as he dipped in the oar.

"Good. But we'll keep it from Grandma. First thing she'd do is come here and try to capture Bushnell. She'd do it, too! Can't you just see her filling him with buckshot?" Justin chuckled and Trent joined in.

They looked at each other and laughed harder.

* * *

Priscilla walked restlessly back and forth in front of the picnic table while the children shouted and laughed and played in the yard. Her short blue skirt flipped about her knees. She ran a finger around the neckline of her plaid blouse. The hot afternoon sun burned down on her, putting her temper on the verge of exploding.

"Want some company?" Noah asked with a grin.

Her heart leaped and she nodded. How handsome he looked in his light gray shirt and dark trousers! His brown hair was parted on the right and slicked back above his ears and back off his forehead. "I thought you were gone for the day."

Gabe Lavery had paid him to come back and play up to Priscilla. He smiled into her eyes. This was going to be an easy, pleasurable job. "I came back early."

"Oh?" She fingered her bobbed hair. "Why?"

"I missed you too much."

His words turned her to jelly and she sank to the bench. "You did?" she whispered.

He sat beside her and took her hand in his. Gabe had said Justin Havlick and all the Havlicks were going to have Gilly's Place and all the other speakeasies shut down, so they had to do everything they could to get the Havlicks' minds off bootlegging and illegal drinking. "Make family problems and they'll soon forget all about other things," Gabe had said. Noah leaned close to Priscilla. "I'm fed up with the way your husband ignores you. I want you to leave him and go away with me."

She gasped. "But I can't!"

"Sure you can."

"But I'm married to Justin."

"So what?"

"I couldn't . . . leave him!"

"Sure you could." Maybe this wasn't going to be as easy as he thought. "You and me and the children could have some good times together."

"Oh my."

"I got some money. We could go far away."

Priscilla's heart fluttered as pictures flashed across her mind of the fun she could have with Noah. "I don't know," she said weakly.

He lifted her hand to his lips and kissed her palm. He liked making her heart beat faster.

A thrill ran through her.

He pressed her hand to his cheek as he looked at her tenderly. "You're a beautiful lady and you deserve to be loved and cared for. You deserve it all! You think about it and let me know."

"I will."

"You're important to me. So are the children. I want to show you the world!" He lowered his voice to a husky whisper. "I want you to know how it feels to have a real man love you."

Her heart lurched. Wasn't this what she'd wanted from him? Then why was she afraid to take what he was offering?

* * *

It was three in the afternoon. Emily took a deep breath and opened the back door to Trent's farmhouse. Rachel stood at her heels. For once she wasn't chattering.

Emily stepped into the enclosed porch that held the washing machine and stack of split wood, then on into the kitchen. A strange smell hung in the air. A breeze ruffled the curtains at the windows. Gabe Lavery had probably left them open to air the house. The room was clean except for a fine dusting of what looked like ground corn in the corners nearest the cast iron range. An oblong oak table with four chairs around it stood in the middle of the large kitchen.

"Did my momma Celine cook at this stove?" Rachel asked, her eyes wide.

Emily nodded.

Rachel touched the tall cupboard with glass doors, the pie

safe, the sideboard, the washstand with a red hand pump. "Celine touched all of this."

"Yes, she did." Emily blinked tears away. Many times she'd worked side by side with Celine in this very kitchen. They'd canned together, baked Christmas goodies together, cooked meals together.

Rachel ran into the dining room just off the kitchen through wide oak pocket doors. She rubbed a hand over the cherry table and counted aloud the eight chairs around it. She patted the matching hutch, buffet, and corner hutch. She studied the fancy dishes and the white china pitcher and bowl with red cabbage roses painted on it sitting on top of the buffet. "I like Celine's things, Emily."

It was hard to speak around the lump in her throat. "So do I."

Rachel slipped her hand in Emily's as they walked into the parlor, the front room, the den, then up the wide stairs to the four huge bedrooms. A wooden cradle stood beside a large bed in the first bedroom.

Rachel touched the cradle and lifted wide dark eyes to Emily. "Was this mine?" she whispered.

Emily's tongue clung to the roof of her mouth and she could only nod. She saw the bed where Celine had given birth to Rachel. She walked around the spot where Celine had crumpled to the floor.

"Is this where Momma died?" Rachel whispered, standing beside the huge bed and looking down at the wooden floor.

"Yes. But she's in heaven now, Rachel."

"I know. She's with Jesus."

Emily stood at the window. She would not have this for the master bedroom! She'd make this into a pleasant sitting room and play room. She'd change the drapes and put in a sofa and rocking chair.

Rachel led the way to the other bedrooms down the wide hall. Two of the bedrooms were empty and the fourth had a four poster walnut bed and dresser that looked old and cherished. It was a bed Freeman's grandfather had passed down. Free had given it to Trent. This would be the bedroom she'd share with Trent. She flushed, turning away quickly before Rachel noticed.

Emily looked out the window, waiting for her brothers to arrive to help her.

"Where will I sleep?" Rachel asked, leaning against Emily.

"You can have the room across the hall from this or the one beside it."

Rachel ran to look out the windows of both rooms. She stayed in the one across the hall. "I can see the river from here. I'll take this room."

"Good. We'll make it pretty for you."

"But not pink!"

Emily laughed. "No, not pink."

Several minutes later Emily's brothers arrived and she had them move the furniture where she wanted it. She took the drapes off the windows in Celine's room and put up the blue and rose floral drapes that had hung in the front room. The boys carried a sofa from the front room and set it against a wall with a low coffee table in front of it. They carried a rocker in from the parlor and Emily laid a rag rug in front of it. She set Rachel's dollhouse and several of her dolls near the window. She found pictures throughout the house that would look nice in the room. Soon the room looked so different it was hard to imagine it had been a bedroom.

The boys put Celine's bedroom furniture in Rachel's room. With a different spread and a different color around it, even the furniture looked different. Rachel lined up three dolls on the pillows, then stood back, satisfied. Her small rocker stood in one corner beside a short table with a kerosene lamp on it.

While Emily worked upstairs Martha, Zoe, and Hannah worked downstairs. They were glad Trent was staying even if only another month. Martha had reminded Emily of what she'd said a few days ago about Trent never leaving. Emily had brushed the idea aside once again.

Soon the house smelled of pie baking and beef stew boiling.

Emily's brothers did the chores, then left for home to do their own chores. Shortly afterward the women said goodbye and left.

Later Emily and Rachel stood in the kitchen at the window. Fire crackled in the range. Outdoors a turkey gobbled.

"Are you sure Daddy's coming?"

"I'm positive."

"What if he goes to Texas without us?"

"He won't." Emily pulled Rachel close as they stood at the window and watched the lane for Trent's blue Dodge. "Maybe we should eat. I'm hungry."

"I guess we could. I did want to wait for Daddy."

"Me too, but he might be really late." Emily dipped stew into two bowls and sliced the bread Lark had sent with them. With Rachel talking only a little, they ate. The stew was delicious, but Emily couldn't enjoy it. She jumped at every little sound.

They walked to the parlor and Rachel tried to play the piano. "I remember hearing Celine play the piano," Rachel said.

Emily smiled gently. "You remember me telling you about her playing."

"I know. I wish I could really remember it."

Several minutes later Trent drove in and stopped near the back door. The last time he'd lived here, he'd driven a buggy instead of an auto. He gripped the steering wheel. Could he get out and walk to the door as if this was just any old house?

Emily and Rachel stepped out the back door and waved.

"Hi, Daddy! I like our house!"

Emily's stomach tightened. She knew it was hard for Trent to walk to them so they walked to him. "We ate supper without you. I hope you don't mind."

"Not at all."

"We waited and waited," Rachel said. "And we got too hungry."

Trent bent down and kissed Rachel's cheek, then turned to Emily. "Sorry I wasn't here sooner. I got held up in town." He and Justin had reported to Agent Lorraine and they'd learned what he planned to do next.

"I like our house, Daddy." Rachel tugged on his hand. "I like the animals, too."

Trent hesitated, almost too weak to step through the back door.

"Everything's in order," Emily said cheerfully as she nudged Trent from behind.

He walked in and stopped near the table. The room was familiar, but also different.

"Your Aunt Hannah baked an apple pie for us," Emily said, pointing to the still warm pie on the top shelf of the pie safe.

"Smells good," Trent said around the lump in his throat. Celine had made delicious apple pies. She favored making cherry pie, but she'd made apple especially for him.

They walked through the house. Outside the master bedroom Trent broke out into a sweat. Emily caught his hand and held it firmly, then pushed open the door and followed Rachel in.

Trent looked around in surprise at the changes. The dull ache of losing Celine was there, but the stabbing agony was gone. "Thank you," he whispered to Emily.

She smiled and nodded.

"Come see my room, Daddy!" Rachel ran down the hall and stopped in the doorway of her room. She pointed across the hall. "You and Emily have that room and I have this one."

Startled, Trent turned to Emily. "Is that right?"

She barely nodded.

A muscle jumped in his jaw. Was he ready for this? He strode down the hall to look in Rachel's room, but his mind was on Emily and on Celine.

Long after Rachel was asleep, Emily slipped into bed, her nerves as tight as the ropes that held the mattresses. Would Trent come to bed with her or stay downstairs? The lamp burned a low flame on the stand beside the bed. She heard every creak in the house and every sound outside the house. She closed her eyes, but they popped open the minute her eyelids covered her eyes.

Finally Trent walked in, blew out the lamp, undressed, and slipped in beside her. He didn't reach out for her or turn to her. "This is hard for both of us," he said in a tight voice. "I would've stayed downstairs, but the couch was too small and the floor too hard."

Emily breathed a sigh of relief. "When the time is right we'll become man and wife."

"Yes. I thought you'd understand." He turned on his side facing away from her and fell asleep.

She listened to him breathe and almost reached out to touch him. Her face flamed and she kept her hands at her sides and her back poker straight.

The next morning when she woke up he was gone.

CHAPTER

12

♦ Yawning, Justin looked through the pile of bills on his office desk. Early morning sunlight shafted through the window behind him. A cup of coffee he'd made himself was at his elbow. He wore a white shirt with a figured tie and dark pants. The bills in his hand crackled. If they didn't get oak for chairs soon, the Wagon Works would be in bad shape—worse than last year. He heard the first men arriving for work. He yawned again. Priscilla had been in one of her moods again last night and wouldn't let him get to sleep.

She'd rested her head on his arm and put her arm across him while he lay on his back. "Justin, let's get somebody to watch the children and then ride the train to Grand Rapids. We could stay a couple of days at the hotel and spend time together, eat in a nice restaurant, and maybe even go to the theater. Could we do that, Justin?"

"I have too much going on," he'd answered, already half asleep.

"Then how about if you come home from work early tomorrow? I'll feed the children early and put them to bed. We could have the whole evening together—just the two of us. Please, Just?"

"I'm bone tired, Pris. Let me get some sleep, will you?" He turned away from her and pretended to sleep. She sobbed quietly into her pillow for a long, long time. He'd almost gathered her in his arms, but he couldn't make himself move. He'd gone to sleep while she was still crying.

Now at his office desk, he yawned again. Things weren't right between him and Priscilla, but he couldn't spend time thinking about it. He had to keep the Wagon Works going, even while he worried about bootleggers and Grandma's dream of Havlick's Wilderness.

The door opened and Trent walked in, his cap in his hand. His blue chambray shirt was buttoned to his throat and at the cuffs. A wide leather belt circled his hips and held up his denim pants. "Anything new from Agent Lorraine?"

Justin stifled another yawn. "Nothing that I know about."

"It's been two days!" Trent paced the small office. He'd slept soundly the night before, just as he had the first night with Emily, and woke at the crack of dawn with his arm around her, just as he had the first night. For a split second he'd thought she was Celine. He'd crept out of bed, dressed, and hurried away before Emily stirred. She did look pretty when she slept—her cheeks rosy and her hair in two braids. Abruptly he pushed thoughts of Emily aside to take care of the business at hand. "I think we should get Bushnell ourselves so we can get the crew out there."

"Maybe so." Justin rubbed a hand across his face. For two nights he hadn't slept well. Priscilla had tossed and turned and even mumbled in her sleep. Well, he couldn't think about her or his lack of sleep now. He had more important issues at hand. "Know where we can get oak right away?"

"Did you try the Havlicks south of Grand Rapids?"

"Yes. Cousin Steven doesn't have any. I've tried all my other sources, but the prices are way out of reach. We can kiln dry the oak in the old growth that we'll cut down, but we can't wait that long. This is serious, Trent. We have orders to fill before the end of July and if we don't get them filled, we might lose the accounts."

Frowning thoughtfully, Trent perched on the corner of Justin's huge walnut desk that was cluttered with papers, drawings of chairs and wagons, a telephone, and a cup of coffee. "Remember old Sam McDaniel near Caledonia?"

Justin narrowed his eyes thoughtfully. "I don't. What about him?"

"We sometimes got oak from him. I'll contact him and see what he has to say."

Justin smiled. "Thanks. It's great not to carry this alone."

Trent shot up. "Don't get used to it. I won't be here long."

Justin's nerves tightened. "I know." He looked back at the mail in his hands. He flipped through it, stopped at an envelope that looked soiled and was addressed with a pencil in a scrawl that could be a child's. "What have we here?"

"What?" Trent leaned over the desk to look.

"It's addressed to both of us." He turned the envelope for Trent to read their names written in inch tall letters. "Somebody dropped it off."

A shiver trickled down Trent's spine. "Open it."

Justin pulled a piece of lined paper from the envelope. He unfolded it and read aloud: "You Havlick twins think you have everything. But you don't. Ask Priscilla how she likes Noah Roswell's romantic attentions." Justin's mouth dried to dust and the letter fell to the desk. His face turned a chalky white.

With an angry cry Trent scooped up the letter and read, "Ask Emily about Bob Lavery's kisses. You Havlick twins are losing your wives and you don't even know it." Trent sank to a chair, his whole insides on fire. He flung the letter to the floor. The words looked bold on the white paper and seemed to jump up for him to see all over again. "Lies!" he said hoarsely.

"What if it's not?" Justin raked his fingers through his dark hair.

"It has to be!"

The door opened and Clay walked in dressed in dark work pants, held up by wide black suspenders, and a green plaid shirt, his cap in his hand. He stopped short. "What's wrong?"

Justin struggled to pull himself together, but couldn't.

Trent turned his face away.

Clay saw the paper on the floor, picked it up, and read it, then savagely balled it up. "Lies! You boys can't believe those lies!"

They looked at each other, at their dad, then nodded.

His brow knit, Clay hauled a chair up near the desk and straddled it. "Tell me what's going on, boys! It seems I've been missing something. Justin, you start."

He flushed, feeling like a boy again. He had to admit it felt good to have Dad take over. Justin talked, too numb to know what to do. "I know Pris likes Noah. He takes time for the children and he talks to her. But I never thought it would go this far."

"Maybe it hasn't!" Clay cleared his throat. "But I have noticed you've been neglecting her."

"But . . ."

Clay lifted his hand to stop Justin. "You know you have. We've talked about this several times already."

Justin raked his fingers through his dark hair. "It doesn't give her any right to two-time me with the hired man! And a kid at that! He's twenty-one years old and she's close to thirty!"

"Don't let your temper make things worse."

Justin growled. If he had Noah Roswell here right now, he'd beat him within an inch of his life!

"Let Trent talk now." His gray brow lifted, Clay turned to Trent. "I know there've been rumors about Emily and Bob Lavery. But that's all it was. I know Emily."

Trent thought of the look on Emily's face when he learned she'd talked to Lavery the day she looked over the property Grandma gave her. That had been a guilty look if ever he had seen one. "You don't know her as well as you think, Dad." A hurt stabbed deep within as Trent told his story.

Justin jumped up, almost spilling his cup of coffee. "I'm going home right now!"

"Sit down!" Clay barked.

Surprised, Justin sat.

Trent sat on the edge of his chair, his muscles bunched, ready to spring up.

Clay's gaze softened. "It's not going to do a bit of good to rush home with your tempers flying and demand an explanation. We got to think this through. We got to pray for wisdom."

Trent sprang up, his fists doubled. "You pray, Dad. I'm going to get the truth out of Emily now!"

Justin shot around the desk and shook his fist at Trent. "It's your fault this happened! If you'd stayed home to help me run the business, I would've had more time."

"Boys! Boys!" Clay gripped Trent's arm and reached for Justin, but he backed away. "You boys have been spoiling for a fight for weeks now. But fighting's not the answer and you both know it. God is the answer."

"I don't want to hear it," Trent snapped, twisting free of Clay. "Preach to Justin. He's the killer of the family!" Trent strode out, slamming the door behind him.

Justin's face was as white as his shirt. Killer! That's exactly what he was. Yet the words burned him, especially coming from Trent after the past several days of working together without fighting.

"Killer? What does Trent mean?" Clay asked, frowning.

"It's between him and me, Dad."

"I want to know so I can help you!"

Justin shook his head. His face set, he grabbed his cap off the peg near the door and stormed from the office, leaving the door wide open.

Clay moaned. Hot tears stinging his eyes, he covered his face with his hands and prayed.

Outdoors Justin ran toward his auto, his mind reeling. He didn't deserve a wife and family, but he couldn't let Noah Roswell steal them!

"Justin!" Trent shouted frantically from his Dodge parked on the side of the street under a maple. "I need you, Justin!"

He looked toward the street to see if he'd heard right. Abel Grant stood at the side of Trent's car while Trent sat in the driver's seat. They were motioning wildly to him. Fear shot through Justin. He veered away from the parking lot and ran to the street, his collar suddenly feeling too tight. "What's wrong?"

"Your grandma took another walk by herself," Abel said in agitation, his ebony face glistening with sweat, his hand on the butt of his revolver.

"And she went to the woods!" Trent slapped the steering wheel in frustration.

"I tried to talk her out of it, but you know your grandma."

"Let's go get her," Justin said gruffly as he ran around and climbed in the passenger seat.

Abel climbed in the back seat of the Dodge and was barely seated when Trent took off. "She was gone this morning when I came down for breakfast. She left me a note. That's why I came after you. I knew I couldn't find my way around the woods like you two can. Your grandpa went away with Tris and Zoe, so I couldn't tell them."

Justin groaned as he braced himself to keep from falling against Trent as they turned a corner. Would Grandma walk to the area where Bushnell had his still? Maybe Agent Lorraine was watching him and would be there to protect Grandma. Justin tried to pray, but the words stuck in his throat. He hadn't been able to pray since the devastating day of Celine's death.

Trent gripped the steering wheel so tightly his knuckles hurt. Would they get to the woods in time to keep Grandma safe? Maybe she wouldn't walk in the area of the still. His heart sank. She'd want to stand where the cabins were going to be built. Bushnell's still was in the ravine several yards from the very spot where one cabin was to be. Driving to Fromberg and rowing across the lake was much quicker than trying to run through the woods with the swamps and briars, not to mention the wild creatures that always meant danger. Grandma would take a gun; she always did. Trent glanced at the glovebox. His revolver was in it. He knew Abel carried one, but Justin didn't.

After what seemed like hours, but was only part of an hour, they tied the boat at the edge of the white pine forest. Trent led the way as they ran silently through the woods from tree to tree like Indians toward the ravine and the still. It had rained the night before and their steps were muted on the fallen leaves and pine needles. They stopped behind a clump of bushes and peered around them down at the ravine. The wind carried the smell of the corn liquor away. No smoke drifted up that they could see. Honey bees swarmed on a low hanging limb of a wild cherry tree. Deeper in the woods a crow cawed. A heckling bluejay darted from bough to bough. The smell of damp leaf mold rose around them.

"Maybe the sheriff or Agent Lorraine already arrested Bushnell," Justin whispered.

Trent caught a movement in the ravine. His nerves jangling, he nudged Justin and Abel and pointed. As they watched, Sheriff Lamont walked into sight, deep in conversation with the man they knew from Agent Lorraine's description was Leroy Bushnell. His face was almost covered with wild, uncombed whiskers and a mustache that hid his mouth. Long shaggy dark hair hung below a wide brimmed hat that looked like he'd worn it since the turn of the century. Why was the sheriff talking to Bushnell as if they were in cahoots? Trent frowned. He and Justin exchanged puzzled looks.

Abel jabbed Justin and motioned to their right. A walking

stick in her hand, Jennet Havlick stepped into full view of the sheriff and Bushnell. She was looking down and didn't see them. A blue bonnet covered her white hair. A revolver hung in the holster strapped around her waist. Her blue and white dress made a splash of color against the dull gray bark of the trees.

Bitter gall rose in Justin's throat, almost choking him as he forced himself to hold back a shout.

A knife-sharp pain stabbed at Trent's stomach. He wanted to call to her, but pressed his lips closed and bunched his muscles, ready to leap to her defense.

Groaning from deep inside, Abel drew his revolver.

Jennet looked up and caught sight of the sheriff and Bushnell. She frowned, then waved, and called, "Sheriff! What brings you out here? And who's that with you?"

The sheriff growled something to Bushnell that Trent couldn't hear, then strode up the incline to where Jennet stood while Bushnell disappeared in the ravine.

"You here alone, Mrs. Havlick?" Sheriff Lamont asked, his face red.

Jennet laughed softly. "I know I shouldn't be, but I have protection."

Lamont wiped a thick hand over his hook nose. "Where's the Negro you hired to guard this side of the woods?"

"At home. He's feeling much better after the dog attacked him, but I didn't want him coming here until he's a little better." Jennet looked down at the ravine. "Who's the man you were talking to? Why's he here?"

"He's working with me to catch the bootleggers. Now, suppose you head back to your place."

A shiver ran down Trent's back. He lifted his brows as he looked at Justin and Abel.

"Liar!" Justin mouthed, his face a dark thundercloud.

Trent and Abel angrily nodded in agreement.

Just then Leroy Bushnell strode up out of the ravine with a double barrel shotgun at his shoulder. He stopped several yards from Jennet and Lamont. "Step aside Lamont."

Trent's blood ran cold as he drew his revolver. He felt fear in Justin and Abel. He saw Abel lift his gun. They didn't know what to do, what with the sheriff there to see that the law was upheld.

"Bushnell, you fool!" the sheriff cried. "You can't shoot her!"

"Who sez?" Bushnell's whiskers bristled and he waved the barrel of the shotgun. "Step aside 'less you want shot deader 'n a skunk!"

Jennet cried out, her hand at her racing heart. She wanted to reach for her revolver at her side, but she knew there wasn't time. Silently she prayed for a miracle. That's what it would take. The man was indeed planning to shoot her, but she didn't know why and she didn't know why the sheriff wasn't doing something about it.

"There's another way, Bushnell!" the sheriff cried, holding out his hand as if he could ward off a slug.

Bushnell sighted the shotgun on Jennet.

The sheriff jumped away from Jennet.

Abel fired at Bushnell. The shot whizzed past Bushnell and he jerked back. The shotgun exploded just as Jennet dropped to the ground.

Jennet's head whirled and she was too frightened to reach for her gun. She lifted her head in time to see the sheriff aiming his gun right at her. "No!" she screamed.

Trent leaped around the bushes, his revolver pointed at the sheriff. "Don't make a move, Lamont, or I'll kill you where you stand!"

"Trent!" Jennet cried, too weak to move.

His face black with anger, Lamont dropped his gun and raised his arms high.

Cursing angrily, Bushnell lifted his shotgun. Abel fired again. The bullet plowed into the man's chest, knocking him back. The shotgun flew from his hands and landed on the ground.

With a strangled cry Justin raced to Jennet and pulled her tight into his arms. She clung to him, trembling.

"Get that gun off me!" the sheriff shouted at Trent. "I'm a law man. I was here to protect your grandma."

"We saw it all," Trent snapped as he strode toward the sheriff. "No story you tell will do you any good." He turned and looked down at Bushnell. "It looks like he's dead."

With lightning speed the sheriff scooped up his gun, but before he could fire at Trent, Justin caught up a branch that looked much like the cudgel his mother had carried while guarding the pines years ago and flung it at the sheriff. It struck his shoulder and the gun fell from his hand.

Justin grinned. He'd thought he wouldn't remember what his mother had taught him. But he had. He'd never been as good as she was with the cudgel, but he'd been good.

"Good move, Just," Trent said, grinning.

Justin smiled back. "Thanks."

Abel found the sheriff's handcuffs and locked them on the man's wrists and sat him against the base of a pine.

"Abel, you stay with Grandma while we check out the still and Bushnell," Trent said.

Abel nodded, his eyes on Jennet.

Trent and Justin walked away, talking about what had just happened.

Jennet shivered and wrapped her arms around herself.

Abel stepped closer to Jennet. "You all right, ma'am?"

Jennet smiled and nodded, then shivered again. "I should've listened to you."

"I know." Abel holstered his gun.

Jennet touched Abel's arm. "You saved my life."

"Now we're even."

"What'd you mean?" Jennet studied him thoughtfully. "You've been acting as if you know me from the time we first met. Suppose you tell me what's going on."

Abel pulled off his cap and looked down at Jennet. "Years ago you helped a slave named Dacia find freedom—Dacia and her newborn baby, Colin."

"Dacia! Yes, I remember. I hid Colin in my laundry basket and had Dacia dress in Freeman's clothes. I took them to my pa and on the way we got stopped by a slave hunter, Blue Newmeyer."

"You gave him a paper he thought was Dacia's identification papers and the only word the man could read was *free*."

Jennet gasped. "How did *you* know!"

Abel laughed. "Colin is my daddy and Dacia, my granny."

Tears welled up in Jennet's eyes. "Your granny?"

"I came to find you to thank you for what you did for us." Jennet held her hands out to Abel.

"I promised Granny I'd find you no matter how long it took and that I'd stay until I helped you to partly repay you for what you did all those years ago when you were no more than a girl yourself."

"I want to hear everything!" For the moment Jennet pushed aside thoughts of Bushnell near the ravine and the sheriff handcuffed several feet away. "How is Dacia?"

"She's doing just fine for her age. She married when she was about eighteen and had eight more children. All of 'em born free just like she wanted." Abel brushed at his eyes.

"And baby Colin?" Jennet whispered around the lump in her throat.

"Grew up to be a fine man—a blacksmith by trade. I know the trade too, but I went to school and became a school master." Abel's voice broke. "All the family got schooling. Even Dacia learned to read and write."

Jennet wiped away a tear. "I never expected to hear from any of the slaves I helped. Thank you for finding me to tell me your story."

While Jennet and Abel talked, Trent and Justin walked down to the ravine. Trent bent over Bushnell. "He's dead."

Justin's stomach rolled and he looked quickly away.

They walked down in the ravine and stood at the side of the still. Behind the still stood a small cabin—four walls and a roof. It housed the sugar and ground corn as well as a cot, a blanket, and a tiny stove with a pot of coffee on it.

"We'll destroy the still and save Agent Lorraine a trip out here," Trent said.

Justin shook his head. "I figure prohibition will be over someday and the tourists that come to Havlick's Wilderness would like to see this still. We'll ruin it so it won't work, but otherwise leave it."

Trent chuckled. "You're always thinking of the angles, Just. I always did admire you for that."

Justin's heart jerked. Once they'd loved each other, been best friends, now they were enemies. All because of him! Couldn't they go back in time and be friends again? With tears in his eyes he turned to Trent. "About that day Celine died."

Trent's jaw tightened. "Don't bring it up. Not ever!" He strode away, blood roaring in his ears.

Justin hung his head, feeling as dead inside as Bushnell. Slowly Justin put out the fire with a couple of shovels of dirt, then tore off a piece of copper tubing that looked like it might be a vital part of the operation. The smell turned his stomach. Nobody would have a chance to rebuild the still and work it again since men were coming to cut down some nearby trees.

Slowly Justin walked up out of the ravine, past Bushnell's body, and to the spot where Abel and Jennet stood. Trent leaned against a tree several feet away with his back to all of them.

Much later Abel walked Jennet home, telling her more of Dacia and Colin and the family.

Ignoring Justin, Trent unlocked the handcuffs and jabbed the sheriff in the back. "Pick up Bushnell and carry him to the boat."

Cursing, Lamont struggled with the body and finally flung it over his shoulder and carried it to the boat.

His mind reeling from Trent's rejection, Justin rowed while Trent kept his gun on the sheriff. The sun beat down on them, glaring off the mirror-smooth lake.

A tight feeling in his chest, Trent looked at the gun in his hand, then at Justin. It would be so easy to point the gun at him and pull the trigger. Then they'd be even. But he couldn't do it. He cursed his own weakness.

He had to get away from Justin—away from his family! He'd take Emily and Rachel and leave for Texas today! With Bushnell dead and the sheriff in custody, the men could build Havlick's Wilderness without a catch.

Agent Lorraine was at the dock ready to get in his boat. Justin handed the sheriff over to him while Trent told him about Bushnell.

"I had my suspicions about you, Lamont," Agent Lorraine said.

"You'll be sorry you interfered," the sheriff barked.

"Nobody will ever know what became of you," said the agent with a chuckle. "I'm taking you away where you can't get in the way of my work here."

"I hope that's the end of this," Trent said grimly.

Agent Lorraine shook his head. "Afraid not. But I can't expect you to do more for me. I appreciate your help with these two."

"We're taking a crew out to start cutting trees tomorrow," Justin said.

"Go right ahead. I hope someday my family and I can visit your Havlick's Wilderness. In the meantime, I've got more bootleggers to find around Blue Creek and a few speakeasies to shut down."

Justin turned to ask Trent about their next move, but the icy hatred in his eyes stopped even the first word.

Rage erupting inside him, Trent ran down the dock to his auto and drove away, leaving Justin behind to find his own way home.

CHAPTER

13

♦ Trent drove like a wild man toward Blue Creek, the rage against Justin seething inside him. Why hadn't he killed that murderer when he'd had the chance? Were either of them thinking the last few weeks together had made a difference? He would not now or ever forget what Justin had done! And he would never forgive him. He would take Emily and Rachel and go to Texas, even if it meant leaving before construction of Havlick's Wilderness was under way.

The thought of Emily brought the note to his mind, and his blood ran cold.

"Emily!" he growled through clenched teeth.

He sped toward home, the Dodge swaying dangerously. Several agonizing minutes later, he jerked to a stop in a cloud of dust near his house. Chickens scattered, squacking and flying low across the yard. He leaped from the auto and strode toward the house.

Alone in the house, since Rachel had gone to Lark's for the day, Emily had heard the automobile approaching. Alarmed at its speed, she ran out the back door. "Trent! What's wrong?" she shrieked. "Has something happened to Rachel?"

Trent gripped Emily's arms, his eyes like smoldering

chunks of coal. "How could you let Bob Lavery kiss you?"

She sagged like a rag doll and her forehead fell against his chest. She could smell his sweat and feel his anger. How had he found out? Had he read her mind? If he had, he would also know she had asked herself the same question many times—how could she let Bob kiss her and how could she enjoy it? The shame she felt seemed boundless.

Trent glared down at Emily and a shudder passed through him. In his heart of hearts he'd believed the note was a cruel hoax, but now he could see it spoke the truth. Emily, the last pure woman he knew, had been dallying with another man. "But she's *my* wife," he thought. "How could she do this to me?"

His silence alarmed her. Weakly she lifted her head and looked into his pale face. His fingers bit through the sleeves of her flowered blouse into her arms. "I . . . didn't mean . . . for it . . . to happen," she whispered.

"I'll kill him." Trent's voice was ice cold steel.

"No!" She gripped the front of his shirt, almost tearing off the buttons. "How can you say such a thing?"

"I . . . will . . . kill . . . him!"

His words sounded like the snarling roar of a wounded bear, and Emily was cold with fear.

"No, Trent! No!"

Their eyes locked and Emily was unable to look away. She'd never seen such pain and rage on a human face.

"Please, Trent," she whispered, her blue eyes wide with pleading. "Please." She stroked his face with her fingers. "Please, don't."

"You love him that much?"

"No. I don't love him." And she realized she'd spoken the truth. She no longer loved Bob. "I don't love him at all."

Trent groaned from deep within and a weakness crept over him. His gaze fixed on a hairpin holding the coil of black hair in place. "Such pretty hair," he thought and longed to remove the hairpin and run his hands through the luxuriant mass as it cascaded down her back. Slowly he wrapped his arms around her and held her close. She pressed her face against his neck and clung to him, her arms tightly around him. He felt his rage drain away. The closeness of her body and the feel of her breath on his skin reminded him of another time, years before, when he had held her close.

It was just a few months after he had caught Celine in his grandpa's barn and kissed her. Since that day, he'd managed to "run into" Celine as often as possible. Emily was always with her. The three of them had become good friends, sharing secrets, laughing, and teasing each other until the girls' faces were red with embarrassment. This day he'd found them walking toward the orphanage, talking and laughing. He reigned up his horse, jumped to the ground, and fell into step with them.

He tried to be nonchalant, not wanting to admit that for more than an hour he'd galloped all over town searching for them. Something very exciting was about to happen to him and he wanted to tell his good friends, Celine and Emily. They were always interested. He was certain they'd be excited when he told them he had a date to court Marybell Astor, the most pursued young lady in town.

But when he proudly lifted his chin, squared his shoulders, and told them his news, they weren't glad. Celine gasped and Emily frowned. Then, her face very pale, Celine turned and ran as fast as she could toward the Orphans Home. Emily remained in front of Trent, her hands on her hips and her face red with anger.

"I don't understand," he said. "I thought she'd be happy for me."

"How could you do that?" Emily shrieked and flew at him, pounding his chest with her fists.

He caught her tight against him to keep her from hitting him again. "What are you talking about?" he asked, completely confused.

"You'll hurt her if you court another girl. Please don't do it."

"But I like Marybell."

Great tears welled in Emily's eyes. "I thought you liked Celine!"

"I do, but Marybell's so pretty."

"So is Celine."

"I know."

"And Celine's a whole lot nicer."

"She is nice."

"I thought you'd wait until she grew up. Then you'd marry her."

Trent was speechless.

"Please don't break her heart. Please!"

His heart was touched deeply. He held Emily close, and promised, "I won't court Marybell Astor. I promise."

Emily smiled. "Thank you, Trent! You won't be sorry!" She hugged him fiercely, then ran off after Celine.

Chuckling, he'd swung up onto his horse. He never did court Marybell Astor. But he did court Celine and, as soon as she was old enough, he married her. On their wedding day he made sure he thanked Emily for helping him.

Now he looked down at Emily, realizing that once again she was helping him. She'd done it many times. Suddenly he was aware of just how much he'd missed her while he was away. He didn't want anything to separate them again. She was his friend, a real friend.

Gently he held her from him and tipped her face up to his. She sighed in relief.

"I don't ever want to see you even passing the time of day with Bob Lavery."

"I won't ignore him on the street, but I won't go out of my way to see him. I promise."

"And if he tries to see you here or anywhere else in private, you'll refuse to see him?"

She nodded, determined more than ever that she would never be alone with Bob.

Trent brushed a strand of her hair off her cheek. "You've always been able to talk sense into me, Emily. Thank you."

She flushed with pleasure. She wanted to talk sense into him about his anger toward Justin, but this wasn't the time to bring it up. "You're a wonderful man, Trent. A man of your word."

Chuckling, he tapped her nose with his finger. "You always could get me to do exactly what you wanted."

"I could?"

"Don't act so surprised. You know you could." He turned her toward the house, his arm around her lightly. "Do you have anything to eat? I'm hungry. I missed breakfast and dinner."

She slipped her arm around his waist as they walked. "I could fry you a steak."

"Or two." He grinned down at her.

Later after they'd eaten and she'd stacked the dishes, she stood beside him at the kitchen window. He was holding a cup of coffee in his hand.

She reached deep for the courage she needed, then asked, "How did you find out . . . about Bob kissing me?"

Instantly Trent was angry again and set the cup on the table with a bang. "From a note left at the Wagon Works."

"Who left it?"

"I don't know." He told her what the note looked like and what it said.

"Priscilla and Noah? I can't believe it!"

Trent nodded.

"Does Justin believe it?"

"I think so. He acted like he did."

"Somebody was certainly trying to cause trouble by sending that note." Emily frowned thoughtfully. "I wonder who and why?"

"Good questions," Trent said grimly.

"Who would know both about me and about Priscilla? Did someone spy on the two of us because we're married to you and Justin? Maybe we should talk to Priscilla and Justin."

Trent stiffened. "I don't want to see him again."

"We have to get to the bottom of this, Trent. If we don't, who knows what else will happen? The Havlicks are fighters, not quitters!"

Trent laughed. "Well, you sure fit right in, don't you?"

She laughed with him. "I guess I do."

"Think what our kids will be like!"

The laugh caught in her throat, and she flushed crimson.

Trent tweeked her chin. "Don't you go getting all embarrassed on me now. Married people do have kids, you know. You are such an innocent!"

"I am not! I know where babies come from."

"But you don't know the pleasure of making one. I'm going to show you about that."

"Can we change the subject, please?"

He chuckled. "I'm sorry, but teasing you is so much fun."

"Oh, you!" She managed to laugh even as she struggled against the strange feelings going on inside her.

Abruptly his mood changed. He strode to the kitchen window and looked out. Wood snapped in the stove. "I wonder who sent that note. Why would someone want Justin and me to know about Lavery and Roswell and our wives?"

Emily sat at the table, her hands folded in front of her. "From simple power of deduction, I'd say it has something to do with Havlick's Wilderness. If your mind is on me, it won't be on getting the project under way."

"Think so?"

"That's why we have to talk to Justin and Priscilla. Instead of drawing apart, the family needs to get closer, stop the enemy, and accomplish our goal."

Trent turned to face Emily and smiled tenderly. "Come here, you. What did I ever do to deserve such a wife?"

His words wrapped around her heart, turning her limp. Slowly she walked to him.

He pulled her close and held her.

She felt the thud of his heart as her own heart beat faster. She smiled up at him and rested her hands at his waist.

A desire to kiss Emily rose in Trent, surprising him. He lowered his head and touched his lips to hers.

The kiss took her by surprise. She kissed him back, surprising herself even more.

He pulled away slightly and looked into her eyes, then down at her trembling lips. "Emily," he whispered hoarsely. He kissed her again, savoring the taste and the feel.

She returned his kiss with a fervor. Never had she experienced such a rush of emotion! Just as she thought she would drown in it, she heard the ugly ooh-ga of an auto horn.

Trent heard it too and reluctantly pulled away, his breathing ragged. He peered out the window, then frowned. "It's my dad! I wonder what he wants."

"Maybe he's bringing Rachel home." Emily struggled to sound normal. But her heart was beating so wildly she was sure it would rattle her words.

"No. He's alone." Trent strode outdoors with Emily hurrying fast to keep up. The sun shone brightly in the blue sky. "Dad, this is a surprise!"

Clay smiled, but his eyes were serious. "Trent, Emily, we are all meeting at the home place at seven tonight. Please come!"

"What's it about?" Trent asked.

"The family," Clay said.

"We'll be there," Emily said.

Trent shot her a look, grinned, and said, "We'll be there. What about Rachel?"

"If it's all right with you, we'll leave her with Lulu in town."

"That's fine."

"Would you like a cup of coffee, Clay?" Emily asked.

"Not this time." Clay smiled as he turned back to his auto. "I'll see you two later."

They stood together and watched Clay drive away, then slowly walked back inside, not touching, both trying to forget what had just happened.

Trent sighed heavily. "I had myself convinced to leave for Texas and forget all about the family."

"I'm glad you changed your mind. We will not let some evil force tear apart the Havlicks!"

* * *

Justin thanked Ben Dreski and dashed toward his Duesenberg. He was outraged at Trent for leaving him without a way home. He had walked for over an hour, getting madder by the minute, looking for someone heading toward Blue Creek who would give him a ride. But now that he was back, he intended to confront Priscilla about the contents of the note. The thought of it made his blood boil again. She would have to give him an explanation—even for a hoax!

As he reached for the doorhandle, a woman's voice called, "Oh, Justin, wait!"

Impatiently he turned.

"You are Justin, aren't you? Not Trent? Someone told me this is your automobile. I've been waiting for you."

She walked toward him, her hips moving provocatively. A short skirt swished around her knees, and a wide brimmed hat rolled in front covered her short, straight blonde hair. Her legs were shapely and her low cut dress hugged her. Heavy makeup covered her cheeks and lips, and he could smell her perfume before she reached him. She looked familiar.

"It's me, Justin—Aggie! Your old flame."

It was Aggie! "I heard you were back in town." Justin forced himself to be polite.

"Yes. My dear husband died and I've come home." She fluttered her eyelashes and toyed with her beads, showing off a large diamond ring.

"Sorry about your husband," Justin murmured. He didn't have time for Aggie, of all people.

"Thank you. But now that I'm back, I expect to see a lot of *you*. In fact, I thought this afternoon I would drive out to see Priscilla. Do you know if she's home? She was always such a dear friend of mine."

Pictures of Priscilla watching Noah flashed through Justin's mind and he tensed, the color draining from his face. He'd been aware of something between them, but he'd been too preoccupied to care. "Today isn't a good time, Aggie," he said, feeling a dread building inside. "Maybe another day. Excuse me; I must hurry." He reached again for the door-handle.

"Is something wrong?" She put her hand on his arm and moved closer to him.

"No, of course not. Why do you ask?" he said as he stepped back.

"You look worried."

"Oh, well, business, you know." He shrugged. "Excuse me." He tried to turn away, but she stepped between him and his automobile.

"I wanted to talk to you about that, too. I hear you need oak for your company, and I know where you can buy some at a good price. Let's go to the cafe. We'll have a cup of coffee, and I'll tell you all about it. Besides, it's been a long time and we need to get reacquainted." She slipped her arm through his and began to move toward the cafe.

Justin took a step and then stopped. He desperately needed oak for the Wagon Works but it was even more important that he get home to Priscilla. And he had the feeling that wouldn't wait.

"I can't," he said.

"Oh, Justin," she cooed, running a finger down his cheek. "I've missed seeing you, and we have so much to talk about." Her voice dropped to a whisper. "I can make you forget all your problems."

His pulse quickened. The burden he was carrying was killing him. He would like to forget it, even for a little while.

"I've returned to Blue Creek to put the sparkle back in your eyes. I'm gonna put fun in your life."

He looked down at Aggie, remembering the carefree days when they were in school. She'd been wild—a girl with a "reputation," the kind of girl that men dally with but never marry. He had found her both appealing and repugnant—appealing because she seemed to have fun and repugnant because she had loose morals. He was looking for a good girl then, one he could truly love and marry, one who had Christian values and would be a good mother to his children. He had found Priscilla. And now he needed to make certain she was still with him.

"Sorry, Aggie. I'm a married man. You'll need to find some other man and put a sparkle in his eyes." He disentangled his arm from her clutch.

"Oh?" she said. "You're turning me down? Well," she fluttered her eyelashes and slowly moistened her lips with the tip of her tongue, "there are other men who appreciate what I can do for them." She paused and trailed her fingers up and down his neck. "Noah appreciates me." She paused again and opened her eyes innocently. "Do you know Noah? Noah Roswell? He's very handsome and young and, ah, vigorous. Of course, he is a teeny bit distracted right now with another woman. . . ." Her voice trailed off and she smiled.

Justin felt like someone had socked him in the stomach. He

stammered, "Gotta go," yanked open the door of his automobile, and jumped in. As the door shut, he could hear Aggie laughing. He switched on the ignition and roared away, her taunting laughter ringing in his ears.

When she was out of sight he slowed. How did Aggie know about Noah? Was the whole town gossiping about his wife and his hired hand? It must be true, else how would Aggie know? The pictures began to flash in his mind again: Priscilla gazing longingly at Noah; Noah winking at Priscilla; Priscilla giggling as Noah whispered in her ear; Priscilla's face flushed and her eyes shining as Noah embraced her; Noah and Priscilla kissing, their arms wrapped tightly around each other.

"No!" he growled. Rage began in his toes and rose until it consumed him. "Cuckold me, will you! I'll kill you, Noah Roswell!"

Justin mashed the accelerator to the floorboard and the Duesenberg careened through curves and around corners until it screeched to a stop behind Priscilla's black Ford.

As he dashed toward the house, he was aware of the windmill squawking, a piglet squealing in the muddy pigpen, and the horses standing quietly in a pen near the barn. Chickens pecking in the yard scurried away from his pounding feet. He threw open the door, yelling, "Priscilla!"

He ran to the kitchen, through the dining room, and into the parlor. The rooms were neatly clean and empty. In the front room, a rag doll lay in a heap beside the rocking chair. He snatched up the doll and roared, "Priscilla!"

He ran to the hall and took the wide stairs two at a time. His steps ringing loudly on the wooden floor, he dashed in and out of the boys' room and the girls' room. The beds were made and the toys lined up neatly on the shelves.

In the bedroom he shared with Priscilla, he stopped. The creamy-colored crocheted spread neatly covered the brass bed. A breeze ruffled the muslin curtains at the open window.

On the dresser, yellow roses were in a milk glass vase next to a framed photograph of Priscilla in her wedding gown. "Priscilla?" he whispered. "Where are you?"

With a groan he opened the chifforobe. Her clothes hung there next to his. He touched the sleeve of her pink robe and pulled it to his face. The scent of her perfume clung to it and he breathed deeply, filling his lungs with Priscilla's perfume. His eyes filled with tears. "Oh, Priscilla, I'm sorry. Please, don't leave me."

Slowly he walked back downstairs, through the open door, and into the yard. As he touched her car, he noticed he was still clutching the rag doll. He set it gently on the hood and gazed across the yard to the big red barn.

Noah! Justin clenched his teeth and strode purposefully toward the barn. He'd find that philanderer, beat him within an inch of his life, and send him packing!

In the barn, pigeons flew among the rafters, and dust particles floated in beams of sunlight. A cat rubbed against Justin's ankle. Noah wasn't there or in his room. Justin found only a pair of denim pants hung on a hook beside the steel-frame bed and a bright afghan, folded neatly at the foot of the bed. Angrily he strode from the barn to the sheds and to the milk house. Noah wasn't anywhere.

Justin stopped short in the middle of the barnyard. The wagon and the work horses were gone! Again pictures of Noah and Priscilla in each other's arms flashed through Justin's mind. He slammed his fist into his palm. A groan of agony rose inside him, leaving him weak.

He'd been a terrible husband. He'd ignored his children and neglected his wife. He'd been surly and short-tempered, angry and sarcastic. He'd been consumed with guilt—that he wouldn't measure up, that he wouldn't succeed the way his father and grandfather had, that he would senselessly cause harm again the way he had caused Celine's death. He had been afraid and had buried himself in the Wagon Works, trying to block all his feelings. He had pushed his wife into the arms of another man.

Standing in the barnyard, looking at his house—the house he'd built for Priscilla and their children, where they would live together all their lives, where they would love each other—he felt bereft.

The sounds of jangling harness and laughter floated across the field. Justin ran to the side of the garage and peeked around it. He saw Noah driving the wagon with Priscilla on the high seat beside him. Blood roared in Justin's ears. Where was his gun? He'd kill Noah Roswell!

He tried to push away from the garage to go after his gun, but his legs wouldn't move. He peeked around the garage again and saw his four children riding in the back of the wagon, laughing happily. Pris hadn't been alone with Noah! Relief swept over Justin.

Noah stopped the team near the barn and jumped to the ground. He reached up to help Priscilla down, then held her by the waist and looked into her smiling face. He held her while the children jumped up to stand in back of the wagon. He held her while the team shook, rattling the harness. He held her while heat washed up over Justin, then washed back down, leaving him icy cold.

"That was a fine picnic," Noah said, still holding her.

"It was fun." Laughing, Priscilla stepped away from him, flushed and pretty.

Justin bit back a groan.

Noah laughed and winked at Priscilla. Then one by one he lifted the children to the ground. And a fire exploded inside Justin.

He stepped into sight and stood perfectly still, his feet apart, his fists on his hips. He saw the shock on Priscilla's face and the look of surprise on Noah's.

"Daddy!" Faith shouted happily and ran to him. Chloe tumbled after her, trying to keep up.

"Daddy! We had a picnic!" Chloe called. They hugged his legs. "It was fun. Noah took us."

Justin patted their backs and the tops of their heads, then squatted down and hugged them.

"Run on in the house," he said, his voice catching. "I need to talk to Mommy. Ted," he called, "take your brother and sisters in the house. You're in charge until we come."

"Yes, Dad," Ted said, sounding very grown-up for his seven years.

Priscilla watched the children until they reached the back porch, then said stiffly, "What brings you home in the middle of the afternoon? Is something wrong?"

"Yes!" Justin barked, his anger rising again at the sight of Priscilla, her face flushed and her hair mussed from the wind, standing with Noah.

Noah moved nervously. "I'll take care of the horses."

"Don't move!" Justin's muscles bunched as he walked to Noah and Priscilla. Without warning, he knotted his fist and struck Noah on the chin, sending him sprawling in the dust. The team moved uneasily, rattling their harness.

Priscilla stifled a scream. She caught at Justin's arm. "What's wrong with you?"

He brushed her aside and hauled Noah to his feet and punched him in the stomach, knocking him hard against the side of the wagon. Justin caught Noah by the front of the shirt and pushed his face close. "Leave my wife alone!"

Priscilla trembled, her hands at her mouth and her eyes wide with fear.

Noah struggled, but couldn't break free. "Let me go! You got no right to hit me!"

"You're fooling around with my wife! I have every right to kill you!" Justin pulled back his fist to strike Noah again.

"Wait!" Noah cried. "Don't hit me again. It was innocent. We just took the children on a picnic."

"I saw you! Smiling at her, winking at her, touching her!" Justin dropped his fist, but continued to glare at Noah.

The color rose in Priscilla's cheeks. She forced herself to look at Justin, at his white skin—pale from spending every day inside, at his shoulders—slightly stooped from bending over his desk for long hours at a time, at the lines in his forehead—put there by worried frowning. She hadn't meant to hurt him, not really. Or had she?

She'd been so lonely and hurt that Justin didn't seem to be aware of her. Noah had made her feel alive, giddy, like a schoolgirl. His winks and whispers had told her she was still attractive, that someone wanted her. She needed to be wanted.

Noah laughed, shrugging. "It was just a joke."

"A joke?" Justin roared.

Noah nodded. "I was spying on you, getting information about you and your brother and what your family's up to with the forest. I didn't want her," he jerked his head toward Priscilla. "I only wanted news and her tongue wags at both ends."

Priscilla gasped. She'd made a fool of herself, and it had been meaningless. Noah hadn't been interested in her. Her heart froze and she couldn't move or speak.

"Why would you spy on us?" Justin asked, balling his fists and tightening his hold on Noah's shirt. "Explain!"

Noah tried to laugh again, but the rage on Justin's face made him blanch. "I don't know for sure, but I think it has to do with bootlegging. Gabe Lavery and his brother Bob been running a still out of Trent's house, and they wanted to keep up with Trent—if he'd want his house back, you know. There's a lot of money in running liquor, you know. They've been paying me for information I got out of your wife. That's all there was to it. I had to keep her happy so's she'd talk."

Humiliated, Priscilla sank to her knees and buried her face in her hands.

"You're fired," Justin growled. "Get out of here before I break you in little pieces and feed you to the hogs."

Noah eased himself away and stumbled toward the barn. He broke into a run and disappeared inside. Justin stared after him until, a few minutes later, Noah ran from the barn with his shabby suitcase, jumped into his pickup, and roared away.

Justin looked down at Priscilla kneeling in the dust, sobbing quietly. He took her arm and gently raised her to her feet. Their eyes locked.

"Priscilla, I'm . . ." Justin's voice was low and she strained to hear him. But his words were drowned out by the noise of an automobile churning gravel in the lane, the horn blowing repeatedly.

Clay drew up beside them and called, "There's a family meeting tonight at Pa's place. Martha Bjoerling will watch your children. Be there at seven!" He jammed the automobile in gear and drove away, leaving behind a cloud of dust.

CHAPTER

14

♦ Her hands locked in her lap, Emily sat beside Trent on Free's front porch, looking at the others. Nervously she rubbed her slightly flared skirt over her knees and touched the beads hanging down on her white blouse. It had a rounded collar embroidered with tiny yellow and blue flowers. Trent had changed into a white shirt and dark pants, the very thing Justin was wearing. Emily watched Trent and Justin exchange frowns before she turned her gaze on Priscilla, who wore a red middy and a knee-length white skirt. Justin and Priscilla looked as tense and nervous as she felt. Clay and Lark were talking softly to each other. Free stood near the screen door, his hands looped around his wide suspenders, a thoughtful look on his lined face. Jennet sat in her white rocking chair, her dark blue cotton dress covering her crossed ankles. Her hands were folded in her lap. She wanted to meet on the porch to catch the cool evening breeze.

The sun was low in the west and had lost its heat. In the pigpen at the far side of a shed, baby pigs squealed and their sow grunted to calm them. A horse nickered behind the big barn. The constant smell of pine filled the air.

Emily glanced down the lane. Were Beaver and Hannah

coming? Where were Tris and Zoe? This was a Havlick family meeting, but not all the family was present. She moved restlessly. She'd sat in on Havlick family meetings before, but this was the first time as a member of the family.

Free cleared his throat and stepped away from the screen door. His pants hung loosely on his lean frame. A gentle breeze ruffled his gray hair. "We didn't ask the whole family to come tonight, because this is something for just the eight of us to settle."

Trent moved uneasily. He hadn't been to a family meeting in ten years, and he dreaded this one. He felt tense and very uncomfortable.

Justin glanced at Trent, then quickly away. He sensed Priscilla's tension and suspected she wished she were at home, away from all of them. He'd often wished the same thing. Frequently he was the target at meetings called to discuss his over-involvement with his work and his under-involvement with his family. He would usually get mad, eventually promise to try harder to be a good husband and proper father, but afterward there would be little change. He glanced again at Priscilla. This time it would be different, regardless of the topic of the meeting.

Free pushed his hands deep in the pockets of his dark pants. "I've told you this many times in the past, but I want to tell you again." He looked at Jennet and she smiled reassuringly. His gaze rested lovingly on each of the others before he continued. "When I was a boy I worshiped the ground my Grandpa Clay walked on. That's why I named my first son after him."

Free smiled at Clay, and Clay smiled broadly in return. At times, when he was working hard to make his own fortune, it had been hard to live up to the image of Great-grandpa Clay, a man of impeccable integrity who was respected by all who knew him.

Free looked off across the field toward their beloved white pines. "Grandpa walked the woods around here when this area was completely covered with timber. With the money he made as a fur trader, he invested in businesses in Grand Rapids and in Detroit, and he bought this land. In his later years he accepted Jesus as his Savior. He began to study the Bible and talk to Jig, his friend, about God. Grandpa learned that through salvation he'd entered into covenant with God. Jesus cut the covenant with God for him and for us and for all mankind. And the most wonderful, comforting promise we know from God is that He will never break it!"

Free's voice faltered and he cleared his throat. "It took me years to learn that, but I finally did, and I taught it to my children, and they to theirs. Trent and Justin, you are to teach it to yours. We are in covenant with God!"

Trent and Justin squirmed guiltily. They had failed to teach their children.

Free smiled. "A covenant is two people filling each other's shoes all the time. All that God is, I am. All that God has is mine. All that I have is His. *I* am His!"

Free brushed moisture from his eyes.

"Every one of you has confessed Jesus as Lord and Savior and, therefore, is in covenant with God and heirs to His promises.

"So," he paused and looked intently at Justin and Trent, "what's going on here? We have had differences of opinion in the past, but this is much more than that. This is deadly! Someone in this family has opened a door and allowed the devil to come in to work against us."

Trent's stomach tightened, and Justin forced back a groan.

Free sighed heavily. "As a result of strife and unforgiveness and our preoccupation with it, we haven't been living in the covenant promises. Strife and unforgiveness are tearing this family apart." Free sank to the edge of his chair and looked around at his family.

Emily bit her lower lip and peeked at Trent. She knew he didn't want to hear what was coming, but she also knew he wouldn't walk away. He respected and loved Free too much for that.

Free motioned to Justin and Trent. "I should've talked to you boys about this long before now." Free reached over and touched Justin's shoulder and tapped Trent's knee. "You boys had a falling out that you must set straight. You two are in strife and have been for ten years. As a result you haven't been living in the blessings of God, and it has affected the whole family. It's killing you! And the family!"

Justin sat very still, his eyes on the gray porch floor. Inside he was crying out to settle the agony he felt, but he didn't let it show on the outside.

A muscle jumped in Trent's jaw. Grandpa had no idea. It wasn't a falling out. It was murder. Justin's self-centeredness had caused Celine's death. Trent tensed. He couldn't forgive that and he couldn't forget it. Justin would have to pay. Trying to pretend it no longer mattered, saying "I forgive you, Justin, for the pain and heartache you've caused, for taking my life from me," would mean that it didn't matter, that Celine's life wasn't important. They'd forget her. It would be like she'd never lived and loved him. She'd given meaning to his life. Without her he was empty, nothing. "No, Grandpa," Trent thought in his mind, "there'll be no setting straight. You'd understand if you knew."

Free leaned forward earnestly. "We're going to build Havlick's Wilderness. But look at the trouble we've faced already. Look at what happened to Rachel and to your grandma. Now today I learned someone is trying to make trouble between you, Trent, and Emily. And between you, Justin, and Priscilla. We can't let the enemy destroy our families!"

Free jumped up, his eyes blazing. "Your marriage vows spoken to each other are a covenant between you. Don't break that covenant! Love each other. Love God with all your beings. We have a dream—to build Havlick's Wilderness for folks everywhere to enjoy. You boys have the Wagon Works to keep going. We each have a family to keep together. Every part of our lives is affected by what's in our hearts. When your heart is right with God, it'll be right with each other. Your marriages will be blessed and happy. *You* will be blessed and happy."

Emily bit her lip to keep from sobbing. She hadn't thought of her marriage as a covenant with Trent. That wasn't why she'd married him.

Free's eyes filled with tears. "If you have unforgiveness in your hearts, forgive. Ask God to help you forgive and to help you be forgiven. If you are harboring bitterness and hatred or are suffering from a broken heart, rely on God's grace. He can do in you what you can't do yourselves." Free studied his grandsons closely.

"Do you love each other?"

Trent kept his eyes down. Justin bit back a groan.

"Justin, do you love Priscilla?" Free asked softly.

Without hesitation, Justin answered, "Yes, Grandpa, I love Priscilla." His voice was level and even. He forced himself to continue. "But because I haven't given her time, I may have lost her."

"Son, have you told her?"

Justin turned to Priscilla. "I've hurt you. I've raged and moaned, and I've neglected you. I've been very selfish. I'm so sorry. I cannot express how sorry I am. Please try to forgive me."

Tears stung Priscilla's eyes.

"Priscilla," Free said, "do you love Justin?"

She hesitated, her eyes locked with Free's. Then she whispered, "Yes, I do. I always have. But I was hurt and lonely and angry. I believed he'd stopped loving me, and I . . . did something that makes me very ashamed."

She dropped her eyes and tears rolled down her cheeks. Justin took her hand in his, kissed her fingers, and held her hand to his heart. She leaned against him weakly.

Free turned toward Trent and Emily.

"You've been married only a short while. There'll be much joy and happiness, some sad and troubling times, too, but God will see you through.

"The most important thing you need to remember is that a marriage is a commitment to honor, respect, and care for each other every day of your life together. It's part of the covenant you've made with God and each other. You honor God and each other and keep the covenant. You'll know a love for each other you've never thought possible. But this won't happen without God."

Free paused and studied their faces: Emily, struggling inside, biting her quivering lower lip; Priscilla, her head down and tears flowing freely; Justin, the anguish on his face tearing at Free; and Trent. His body tense, his hands balled into fists, his jaw set, Trent stared straight ahead through dark, clouded eyes.

"Trent, son, if you leave us, do it because it's what God wants in your life, not because you're angry or grieving or want to run away from pain."

Free cleared his throat. Had he said enough or gone too far? It was hard to know when a parent, or a grandparent, moves from compassionate, loving involvement to meddling. In his heart, Free prayed for guidance.

"Now, we're going to pray about this," Free said. "We're going to ask God to help us with it. Without Him none of us will make it." Free closed his eyes and, his face lifted toward the heavens, began to pray.

"O God, maker of all things, creator of the universe, thank You for being with us here, right now. . . ."

Priscilla bowed her head and listened to Free in his gentle way ask God to heal their hurts and bless their marriages. She hadn't prayed for a long time. She'd thought she'd forgotten how. But Free's simple words encouraged her to try. Silently she begged for patience and the kind of love that forgives.

As Free asked that God give them wisdom, Emily silently confessed that she had been foolish in dreaming about and longing for a man she couldn't have. She had let that disappointment interfere with her daily walk. She asked God to take away her feelings for Bob. "Forgive me, Lord," she breathed. "I was wrong. Now show me how to love Trent the way a wife should."

When Free begged that their sins be forgiven, Justin knew he wanted forgiveness. In his heart, he asked God to help him make amends for the hurts he'd caused Priscilla. But when he thought of Celine, he knew that could never be forgiven—not even by God.

Trent's heart and mind were troubled. He hadn't prayed since Celine died. He hadn't wanted to talk to God. But he couldn't shut out Free's prayer asking God to open their hearts and dwell in them. In his mind, Trent heard a soft voice, saying, "My child, I am with you," but he couldn't respond.

The voice said, "It's time to let Celine go."

"No!" Trent felt it like a scream, exploding through his body, reverberating through the fields, echoing through the forest. "I can't let her go! She's my life!"

"I will give you new life."

Free ended his prayer by saying, "As always, Father, thank You for Your great love."

"Amen," Clay said, and together Jennet and Lark said, "Amen."

Free blew his nose and Jennet and Lark dabbed at their tears.

"God is good," Clay whispered.

"And faithful," Lark said.

"Yes, yes," Jennet murmured.

They sat in silence, each lost in personal communion.

"We must talk about this note." Clay took the folded paper from his pocket. "We need to figure out who sent it to Justin and Trent and why. Each of you look at the handwriting to see if you recognize it."

"Emily may have guessed the reason behind this," Trent

said as they passed the paper from one to another. He looked quickly at her and a smile passed between them. "If I have my attention on trouble with my wife, I can't pay attention to building Havlick's Wilderness."

"But why would anyone want to stop you from building a nature preserve?" Lark asked. "That's a good thing and will benefit everyone."

"I think it has to do with bootlegging, Mom," Justin said, a new fire in his eyes.

"Bootlegging?" Jennet's face was a study in shock. "There's no bootlegging around here, and if there were, what would it have to do with our family?"

"It isn't just bootlegging, Grandma," Justin said gently. "It's illegal stills, too! And it's been happening on Havlick property."

Jennet gasped and looked at Free who threw up his hands and said, "I don't know what the boy is talking about."

"Grandpa, this afternoon we learned from Noah—by the way, Noah Roswell is no longer working for us!—that Gabe Lavery, while he was caretaking at Trent's place, was operating a still in Trent's house. He and Bob have been running liquor all over the area.

"Naturally they didn't want Trent to stay here—he'd want his place back and they'd have nowhere to hide their still. So they paid Noah to play up to Priscilla and get information from her."

Priscilla's face flushed beet red as she remembered the humiliation she'd felt when she learned Noah had made a fool of her.

Emily was so shocked to learn that Bob—the man she'd tried so hard to love—was involved in such evil, she thought she might faint.

Trent remembered Martha had mentioned, after she helped Emily move into his house, that the place was in good order and clean, except for mysterious piles of grainy dust in the corners of the kitchen. "Corn," he thought. Anger surged through him.

"But Trent and Emily and Rachel are living there now," Clay said.

"I expect they want them to leave again," Free said.

"As bad as all that sounds," Jennet said, "what would it have to do with Havlick's Wilderness? The man that shot Rachel said not to build it."

"Our forest is very big, Grandma. Someone hid a still there, too. If we were to bring in loggers and construction crews, we'd be sure to find it. They had to stop us. But we found it and the man who was running it. And we learned the sheriff was involved."

"Get us fighting among ourselves and maybe we'd have to give it up!" Free slapped his knee. "I believe you've got it, Justin. But is it only the Laverys and the sheriff? Is there anyone else involved?"

"Until we know, we've got to be very careful," Clay said. "Like Pa said, this is deadly business."

"Whoever they are," Free said, "they've picked on the wrong family! No one will destroy the Havlicks."

"Anybody recognize that handwriting?" Clay asked.

"I think I do," Priscilla answered. "There's something about the *i*'s and the *e*'s that is familiar. The *i*'s are open when they should be closed, and the *e*'s are closed when they should be open. Aggie Karin used to write notes to Gabe when we were in school, and she would show them to me. I think this looks like her handwriting."

"Aggie?" Justin asked, remembering his encounter with her that afternoon. "I saw her today. She was definitely trying to work on me."

"Gabe and Bob and Aggie and the sheriff," Clay said. "I wonder who else is involved."

Emily looked up at the full moon as she walked toward their house with Trent. A dog howled in the distance. A horse nickered in the pen beside the barn. The quiet sounds of the forest added to her sense of peace. She wanted to ask Trent why he hadn't settled his quarrel with Justin, but she couldn't bring herself to speak of it. She wondered if he felt the peace, too?

Trent stopped near the back door and rested his hands on Emily's shoulders. "Do you think you'll ever stop loving Bob Lavery?"

She looked in her heart and found the feeling was gone. "I've stopped loving him already."

"For a fact?" Trent asked in surprise.

Emily laughed breathlessly, glad to be free of her guilt. "I don't know when it happened, but it's gone." She rested her hands on Trent's waist. "Tonight I asked God to take that away and forgive me for it. And I also asked Him to fill me with love for you—the love a wife should have for her husband."

Trent's heart jerked. Emily's honesty always took him by surprise. "I wish I could love you the way a husband should love his wife."

"Your grandpa said marriage is a commitment. And you're committed to me. Now all you need is the feeling."

Trent pecked Emily on the cheek. "Sometimes I think my feelings are dead."

"God is a God of miracles," she whispered.

They walked into the kitchen and Trent lit the lamp. The smell of sulfur and kerosene stung his nose. He turned down the flame to keep it from blackening the globe. The lamp cast a soft glow over the room.

"I wonder how long it'll take to get electricity out in the country," he mused, but he didn't want to talk about electricity. He wanted to ask if she was ready for them to become truly married now that her love for Bob was gone.

"I heard that someday in the future every farm and every home would have electric lights. That's hard to imagine."

Trent chuckled. "Well, that subject's boring. How about talking about something we're both thinking about." His pulse quickened. "Us."

"All right. You start."

He walked to the window and stood looking out at the bright moon, his back to Emily. "I don't know how to start."

Emily's heart sank. He didn't want her near him! "Since Rachel's not here I could sleep in her bed tonight if you want," Emily said just above a whisper.

"Is that what you want?" He held his breath, waiting for her answer. Slowly he turned to face her.

She hesitated, then with her cheeks crimson, she lifted her chin and said, "No. We are married and we should share a bed. That's what I want."

Once again she'd taken him by surprise. He'd expected her to be too shy to agree to share his bed after their kisses that afternoon.

Gently he took her in his arms. He thought of his wedding night with Celine, how shy she'd been and how he'd had to tenderly, gently coax her out of her fear.

"You're the only man for me," Celine had said in the safety of his arms.

"You're the only woman for me," he'd whispered with his lips against hers.

Abruptly Emily pulled away. "You're thinking of Celine, aren't you?"

He nodded slightly.

Emily locked her fingers together in front of her. "I thought I could handle this, but I can't. I can't have you touching me, holding me, kissing me, while thinking about Celine." Tears filled Emily's eyes. "I can't, Trent."

"You knew how it'd be when you married me."

"Yes, but I didn't know it'd be too hard for me."

"I'm sorry. I don't want to hurt you."

"I know." She gripped the back of a chair. A cricket sang in a corner in back of the woodbox. "Maybe it'll be different in Texas. Maybe we should wait until then."

"If that's what you want."

"It's not, Trent, but I can't take Celine's place in your bed." She moistened her dry lips with the tip of her tongue and lifted her chin. "I will share your bed the way we've done the last two nights."

He picked up the lamp and silently they walked side by side up the wide stairs to their bedroom.

She pulled back the spread, then turned down the sheet and cover. She took her nightgown from the chifforobe and dropped it on the bed. Too shy to undress in front of him, she said, "You can blow out the lamp now."

He smiled as he turned down the wick and blew out the flame. He walked to her and slipped his arms around her. He reminded himself that he really should feel guilty, but he didn't. He wanted her.

She stiffened and gasped. "Trent! We agreed."

He laughed gently. "You said it, but I didn't agree."

She struggled to free herself.

Catching her face with his hands, he looked deeply into her eyes. "I'm not thinking about Celine now. I'm thinking only about you. Celine's gone." And she was. He could see her face and hear her laughter. But his longing for her was gone.

Emily stood very still, her heart thundering.

He lifted her face with his fingers under her chin and kissed her.

She swayed against him and clung to him. She returned his kiss. A fire she never knew was locked inside her burst into flame. Her passion ignited his.

"Emily, Emily," he whispered huskily as he gathered her closer.

* * *

In his stocking feet, Justin paced the bedroom. Priscilla walked into the room and stopped short. She was ready for bed, wearing a long yellow nightgown. She'd checked to see that the children were asleep and covered and kissed them tenderly. She had prayed silently for them. She hadn't heard Justin come into the house or walk upstairs.

"I thought you were going to sleep in the barn."

"I changed my mind."

"Oh." Trembling, Priscilla set the lamp she was holding on the dresser beside her silver brush and comb set.

Justin raked his fingers through his hair. "We can't let our marriage crumble because of what either of us has done. We're a family. We can't let anything or anybody break us up."

Priscilla sank weakly to the edge of the bed. "I didn't think I'd ever hear you say that! I fell in love with you and married you because you believed so strongly in the Lord. I wanted a marriage like your parents and grandparents had. After Celine died and Trent left, you changed so much you were someone else. A stranger."

He knelt beside her and rested his head in her lap. "Forgive me, Pris. I know I get caught up in my work and forget everything and everybody. I am going to try to do better. With your help and with God's help, I'm going to change. I'm going to try to make it up to you."

She stroked his head. His hair was as soft as their children's asleep down the hall. "We'll all help you remember us. We need you." She bit her lip. "I said I wouldn't say that again, but it's true. I love you and I need you."

He stood and pulled her into his arms. "I almost lost you. I don't know what I would've done if I had."

"Forgive me for turning to Noah."

"I already have. Grandpa showed me the way." Justin stroked her hair. "I'm sorry for what I've put you through. Please forgive me."

She smiled and nodded. "I already have."

"Oh, Pris! I do love you!" He kissed her as if he'd never let her go.

CHAPTER

15

♦ Trent hesitated at the office door. He knew Justin and Dad were waiting for him inside, eager to get things under way for Havlick's Wilderness. He heard a voice he didn't recognize and slowly opened the door. Agent Lorraine sat beside Clay. He was talking about closing down Gilly's Place. He stopped when he saw Trent and nodded with a smile.

"Come in and sit," Clay said, motioning to the only empty chair.

"Sorry to interrupt your story, Agent Lorraine." As Trent sat down, he glanced at Justin. Once again they'd dressed alike in dark pants and plain shirts. Their eyes locked; then they looked quickly away.

Agent Lorraine, looking very pleased with himself, held his hat in his hands. "We've closed down a couple of other places in the area even though we couldn't close Gilly's place. I went there again last night to shut it down, but the patrons were only dancing. No one was drinking. I couldn't find a drop of liquor on the premises. Somehow they knew we were coming. Too many folks around here are against prohibition." He shook his head helplessly. "The deputy sheriff, Steve Brison, will take over the sheriff's job. He can be trusted to stop any small-

222

scale bootlegging going on. I told him to keep an eye on Gilly's Place. He said he would."

"What about the lead we gave you?" Trent asked.

"On Gabe and Bob Lavery," Justin said.

"Sorry, but I couldn't get anything on them." Agent Lorraine stood. "So, I'll head back to Lansing. But if you ever need me, call." He shook hands all around, clamped on his hat, and said goodbye. At the door he said, "I'll bring my family to visit Havlick's Wilderness when it's finished."

"You do that," Clay said, smiling.

Agent Lorraine left, closing the door after him. Sounds of hammering and sawing seeped in around the door. The faint smell of paint drifted in.

Clay smiled at his sons. "We aren't going to do anything about Gabe Lavery at the moment, but we'll always be on the lookout in case he tries anything."

Trent wanted to do something about the Laverys immediately, but he couldn't say that to his dad. As Clay continued talking of their plans for the morning, Trent turned to Justin and lifted his hand in a salute, their secret message to meet together without Dad knowing. Justin saluted at the same moment. They grinned at each other, then quickly looked away.

Clay stood. "And we're going to take a crew to the forest this morning to begin the work on Havlick's Wilderness."

"I have some business to take care of before going out," Justin said. He didn't look at Trent, afraid he would chuckle.

"Me too," Trent said, holding back a laugh. It had been a long time since he and Justin had had the same thought at the same moment. He knew their business was the same—Gabe and Bob Lavery.

"Then I'll get the men and be on my way," Clay said, smiling. "Ma and Pa are going to meet us there. They want to watch the first tree fall that'll mark the beginning of Havlick's Wilderness. Your mother's not really looking forward to it. It hurts her deeply to see a tree cut." He put his cap on and opened the door. "See you later."

The minute the door closed behind him, Trent said, "What's the plan?"

"To knock Gabe into next week." Justin jumped up.

Trent chuckled and Justin joined in. "Your auto or mine?"

Justin shrugged as he lifted his hat off the hook. "This time let's take mine."

Side by side they walked outdoors toward Justin's Duesenberg. The sun was already warm in the sky even though it was early. A pickup truck drove past, briefly covering the factory noises. Trent opened his door. "But we won't drive up his lane and give him warning. We'll park along the road and walk to his farmhouse. And after we're finished with him, we'll go after Bob Lavery."

Justin nodded. "They'll both be sorry they messed with the Havlick twins and their wives!"

"You bet!" Justin started the engine and Trent burst into song as they drove away from the Wagon Works. "The yanks are comin', the yanks are comin'!"

"You're in a good mood," Justin said, chuckling. He longed for it to last.

"That's because I have a wonderful wife and I'm off to defend her honor."

"Well, then, let's keep singing." Justin sang "Yankee Doodle Dandy" and Trent joined in. It was like old times and Justin didn't want it to end.

Several minutes later they pulled off the road into the underbrush. A cottontail rabbit frantically hopped for cover in taller grass. Trent turned to Justin with a serious look on his face. "We don't know what we're up against, so be careful."

"I will. You be careful, too."

Trent nodded as he climbed from the auto. Further up the dirt road, crows sat in the middle pecking away at a dead animal. A hawk soared in the summer-blue sky.

Instead of walking down the lane to the farmhouse, they cut across a pasture. They ran from tree to tree, pausing behind each and looking out carefully to see if they'd been spotted. As they got closer to the farmyard, Trent noticed Bob Lavery's pickup in the yard beside Gabe's. "We'll kill two birds with one stone," he whispered grimly.

Justin hesitated. "You can't kill them, Trent."

"No, of course not. I didn't mean it that way. But I can make their lives miserable."

Trent ducked behind a large maple and peered around it while Justin hid behind an oak. The house was small and needed paint. The big red barn and the sheds around the place were in good repair. The windmill blades whirled in the wind as water gushed from a pipe into a horse watering tank. Chickens scratched around the yard. Pigs rolled in the muddy pigpen. Cattle and sheep grazed together in a pasture behind the barn.

"Is Gabe married?" Trent asked in a whisper.

"No. He never got married. Maybe he's still hung up on Aggie."

Just then, Gabe and Bob walked out of the house, talking loudly and angrily.

"Let's go," Trent whispered.

He ran across the space with Justin beside him.

Gabe and Bob stopped in surprise.

Justin shot past Trent and knocked Gabe down hard.

"What the . . ." Bob cried.

Trent slammed his fist into Bob's face, bloodying his nose. "That's for touching my wife! You stay away from her!"

Bob stumbled back against his pickup, holding his nose. He made no effort to fight back.

Gabe rolled away from Justin and jumped to his feet, his fists doubled and fire shooting from his eyes. He lunged at Justin, but Justin stepped aside and landed a blow to Gabe's eye.

Trent wanted to jump in and help Justin, but he knew Justin

could take care of himself. Trent kept an eye on Bob even as he watched the fight.

With one mighty blow to the stomach, Justin knocked Gabe to the ground, then stood over him, daring him to get up. "We know what you did!" Justin snarled. "I ought to kill you right here!"

"No, don't." Gabe's face was white with fear. "I didn't mean to shoot the little girl. It was an accident!"

Aghast at what he'd heard, Trent leaped forward and hauled Gabe to his feet. He slammed his fist hard into Gabe's stomach. "That's for Rachel!"

Gabe crumpled to the ground and groaned in pain.

"We want the whole story, now," Trent said grimly as he stood over Gabe with Justin beside him.

The back door of the house burst open and Aggie Beaumont ran out. "Get away from him!" She yelled, and flung herself at Justin. "Don't hurt him!"

Justin pushed her away.

She dropped to her knees beside Gabe and cradled his head in her lap. "Are you all right?"

"He won't be if he doesn't start talking right now," Trent said sharply.

"We didn't mean for your girl to get hurt," Bob mumbled through his bloody lips.

"I only wanted to get your attention," Gabe said, struggling to sit up.

Trent and Justin stood over the Laverys and Aggie as the brothers told about bootlegging to pay off their farms.

"Aggie said she'd marry me once my place was paid off and making money," Gabe said. "She would've married me years ago if it hadn't been for you Havlicks! You and your money!"

"Money's not everything," Trent and Justin said at the same time. They looked at each other and quickly away. In the past they'd often said the same thing at the same time. Were they connecting again the way they had long ago?

"What're you going to do with us?" Bob asked as he slowly stood.

"We'll let the law deal with you," Trent snapped.

Bob shook his head. "Don't! I got a baby on the way. We've stopped bootlegging. The federal agent working the area made that too dangerous, and when you took your house back, we didn't have a place for the still. We're out of business now and we'll leave you and your family alone."

"You'll leave my wife alone, that's for sure!" Trent growled.

"I only kissed her so she wouldn't snoop around the house where we had the still going."

Trent rammed his fist into Bob's stomach. "That's for taking advantage of that innocent woman!" And he slammed his other fist into Bob's chin. "And that's for using my house to make liquor!"

Justin stood with his hands on his lean hips. "We're not going to turn you in this time, but we'll keep an eye on you. If you ever cause any problems for our family or if you start bootlegging again, we will turn you in. Is that clear?"

Gabe nodded and Bob muttered, "Yes."

Several minutes later Trent and Justin climbed back in Justin's auto. They looked at each other and chuckled. "We took care of them," they said together, then laughed, sounding just alike.

"Think we should have turned them over to the deputy?" Trent asked. "After all, they were doing some serious things, especially when they shot at us. They might have killed Rachel."

"I think they've learned their lesson," Justin answered. "Greed's a powerful teacher. I think we ought to give them a chance to redeem themselves." As he thought of giving Bob and Gabe a second chance, he wished that were possible for him.

"Then let's get out to the forest and watch history being made," Trent said.

"Havlick history," Justin said with a nod.

* * *

At the edge of the forest, Trent and Justin left the boat and walked uphill toward the family. Four men were sawing a huge oak with a crosscut. The tree had already been notched with a deep undercut so it would fall where they wanted it to. Justin hurried on ahead and stopped beside Priscilla. He slipped his arm around her waist, and she smiled up at him. His pulse quickened.

"I'm glad you made it," she said, snuggling close to him.

Trent glanced over the cluster of people watching the workers until he found Emily. She was wearing a plaid blouse and green skirt and hightop walking shoes. Just as he spotted her, she turned toward him. Her face lit up and she smiled. The rush of emotion he felt surprised him. She ran to him and caught his hand.

"Hi," she whispered, her eyes glowing with happiness.

"Hi." He felt awkward as he walked her back to stand with the family. Her hand in his felt warm and pleasant.

She leaned close and whispered, "I missed you."

He smiled at her, not knowing how to reply. The feelings for Emily surging in him were new and strange.

"Timber!" a sawer shouted. The great oak trembled, swayed, and with a loud crack and swish fell to the ground, breaking branches from nearby trees. As the tree slammed against the ground, twigs and dust shot high into the air.

"I can't bear to watch," Lark said tearfully as she turned her face against Clay's arm.

"That's the beginning of our dream," Jennet said with a catch in her voice.

Emily barely noticed the tree falling. Her heart was singing. The night before had changed her. Passionate love for Trent had burst into full bloom. She'd never known love could be so all-consuming. This morning as she'd worked in the garden, milked the cow, and fed the animals her heart had been so full of love for Trent that she'd told every living creature around her. When she'd met Free and Jennet to ride into the woods with them, she'd told them, and they'd been overjoyed.

Now he seemed shy and distant. Did that mean he didn't really love her even though she loved him with every fiber of her being? She tugged her hand free in the pretense of brushing back her hair, and she didn't slip her hand back in Trent's. She thought he didn't seem to notice.

Trent felt Emily pull away, and, thinking she'd suddenly turned shy, he smiled. She'd been far from shy during the night. He didn't reach for her hand or slip his arm around her the way he wanted to because he didn't want to embarrass her in front of the family. He turned his attention back to the men cutting the branches off the fallen oak. He knew Justin was figuring how many chairs he could make once the lumber was dried. The smaller oaks they'd selected for cutting would be used to build the log cabins.

A thrill ran through Trent. Havlick's Wilderness was actually getting under way! He'd thought it didn't matter to him, but it did. The log cabins would have fireplaces made of stones taken from the ground right here in the forest. Each cabin would have front and back windows, a loft, and puncheon floors. Grandma wanted the doors made from split logs and hung by leather hinges just like they were done in the past. Maybe he and Emily and Rachel could come for a visit sometime and stay in a log cabin.

He chuckled under his breath, thinking about the first time he spent a night in a log cabin. He and Justin were nine years old and, both pretending to be brave, they'd spent the night in Jig's old cabin. They'd heard every sound in the woods and some that they'd only imagined. They didn't sleep, but that hadn't mattered. They'd made it through the night. They had spent the night in the log cabin and they'd survived!

Trent glanced at Justin to see if he was having the same

remembrance, then frowned. Their fight together with the Laverys would not make a difference in how he felt about Justin. He and Justin would never have the same thoughts again if he had anything to do about it. Justin had ripped them apart ten years ago and nothing could put them back together.

He waited for the familiar rise of rage to wash over him. When it didn't come, he reached for it. But he felt only peace. He frowned thoughtfully, remembering Grandpa's prayer and the voice that spoke to him.

The voice spoke again. "I told you I would give you new life."

Trent bent down to Emily and whispered, "Come with me." He held out his hand and she slipped hers in his. He squeezed her hand and bent down and kissed her.

Her heart leaped and she hugged his arm as they walked together toward the water. In the boat he told her about the meeting with Gabe and Bob Lavery.

"I'm surprised Aggie wants Gabe. She said she was going to marry another rich man. She even said she was going after you and Justin."

"Too bad for her." Trent chuckled as he dipped the oars. "We're both married men."

"And don't you ever forget it," Emily said sharply.

Trent laughed with his head back. His laughter floated out over the blue lake and up to the blue sky.

* * *

Early in the morning on the last day of August, Trent stood on the spot where the cook camp would be built. The other buildings would be nearby, just as in a real lumber camp. The sun was already hot, even in the shade of the forest. He and Justin had agreed to meet to make their inspection. They'd worked together all summer, planning and supervising the construction, laying out paths through the forest, listening to Grandma Jennet describe her dream for Havlick's Wilderness in greater detail, and trying to make the dream a reality. They'd also worked side by side at the Wagon Works, each running the part of the business he knew best. They'd done it mostly without speaking unless they had to. But there had been times when they'd had the same thoughts or when something made them laugh together. There were times when they felt like brothers again, but that didn't happen often. But times change and circumstances alter, Trent thought.

He put his hand in his pocket and fingered the letter. When he'd stopped at the post office that morning it was waiting for him. Trent didn't need to look at it to remember what the letter said. He had memorized it.

"Dear Trent, I've had a good offer from a man up in Abilene to buy the ranch. He wants to take over right away, but I told him the place is yours if you still want it. I'm not putting pressure on you, but I need to know what you're planning by the first of October. I don't want to lose this chance to sell if you've changed your mind. I know you are a man of your word, but sometimes things don't work out the way we thought they would. Your friend, Cactus Pete."

"Morning," Justin said, stopping a few feet from Trent. His face bore the agony that had become so familiar.

Trent's heart lurched at Justin's grief, and he remembered two ten-year-old boys, pricking their fingers, pressing blood to blood, and vowing a covenant with each other. Just like Jonathan and David in the Bible, they vowed to take care of and love each other all the days of their lives.

"Ready?" Justin asked.

"In a minute," Trent said. "I have something to show you." Trent took the letter from his pocket, offered it to Justin, and waited quietly while Justin read it. Justin's shoulders sagged and he took a ragged breath, then his temper flared.

"You got the oak I needed to make the chairs and now you think your duty is over at the Wagon Works! It's not! I need you there."

"You knew we'd be leaving."

"I thought you'd accept your responsibility and stay!" Justin had really thought they were finally going to be brothers and friends again, especially after Grandpa's talk and prayer. He and Trent had gotten along well the past few weeks. He looked Trent squarely in the eyes. "I thought you were over Celine's death."

"Death? Murder, you mean!" His fists doubled, Trent sprang forward to strike Justin, but he couldn't do it. His hand fell to his side. What was wrong with him?

Justin doubled his fists, but he didn't move. His mind flashed back to when they were ten and they had pricked their fingers and pressed blood to blood and vowed a vow that they'd take care of each other forever, that they'd love each other forever. He opened his hands and pressed his palms against his legs.

Trent remembered the covenant again. Justin had said he was Jonathan and Trent had said he was David—blood brothers. He'd forgotten the promises they made. With a strangled cry Trent bowed his head and wept, the tears coming from deep inside where he'd locked them ten years ago.

Justin groaned in agony, then tears filled his eyes and poured down his cheeks. He laid his hand on Trent's shoulder and sobbed harder. After a long time Justin said hoarsely, "Trent, forgive me! I'm sorry, so sorry for killing Celine! I am so sorry! Forgive me!"

Trent flung his arms around Justin. "I do!"

"Thank you," Justin whispered hoarsely. He held Trent as if he'd never let him go.

Finally they broke apart and looked searchingly at each other.

"I guess this means you'll be leaving soon," Justin said.

"That's always been my plan. You know that. Just yesterday I hired Emily's brother Lars to take care of my place—live in the house and share the profits from the land—and I told Emily and Rachel to get ready to leave Saturday morning."

Justin's eyes sought solace deep in the forest. "I'd hoped you would stay. I need you at the Wagon Works."

Trent studied Justin's face. All the agony was gone from inside Trent—all the hatred. "I went over and looked at the land Grandma gave Emily and I could see cattle grazing there, and drinking from that clear stream. I could see us harvesting the second growth trees and using the lumber at the Wagon Works, then replanting for future Havlicks to harvest, or leave if they want. I could see my children growing up with yours and learning to love and care for Havlick's Wilderness and each other, but I refused to accept it. But now, Just, I can't imagine not being here. I'll send Cactus Pete a telegram and say, 'If it's a good deal, take it. If it's not, I'm still a man of my word.'"

"But I'll be here." Justin's throat felt like he would strangle. "Will you be able to stand that?"

Trent's eyes sought Justin's but Justin couldn't return the look. "Of course, you'll be here."

"Can you stand it, seeing me every day, knowing what I did?"

"Yes."

Pain tightened Justin's stomach, then his temper flared. "You're just going to stay here and make me as miserable as possible, punishing me every day."

"No, that's not it. I want to stay." Trent raked his fingers through his hair.

"Something much bigger than I am has been working on me." Trent's voice was low. "I vowed I would never forgive you for Celine's death, and I vowed I would never forget what you did. I intended to hate you with a vengeance for the rest of my life. I would hate you and torment you until you wanted to die, but I wouldn't let you die. You had to live and suffer!

"Then God began to speak to me. The first time was during

Grandpa's prayer at that family meeting. That time I thought I could hear it the way I hear you when you talk to me. But it was just in my mind. Then later it was like thoughts coming to me. It's so clear to me now!

"It honestly was God, Justin—teaching me, caring for me, loving me, and telling me that my hatred for you was killing me.

"And it was. It separated me from Rachel and I lost ten years of her life. It separated me from my family and my friends who could have helped me with my grief. It separated me from you. It separated me from my Lord. Until that night on Grandpa's porch when he prayed for all of us, I hadn't prayed—not once, and I hadn't read one word in my Bible. Grandpa was right. I'd broken the covenant. But most of all, it separated me from myself.

"As long as I could hate you and blame you for Celine's death, I didn't have to face my part in it. I didn't have to admit that I was to blame, too."

"You? What did you do?"

"I left her. Knowing full well that a contract wasn't worth her life, I left her. Then you asked me to talk Gabe Ingersoll out of cancelling the contract, promising you'd go out and stay with her, and I knew you would forget. But I got a little puffed up with pride. I was the brother who could save the contract and save the company!

"I was as much to blame as you were."

Justin put his arm around Trent's shoulder. "You're being too hard on yourself. It was my fault."

"No. We both did it."

"Are you trying to make me feel better?" Justin was angry again.

"I'm trying to tell you that me forgiving you won't work. You have to forgive yourself. I know God will forgive you."

"How could He, for something so bad?"

"I don't know. I just know that He will if you let Him. Actually He's already forgiven you. You just don't know it. And He'll help you forgive yourself. That's what He's done for me. He's given me new life. I guess I was like the prodigal son—I was dead and now I'm alive again.

"I want you to know that peace, too."

Justin struggled with the agony that had gripped him for years and finally released it. He smiled at Trent.

"You're free, Just!"

Justin pointed toward Jig's cabin. "Remember when we spent the night? We were scared of everything and trying hard to be brave. It was the next morning, right there by the door, that we made our covenant."

"I remembered it while I was waiting for you."

"Let's make a new covenant and this one I'll never break!"

Trent hesitated, then nodded. "Brothers again, Just!"

Later they walked their rounds together. They chuckled. Throwing their heads back, they laughed, the sounds ringing out in the clearing and echoing through the forest. At last they were free!

"Brothers again," Trent said again just as Justin said it.

"What will Emily say when you tell her you're staying?" Justin asked.

"I don't know. Be happy, I hope."

* * *

Later Trent climbed in his Dodge and drove slowly to his farm, singing at the top of his lungs. He parked in his usual spot and looked around. He'd work at the Wagon Works, but he'd raise cattle, too. He'd have Lars work the farm as they'd planned. Lars and Suzie were talking about getting married, and they'd need a house. They could build one south of his home with a lane of its own.

"Daddy!" Rachel called as she ran from the garden where she'd been working. Her red braids bounced on her shoulders. Her legs and hands were dirty. A smear of dirt covered her cheek, but she didn't seem to care. She liked working as much as the other Havlicks.

Trent gathered her close and kissed her clean cheek. "Where's Emily?"

Rachel frowned and shook her finger at him. "Mom, you mean?"

Trent grinned and nodded. "Sorry, I'm having a little trouble remembering her new name."

"Children don't call their mothers by their names," Rachel said. "She's my mom."

"That she is. Where is she?"

"In the house. She's packing and crying."

Trent stiffened. "Crying? How come?"

"I don't know."

"You go back to the garden to work and let me talk to her alone, will you?"

"Sure. But I'm almost done."

"Stay out until I call you."

"I will." Rachel squeezed Trent's hand. "You can make her feel better."

"You think so, do you?"

"Of course! She loves you."

Trent's heart leaped. "Did she tell you that?"

"Yes."

She hadn't told him in words yet, but maybe now she would. He'd longed to hear her say, "I love you." He kissed Rachel again. "I'll give you a call when you can come in."

She nodded and ran to the garden. The chickens squawked and ran out of her way.

Trent took a deep breath and slowly walked inside. The kitchen smelled like fresh baked bread. He hung his cap on the peg near the door. "I'm home, Em!"

She ran from the front room and flung herself in his arms, sobbing hard.

Love for her rose inside him until he thought his heart would explode. When had he started loving her this way? It had snuck up on him and caught him unaware. He gathered her closer and held her fiercely. "What's wrong?" he asked softly.

She lifted red-rimmed eyes to him. "I know I said I wouldn't ask again, but I have to! Please, please, let us stay here to live! Don't move us to Texas. Please!"

He held back a chuckle.

"All right," he said, trying to look serious.

She gasped and her tears dried instantly. "All right?"

"All right. We'll stay."

"Oh, Trent!" She hugged him again and kissed him all over his face in between her thank you's.

He held her close, enjoying every kiss. His lips burned to kiss her. He caught her face between his hands and kissed her deeply, hungrily.

She grew still, sensing a difference in him.

He lifted his head and smiled. "Emily Havlick, I love you."

Her eyes widened. "Oh, Trent!"

"I love the way you smile, the way you walk, the way you kiss me. I love *you*. You fill me with happiness." Gently he kissed her again.

The world was spinning and she had to hold him tighter to keep from falling. He loved her! Her prayers had been answered! "I love you, my darling Trent," she said against his lips. She pulled away slightly and said again, "I love you! I will always and forever love you!"

Afterword

♦

May 27, 1923, Emily stood beside Trent with all the Havlick family nearby. It was the family's day to go through Havlick's Wilderness and the next day it would open to the public. Already people from as far away as Washington, D.C., had made reservations. Smoke drifted up the chimney of the cookshack where two men were cooking dinner for the family. The bunkhouse, with rows of bunks built so close together the lumberjacks, once called shanty boys, had to slip in them like a slice of meat between two pieces of bread, stood closer to the forest. Farther away were the stable, the blacksmith shop, the company store, and the small shacks where the foreman, the bookkeeper, and the cook lived. The furnishings inside the buildings were exactly like they'd been when Freeman had been a shanty boy back before the Civil War. His red sash, enclosed in a glass frame, hung for all to see with a write-up about how all the shanty boys/lumberjacks wore the red sash to show who they were.

Emily stepped closer to Trent as Freeman made the speech he'd make tomorrow about lumbering. Trent smiled at her just as the baby moved inside her. In the fall they'd have their first child. She wanted a boy and she knew Trent did, too, but they really didn't care. They'd love a girl just as much.

Rachel leaned against Emily and whispered, "Mom, I'm hungry."

Emily bent down to her. "As soon as Grandpa Free is done talking we'll all have the giant raisin cookies he told us about." They were as big as stove lids and the lumberjacks loved them. Emily felt hungry enough to eat two of them.

Emily saw Ruth and her family. Clay and Lark had adopted Ruth when she was left as an infant at the orphanage. She'd come from Grand Rapids with her husband, Tom, and their seven children. Their daughter Nan was Rachel's age and they'd become best friends instantly. They reminded Emily of Celine and herself.

Celine. Emily smiled. She, Trent, and Rachel talked about her freely. There was room in their hearts for Celine just as before.

Emily dragged her attention back to what Free was saying. She knew he was happy that all his children were present along with their children and grandchildren. Freeman's brother Wexal and sister Anne had come with their families.

"There are a lot of Havlicks here," Trent whispered.

Emily laughed softly. "Think what it'll be like in twenty years! Fifty years!"

"We're leaving our mark, that's for sure. And I don't mean just Havlick's Wilderness. I mean this whole enormous family is making a difference in our part of the world." Trent gently touched Emily's stomach. "And this new Havlick will make a difference too."

Emily leaned her head on Trent's arm and smiled proudly.

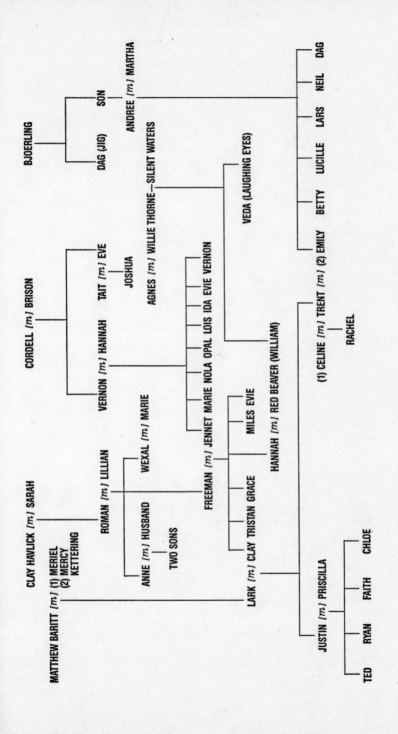

About the Author

♦

Hilda Stahl is a writer, teacher, and speaker, who offers writers' seminars and lectures to both schools and organizations across the country. To date there are over one hundred Hilda Stahl titles in print, published in eight foreign languages, as well as English. In addition she has written and published more than 450 short stories and articles.

She belongs to the Society of Children's Book Writers and is listed in many publications, including *Foremost Women of the 20th Century, International Authors, Writers Who's Who,* and *The World's Who's Who of Women.*

The Stahls, Hilda and Norman, live in Michigan on what they call "eighty beautiful acres." They have seven children and seven grandchildren.